S0-BQZ-971

The Running Iron

The
Running Iron

A Western Story

Lauran Paine

Thorndike Press • Chivers Press
Waterville, Maine USA   Bath, England

This Large Print edition is published by Thorndike Press, USA and by Chivers Press, England.

Published in 2001 in the U.S. by arrangement with Golden West Literary Agency.

Published in 2001 in the U.K. by arrangement with Golden West Literary Agency.

U.S. Hardcover 0-7862-2131-3 (Western Series Edition)
U.K. Hardcover 0-7540-4714-8 (Chivers Large Print)
U.K. Softcover 0-7540-4715-6 (Camden Large Print)

Copyright © 2000 by Lauran Paine

All rights reserved.

The text of this Large Print edition is unabridged.
Other aspects of the book may vary from the original edition.

Set in 16 pt. Plantin by Christina S. Huff.

Printed in the United States on permanent paper.

British Library Cataloguing-in-Publication Data available

Library of Congress Cataloging-in-Publication Data

Paine, Lauran.
    The running iron : a western story / by Lauran Paine.
        p.   cm.
    ISBN 0-7862-2131-3 (lg. print : hc : alk. paper)
    1. Large type books.   I. Title.
PS3566.A34 R8 2001
    813´.54—dc21   2001041508

The Running Iron

A Western Story

Chapter One

An Old Man's Passing

Old Joseph Jessup had been a buffalo hunter. When those times passed, he settled on a stretch of land and went into the cattle business, creating the Lazy J, and by the time he died he was well off and comfortable. He had built May, his Pawnee wife, the finest house he could imagine, which was modest by most standards. And he had bought her the prettiest chestnut mare he had ever seen. He had bought Young Joe the second finest horse he could find.

Every year, during the time of making meat, the three Jessups traveled north to the mountains adjacent to the ranch to join May's tribesmen, the up yonders. The up yonders were a mixed band of hideout Indians scattered throughout the mountainous country — renegade tomahawks who had come together singly and in fugitive groups from as far north as Canada and as far south as the desert country below Albuquerque.

Their rituals and traditions were an amalgam of the representative tribes who, although enemies for many generations, had joined together in a sort of brotherhood when faced with the overwhelming power of the blue coats, their wheeled gun, and the threat of reservation life.

The Jessups would stay with the up yonders for several days when they would visit. During their absence Bart Mather tended to things around the ranch. Mather had been a manhunter for most of his earlier days. But as a result of having been shot and increasing age, there were things Mather couldn't do in recent years. Still, nothing kept him from trying.

At Old Joe's burial Mather stayed to himself with an expressionless face. Earlier there had been a few tears shed in the seclusion of the cabin the two had built together. How he had come to live on the ranch neither Mather nor Old Joe had ever discussed. The same had applied to Young Joe. Old Joe had found him scavenging in some garbage during one of his trips to Cumberland. When asked his name, the boy had said he didn't have one. That had suited Old Joe. He told the scrawny, unwanted boy he would give him a home and his name, and up until Old Joe died that was the only distinction. One was

Old Joe; the other one was Young Joe.

Young Joe was not talkative, especially about his past, before Old Joe found him and brought him home. He and Mather were close, particularly after Old Joe went Up There.

After Old Joe was buried, his wife, May, disappeared for three days. She reappeared as though she hadn't been away, cooked a big breakfast for Joe and Mather, and did not say a word until the next day, when she met Young Joe in the big, log barn readying a buckskin horse for a ride.

She smiled and leaned toward him. He kissed her on the cheek. She was his mother like Old Joe had been his father. She held out a fist and slowly opened it. "She send this for you. Take."

Joe took the buckskin-bound prayer feathers and smiled. "Will she come?" he asked.

May smiled, too. "You know. She 'fraid to come."

He pocketed the symbolic feathers and returned to rigging the buckskin.

May lingered, watching, before she finally spoke again. "Someday you go to her?"

Joe fumbled the latigo and had to re-loop it.

"She good, Joe."

He turned and smiled. "Pretty."

"Much pretty."

"We missed you, Ma."

"I go find the right place to dig to put the hurt."

The lanky lad nodded. "I'll be up by the creek."

She stood in the wide barn opening, watching him ride northwest of the ranch, then returned to the house to get things ready for supper. Supper had been her husband's favorite meal. Supper, his pipe by the fire afterward, and talking dialect with his woman.

Mather was there where Young Joe expected him to be, fishing in the large pond close enough to the timber country to be able to hear the nesting birds scolding potential intruders.

At Joe's approach Mather held up his forked stick. Six Dolly Varden trout were hooked on it. He said: "Your ma'll do justice to 'em, boy. I'm glad she's back."

"She went to do a Indian thing. Bury the hurt in her over Pa dyin'."

Mather rose, flipped the fish line around the pole, and stretched as high as he could reach to place the pole in the crotch of a tree. He brought his horse in from a tiny meadow and talked while saddling. "It's goin' to be different, boy. Just the pair of us."

Joe watched from the saddle. "You like this spot, Bart?"

The older man jutted his jaw Indian fashion. "None better. That's breakfast, boy." Mather mounted his saddle, and said: "They go back. Did you know that? They make their mourning an' stay up there."

Joe rode stirrup to stirrup with the old man. "She wouldn't leave us, Bart. I can't cook. She knows we wouldn't make out without her."

"Boy, it's their custom. They live accordin' to signs an' customs."

"I sure don't want her to go, Bart."

The old man smiled. "Me, too. We'll wait an' see." He stood in his stirrups. "There's a buggy by the house. You see it?" He slumped in his saddle and growled. "That's Nicholson's rig." Mather snorted. "Them damn' bankers, don't even let folks get cold, do they?"

"What do you mean?"

"Your pa's dead, your mother's in mourning. His kind don't let the dust settle before they want to see your pa's will." At his companion's blank look he added: "A will is what folks write out so's, when they die, folks they leave behind'll know what they want done with their leavings."

"Pa'd leave things to the banker?"

"Let's go find out. Boy, kick that lazy damn' buckskin into a lope."

They covered the last half mile with a dust banner in their wake. When they dismounted at the hitching rack in front of the house, Joe said: "I'll care for 'em. You go see what's what, Bart."

"No. The horses will keep. You come with me."

When they reached the porch, they could hear Nicholson talking inside. "Now then, I'll just hold your fingers, sort of guide 'em along. You understand, May?"

Mather stepped just inside the doorway, and May smiled at him. He did not return the smile but, instead, addressed the large man with the unlighted cigar in his mouth. "She can't sign nothin', Nicholson. She can't write nor read."

The large man reddened. "I was goin' to help her."

Mather crossed the room. "Help her what? What's that paper say?"

Nicholson turned beet red and stammered: "Just makes it legal. Joe give the ranch to me two years ago."

Mather took the paper, read it, went to the smoldering coals in the fireplace, and dropped it in.

The large man exploded. "You got no call to do that! It's legal an' all. Now I got to get another fee lawyer to make me up another one."

Mather's hazel gaze blazed as hot as the fire. He addressed the dignified woman: "You want him to stay for supper, May?"

The banker's expression was murderous. "Who'n hell do you think you are? Lazy damned old drifter . . . you been livin' off these folks like a damned Indian!"

Young Joe spoke for the first time. "We got to figure things, Ma."

May crossed the room to pat Joe's cheek. "Supper be ready soon." She went into the kitchen and did not reappear.

Mather's anger was obvious when he leveled a stiff and gnarled finger in the townsman's direction. "Sorry, Nicholson. I don't think she'll want you to stay for supper, after all."

In his matching coat and britches, Nicholson scooped up his hat, dropped it on, and started to the door, where he stopped abruptly. He and Mather faced each other from a distance of not more than ten feet. The banker spoke in a low tone. "I'll have you off this place as soon as I can find Forbes an' sign a warrant against you for . . . cattle stealing!"

He left the house without closing the door and walked stiffly to his buggy. Climbing in, Nicholson swore at the buggy mare and left the yard in the direction of Cumberland, the only town for miles in any direction.

In the kitchen, Mather stared at May Jessup, thinking of what Old Joe had once told him. Joe had first seen her in March. In April he sat across from Blue Barrel by a fire late into the night. Blue Barrel was lined and scarred, the survivor of dozens of battles and discussions. He had yielded when dawn was breaking, taking Old Joe at his word that the cattle would be delivered to the foothills where tribesmen would herd them the rest of the way. Six good horses. No guns, no bullets, but something for the old mother. That had been the hard part. The old woman only had one daughter. She had shed tears without making a sound, when she held out her hand. Joe wasn't allowed to come for his bride until May. That accounted for her name.

Mather shook off his reverie, guided May out front to the porch, sat her in a chair, and talked for a solid half hour about Old Joe with May smiling in her gentle way and occasionally nodding that she understood.

The following day Mather told Young Joe to meet him at the cottonwood spring and left the yard, alone and troubled.

When Young Joe came out from the barn, May was on the porch in the rocker her husband had made for her. He returned her trilled greeting and settled on a bench near her, where he sat looking at his hands.

May said: "Bart is good."

Young Joe nodded without looking up. "He's old, Ma."

She understood. "He go some day. You go. I go some day. Not too long. Miss your father."

The tall, lanky lad had a spell of blurry vision before he spoke. "Bart don't want you to sign any papers." She nodded. "He worries, Ma. It's not like when Pa was here."

"He keep watch. Tell Bart no worry."

Young Joe was late getting started. He did not reach the solitary, shaggy, old cottonwood tree by the spring before the sun was slanting off center.

Mather didn't growl as Joe had expected. He waited until the horse had been hobbled and off-saddled before speaking. "It just kind of worries me, boy. It's hers . . . an' yours, I guess . . . but it's worth a heap of money. Nicholson won't be the last."

Joe settled cross-legged in the shade on the grass. He plucked a stalk and chewed it.

15

"She said for you not to worry, Bart."

The old man snorted. "Easy to say, boy. You 'n' me got to keep her away from town fellers. I guess in a way we're lucky she can't read nor write."

Joe spit out the stalk of grass and leaned against his upended saddle, considering the pool of water. Track marks showed where animals had stopped to drink. "You know Jem Whitmore?"

Mather nodded. Everyone knew Jem Whitmore. He, too, was old, but it didn't show, and he never favored a leg or a foot even when it hurt.

"What about him, boy?"

"He grows a big garden out behind his house. Him 'n' I talked a lot the day of the funeral."

Mather leaned against the old tree and positioned his hat so the sun couldn't get in his eyes. "He's done a lot of things, boy. Hunter, soldier scout, blacksmith, tans hides, talks some Indian. Years back I run onto a feller who knew Jem in the old days. He told me Jem was the best man with a pistol he ever knew. Did he talk to you about guns?"

"No. He told me what with Pa dead and Ma so ignorant I should stick to her like a flea. He said there'd be rustlin' . . . critters stole off the range. He said Ma needs a fee lawyer to make sure she keeps things."

Mather rummaged for a plug, worried off a corner, and re-pocketed the tobacco. "Jem's likely right. But a fee lawyer, I don't know. You gotta remember that one that just about cleaned out Zelda Evans after her Jessie was killed."

Joe considered the lowering sun. "There's no fee lawyer in Cumberland, is there?"

Mather stirred. "I never heard of one in town. I expect a person'd have to go to a city to find one."

"Jem might know. He could write a letter. How much do you expect it'd take to get one down here?"

Mather had no idea nor did he reply. While they were saddling up for the ride back to the Lazy J, he did mention something else. "It'll be sell-off time soon. I'm not sure you 'n' me can do all that's got to be done."

Joe squeezed his horse with both knees as he said: "There's names for hire on the board at Murphy's saloon."

Mather got rid of his cud, tongued a couple of times before expectorating, and said: "It's somethin' to ponder about for you 'n' me. I expect we'll miss your pa real bad when gatherin' time comes."

"Pa used to hire Indian bucks, Bart."

"I know. And folks didn't like that one bit."

Joe's attention was diverted by a small band of pronghorn antelope doing their jumping-in-the-air flight at the sight of the mounted men.

Mather said: "Good eatin'. I expect I've ate more pronghorns than cattle. Joe?"

"Yes."

"One of these days we'll talk serious. I figured we might do it today, but you come out too late."

"Talk about what, Bart? Somethin' special?"

"Real special, boy. I'll let you know when it's time. I think I'll ride to town tomorrow, see if Jem can write a fee lawyer. I don't like puttin' things off."

Joe barely smiled. "Pa used to say you couldn't ever stand leavin' things be."

Mather laughed, squinted his eyes in the direction of the distant yard, and lapsed into a silence that lasted until they were home.

They were no sooner done tending their horses and settling in to a couple of minutes of relaxation when May banged the triangle, meaning supper was about ready.

The meal was filling. Both Joe and Mather believed meat should be cooked plumb through. As for the cabbage, it wasn't really cabbage but some near-thing May pulled up, roots and all, from one of her horseback excursions into the brush country. They all sat on the porch for a while before turning in for the night.

When they were alone, like this morning, May liked to tease Young Joe. Joe was usually good-natured about it, laughing not so much at her remarks as at the way she misused words. Old Joe had spent many a bitter winter night teaching her, and she had learned fast. She didn't bite off words any more as many Indians did, but she had trouble placing words where they should go and remembering the little ones that went in between the big ones.

This morning, though, Joe wasn't in the mood to play the teasing game. He appeared irritated throughout breakfast, and then muttered he was going to tend to the chores. Old Joe had taught him everything he knew, it seemed. Young Joe was a fast learner, and rarely had to be told anything twice. Some folks just naturally came to minding critters, fixing things. Young Joe was such a person. When he was done with the chores, he saddled up and went to check the west range, counting cattle in preparation for the upcoming roundup. Along the way he lost track of time.

It was close to sundown before he returned to the yard. Supper was over. May and Mather were on the porch — the man with an after supper cud tucked into one cheek, the woman pinching peas out of their pods into a bowl in her lap.

Joe waved from the barn, cared for his animal, washed up at the stone trough out back, and gathered a hatful of eggs from the mangers before crossing to the porch. He glanced at Bart and stopped stone still at the base of the bottom step.

Neither of the two looked at him or spoke.

He climbed the steps, put his hatful of eggs on top of the peas in May's lap, hooked his haunch over the peeled, log railing in front of Mather, and said: "Horse buck you off, Bart?"

It was one of those questions folks should never ask a person who'd spent their life straddling horses. Mather leaned out, got rid of his cud, eased back, and answered tartly: "Boy, no damned animal never saw the day he could jump me off of him. I got into a fight in town. Was two of 'em. Range men. Pretty good-sized boys, maybe a tad older'n you. Twenty, maybe."

"What was it about?" Joe asked, and got

another clipped reply.

"Indians, boy. Bein' cussed out for bein' an Indian lover."

Joe nodded. It was all the answer he needed. He'd heard it often enough himself behind his back when he'd been in town. Old Joe had told him to ignore it, that it just came natural for some folks who didn't have the guts to say things to a man's face to spout insults from behind.

May took the bowl of peas and eggs inside, telling Joe over her shoulder she'd kept his supper in the oven.

After she left, Joe said: "More'n two, Bart?"

"Just two, boy. And I'm too long in the tooth to handle two at a time any more."

"Was one of 'em a Colson?"

"Yep. The tow-headed one, Harland. Didn't recognize the other. They done a fair job. I got up, but I couldn't stay up."

"Didn't Forbes try to break it up?"

Mather snorted. "Hell, Emmet wasn't around. The law's never around when you need 'em."

Young Joe pondered what Mather was telling him. When May called, he went inside to eat.

Once Mather was alone, he opened his shirt, probed his left side, caught his breath, and quietly announced: "Two cracked ribs."

When Joe eventually returned to the porch, there was no sign of the old man. May stood in the doorway and spoke softly: "You stay home."

He looked out toward the horizon, sat down on the uppermost step, and responded: "He's an old man, Ma, and getting older."

"You stay home. Your pa tell you same."

"I expect he would." Joe rose, went to the creek to wash, and lingered there, thinking again about what Mather had told him. He knew the older Colson son was a bully. His name was Harland. During their school years together, Young Joe Jessup and Harland Colson had locked horns plenty of times. Since those days they'd encountered one another but always stayed clear. Harland had grown bigger and heavier; Young Joe Jessup had gotten taller but not much heftier.

Chapter Two

Moving On

Often these days, Mather rode with Joe to get an idea how many head there would be when gathering time arrived. It was impossible to get an accurate count with cattle spread over miles of graze. Sometimes May accompanied them. On those occasions, they made a point of using cattle talk for May's benefit. They agreed that, with Old Joe gone, May would have to learn more than cooking and washing.

The day after one such trip, May refused to ride out with them again. That was when she both surprised and embarrassed Mather. She told him she knew what they were doing — teaching her. Mather didn't deny it; he just laughed and went down to his cabin.

May rode out by herself. Mather and Joe shared a confidential suspicion about that. She was going north, and she would meet tribesmen.

Joe was able to fault her for that, but

Mather smiled it off. "Boy, she's Indian. They're clanny. She's only been down here since she married your pa. Otherwise, she spent her whole life with them."

Two days later, at the supper table, she said: "Horses gone."

Both men looked up from their platters.

Mather said: "Horses are gone, May?"

"Yes. Band that watered at Willow Creek. No shoes."

Mather nodded. When it was time to turn out horses, their shoes were pulled.

She paused, raised her head. "Made gone by shod horses."

Mather finished his meal and went out to the porch to settle his cud. When Joe came out, Mather said: "We better get out there."

Joe nodded. Both men had the same thought. It was starting. A boy, an old man, and a tomahawk woman were what would have to fight them off.

Mather mentioned this on the ride out. Joe was quiet until they reached the pond and circled it, looking for the shod horse sign. They found the tracks and followed to within a mile or so of the town before turning back.

Mather cursed to himself. He was too old for what lay ahead. When Joe asked questions, Mather growled his answers and finished up by saying: "It's up to her, Joe, but they'll raid us again. We need a couple of hired hands. Young 'n' fit. Even if you 'n' me could do it, them shod horse tracks was from three riders."

"She'll agree, Bart, you're right."

Mather scowled in the direction of his companion. "No Indians."

Joe looked surprised. "She'd want to hire Indians?"

"Not her, you. You been plenty close to some of the young bucks."

"They can track a fly over glass, Bart."

"Boy, no Indians! Folks we'll need for friends will dig in their heels, if we bring Indians along with us."

Joe said nothing more on that subject, but, when they had the yard in sight, he began to feel uncomfortable, and, once they were in the yard, he dismounted first and held out his hand for Mather's reins.

"I'll take care of 'em. You go tell Ma."

Mather put a mildly caustic look on Joe but said nothing. He was gone a full hour, and, when he came back, Joe was sitting on a little nail keg in the barn, whittling.

Mather leaned on a snubbing post. Lately his back had commenced to hurt if he spent a long time in the saddle.

Joe said: "Well?"

Mather shifted his cud from one cheek to the other, which delayed his reply. "It's your pa's fault. He always used 'em. I never knew her to be stubborn, but, boy, she sure is."

"She wants to hire bucks?"

"Yes, an' she named 'em. Four bucks, beginnin' with that one your pa called C.L."

Joe pocketed his clasp knife and tossed the stick away. "Did he ever tell you why he called him that?"

"Well, one time he started to but we got called to supper. It had somethin' to do with *pawhuska.*"

Joe nodded. "Long Hair Custer. He trailed the *ozu we tawatas,* saw the fight, and rode home to warn the people it was time to scatter an' hide."

"Boy, I know that Indian, C.L. He hates whites. If we use him for gatherin', an' folks learn of it, they'll show up loaded for bear." Mather peered at Joe from beneath his lowered hat brim. "You talk to her."

Joe stood up, went as far as the barn opening, and stood gazing toward the house. After a time he spoke without facing around. "It's her call, Bart. Near as I know she's taken Pa's place."

Mather continued to lean, but he eyed the vacated little nail barrel. "Boy, she'll likely listen to you. You're next in line, now, with your pa gone."

Joe turned. "She's next with Pa gone."

Mather did not push this discussion further. "You're her son like you was your pa's son. Boy, go try. If she refuses, I got to roll my blankets and get to ridin'."

Joe continued to eye the old man. What Joe had just heard hit him almost as hard as when his pa had died. He weakly said — "I'll try." — and pushed clear of the doorjamb, heading in the direction of the house.

Mather moved to the little keg, thinking he might whittle. Where he'd grown up, only townsfolk carried those clasp knives. He carried the same wicked-bladed boot knife an uncle had given him something like fifty years earlier.

Joe found May in her rocker by the fire in the parlor, knitting. A trader's wife had taught her years back. She'd been knitting the same sweater for Young Joe since before his pa had died, and she'd had to unravel and start over at least six times.

She looked up, put the yarn and needles aside, and smiled. She loved the boy not entirely because her man had loved him, but that was part of it. She said: "You hungry?"

Joe dropped his hat beside the battered

27

old leather chair that had been his father's favorite indoor place to sit.

She gestured toward the chair. "You sit."

Joe sat. They looked at each other. Her telling him where to sit was more Indian stuff — when a spokesman was dead, his next in line took over.

She spoke after Joe sat in the old leather chair. "*Dina sica*. We pay with beef. Money in box."

Joe reached for his hat and began turning it around by its beaded edge. "There's a fair amount of money in the box, is there?"

"Yes. Old Joe say all time don't touch. Add to, no take any out."

Joe let go a soundless sigh. "Ma, we all gather at the same time. The Colsons an' others will be huntin' strays among our cattle."

She nodded. She knew all this and more.

"Ma, one of 'em'll come onto broncho Indians, an' it'll scare the whey out of 'em."

Her smile was genuine and fixed in place. "You talk like Bart. Old Joe say we take on anyone we want. On our land we not have to make talk with anyone."

Joe decided on a direct appeal. If she still refused, it would put him in a position where he'd have to leave. He did it anyway. "Ma . . . do this for me. Your son. Pa's son.

For Bart. I never asked for much. Do this for me."

Her smile did not fade, but it appeared to have congealed until it had no meaning.

He continued slowly to turn the hat. He sat forward in the old leather chair. "It's for the best. It's for you an' me an' Bart."

She said: "Come here." He moved to her side. "Good. Now turn back." She held up as much of the sweater as she had finished, laying it across his back, measuring here and there. She pulled it off, saying: "Damn! Do it no more time."

Joe returned to the chair but stood beside it, holding his hat.

"We take three beefs up yonder," she said. "Tell them take meat, not come."

A gentle wave of relief passed through Joe as he crossed toward her. When she raised her head, he kissed her hard on the cheek.

His mother's smile returned. She said: "When?"

"When? When do we cut out the cattle an' drive 'em up?"

"Yes. When?"

He shifted his stance. Bart would have the answer. He faced her head on. "Three days from now?"

May groped for the needles and yarn and

replied without looking at him. "Three days. You tell Bart."

After he had left the house, May worked the needles for a moment or two before throwing as much of the sweater as she had finished into the fireplace where eager flames sprang to consume it.

Mather was in his cabin when Joe went over and rattled the door. When Bart opened it, Joe said: "Three days from now we cut out an' drive cattle to the *ranchería* to pay for them *not* helping us."

Mather held the door wider, and, when Joe entered, he was nearly overcome by the smell of meat that had been fried too long.

Mather removed the large iron fry pan from the fire, tipped up a scant two fingers worth of whisky from his secret bottle, handed one tin cup to Joe, kept the other tin cup, and raised it. "You are her son, boy. Besides that, if she'd stuck to her guns, there'd have been hell to pay. I seen it almost come to shootin' a couple of times when your pa pushed the gather to join the others for the whole drive to head south . . . because he had a couple of Indians along. Have you eaten?"

"Soon," Joe said, setting down the untouched coffee and walking as far as the door. He stopped and said: "You goin' to

30

town an' see if you can hire a couple of men tomorrow?"

Mather nodded, waited until his guest was gone. He closed the door, retrieved the secret bottle, and put it on the table next to his tin plate.

It was their custom to select three critters from whatever herd they found near the upland timber country. This time May pointed them out. She helped to separate them from the other animals. Her choice was good. Two were steers. One was a dry cow — if she'd calved this year, it had been long ago; her bag was as slack as an old croaker sack.

The largest steer turned up the best of numerous trails; his companions fell in behind. It had been done this way since Young Joe'd been a pup. Sometimes they had trouble with a cutback. But not this time. With May riding point, the cattle trooped along behind her horse without even looking back.

The sun hadn't shone until after they had made the cut and had started uphill with it. Once on top, they were only visible when they crossed a clearing. Still, none of them was surprised when an Indian worked his way onto the trail, called out to May.

May replied with a wide smile.

The Indian barely acknowledged the

presence of Joe and Mather. He and May carried on an intermittent conversation in a language of which Mather and Joe could only pick up an occasional word.

Somewhere ahead through a mass of pine and fir trees someone howled.

The Indian rode ahead of May and disappeared. Mather fished out his plug, worried off a cud, spat once, and addressed Joe: "When somethin' unexpected happens, they're noisier'n a herd of geese."

May left the trail, weaving among the forest timbers.

Joe and Mather, anticipating trouble, were ready when the big lead steer balked. Mather made a run at him, but the steer followed May as though he'd never intended to do anything else.

The up yonders maintained a number of *rancherías,* one for each period of the year. The large topout ahead seemed to cover miles of grass and grazing land. Once there had been many trees; now there were stumps, mostly charred. Lightning strikes caused sizable burns. This camp, the summer one, had brush shelters, hide houses, two creeks, and knee-high green feed. Grazing critters had taken it down, more so near the creeks than at places farther from the water.

There were children, women skiving hides,

older men resting in shady places, younger men like statues watching May's party start across in the direction of several houses where a group of people had congregated. A half-grown buck ran in front of the trio, spooking the cattle that bawled and fled amid the angry shouts.

An old woman on the ground, pounding seeds in a hollowed-out stone, screeched and hurled rocks to divert the cattle. May made a sound of greeting, a high, trilling rattle that turned the older woman to stone. Then May flung herself off her horse and embraced her mother. They went inside the brush shelter. May was home.

The young ones made a sport of cornering the cattle. An old man came forward, speaking harshly.

Joe looked at Bart who said — "Wilder'n a damned March hare." — and reined to intercept the angry man. Mather called a greeting. The old Indian replied while glaring in the direction of the teasing children.

Joe went to creek side, dumped his outfit in the grass, hobbled his horse, and turned slowly, smiling.

The girl was attired in smoke-tans. She had made a frenzied change when she'd heard that May and Joe were coming. The change had been so precipitous she hadn't had time to arrange her hair. She knew good English. She had just completed her third year at the Red Cloud Indian School. She had two names. One was Natali for Sister Natali Rose at the school. The other name was Crow and difficult to pronounce, so the Jessup clan had decided to call her Donna, as close to the Indian version of Madonna as they could get. She was tall and carried herself well. Like May she was Pawnee, and the Pawnees were a tall people. She held out both hands.

Joe took them, color rising in his face.

"You made us a surprise, Joe."

"It was May's idea."

Her dark eyes sparkled. "She bring you to marry me?"

Joe stood sweating in the shade.

She read his face. "Not this time?"

"Donna. . . ."

"Maybe next time, Joe? I wait."

This time he gave her no opportunity to override him. "We brought meat. Three head."

"It's early, Joe." She held one of his hands and gently tugged. "Walk with me."

The *rancherías* were open. The only privacy was within the person, or within the dwelling place, or in secret places on moonless nights.

She took him to the creek with its dense

willow growth. They sat. Nearby horses watched them. He gave her a gift, a Navajo bracelet for her wrist. For most of the time together, she kept her attention away from his face, but when someone called for her, she turned to look at him and smile. "The sisters taught us to plan. Always to plan."

Donna stood up, took his hand, and pulled him to his feet. "Someday, Joe?"

He forced his eyes to meet her gaze. "Someday, Donna."

"Soon . . . ?"

The call for Donna came more insistent. She squeezed his fingers and pushed clear of the willows to call back.

He sat on a smooth large boulder.

Some time passed. May appeared and said: "We go back."

He pushed up off the rock. "They understood?"

"No, but now they make meat. It keep them busy." May moved as if to leave, then stopped. "There been scouts. They move soon. Come along. Bart waiting."

Neither of them spoke as they went where Bart stood with their horses. As they approached, he looked hard at Joe.

Two spokesmen came to see them off. May spoke. The older man smiled. They seemed to be studying Joe particularly. Joe felt their eyes boring into him. From the shadows of a hide house, Donna watched, also. She covered her face with both hands, when an old woman close to her ordered her away from the doorway.

The ride back was mostly downhill. They broke clear of the shadowy uplands, loped for a mile. When they had the Lazy J in sight, Mather let May get ahead so he could ride beside Joe. Mather began with — "Boy, you think . . . ?" — then stopped. After several seconds of silence, he added: "I wish your pa was here."

They reached the yard where Mather volunteered to mind the horses. Joe and May crossed to the main house and disappeared inside. The house was cool; it was always cool during the hot months as it was warm in the cold months. May sent Joe for two buckets of water, and, during his absence, she unwrapped the medicine bundle and held its contents to her cheeks.

Later, during the meal, Mather tried to get a conversation going, but neither Joe nor May would co-operate. Eventually Mather concentrated on his supper.

In the morning Mather was gone. May came to the shoeing shed where Joe was working, shirtless, in the heat. She had

36

brought him a jar of sweetened apple juice and told him he was as good at horseshoeing as his father had been.

His response was solemn. "I'll never be that good. I wonder what Bart'll find in town?"

"He offer twelve dollars and found."

Joe was positioned to smooth the outer hoof of a chestnut mare with a flaxen mane and tail. She was an old horse. Her chin was flat, and the hollow above each eye was deep. She had been May's wedding present, still ridable, but she worked best hitched to a light buggy. It had been many years.

Joe finished his drink, handed back the bottle, and smiled. "That was good."

"More?"

"No. That was plenty. Ma?" Joe hesitated. "She's lost most of her grinders."

May went over to put her cheek against the mare's neck. "Soon, Joe?"

"Well . . . before winter. She can't grow winter hair no more. She'll suffer bad when it gets real cold."

May returned to the house, carrying the empty jar. Joe finished with the mare, talked to her, led her to a fenced field, and turned her loose. She ran to the other horses and nickered. Joe lingered at the gate, looking northward.

It was late when Mather returned. He had a pair of range men with him. Joe thought one of them looked familiar. He couldn't put a name to the man, not even at the bunkhouse when Mather introduced them. One was named Colley Bowman, the other Fred Harper. According to what they'd told Mather at the saloon in town, they both had ridden for some big outfits up in Montana and down south in New Mexico. At supper they shared their experiences. May was satisfied; so was Joe. Mather settled them in the old bunkhouse and left them to doctor some sore places in his own hutment.

May sat on the porch with Joe, asking questions. She wanted to know what he thought of the two men. All he could tell her was that, until he'd worked with the new hands for a few days, he couldn't form an opinion. And what Bart had said about the hirings was that, judging from their outfits, they'd been stockmen for a long while.

The first real inkling Joe had that Bowman and Harper were top hands was when three days into the job he'd been out with them and had come upon an orry-eyed cow with a bloody muzzle where she had met up with a porcupine. The pain made her willing to fight.

Colley Bowman took down his rope and called to Harper: "I'll head her." Harper waited. When the rope snugged up, the old girl bawled, pawed dirt, and charged. Fred Harper moved in, made a low cast that caught both hind legs. They stretched her, still fighting, and called for Joe to pull out the quills. It was hazardous work, but Joe managed to dislodge every quill he could find, then moved clear.

Harper, being the header, had the worst end of it. The heeler's job was easier. Bowman snapped slack several times until the old girl set back hard and came out of the lariat. Harper snapped slack, teased the cow to come around, snapped more slack, and she kicked plumb loose.

After supper that evening Joe gave May his honest opinion. "They're top hands," he said, and explained why he thought so. He also told Mather about the porcupined cow, and Mather grinned from ear to ear. "Boy, a man can't live as long as I have an' not know the best ones from the others."

Joe had to be satisfied, but it stuck in his craw that top hands worth twenty-five dollars a month would hire on for twelve dollars.

Chapter Three

A Bushwhack

Mather felt better about going horse hunting when there were four of them. As they put the yard behind them, he explained to the two new men about the missing horses and their tracks — three sets of them.

Neither of the new hands commented, but they followed Joe and Mather to the point where it was possible to pick up the tracks. They surprised Joe and Mather by gesturing to the northwest. They were right: the horse thieves had driven in that direction. Joe's curiosity about how the new men had guessed which way the rustlers had taken their horses was soon forgotten as they picked up speed.

When they passed a gnarled old tree with a circled C burned into it, they were on Colson range, an area his pa had told him not to ride over without first letting Crow Colson or his range boss know why it was necessary.

Mather didn't slouch along. He rode straight up, alternately watching the sign and the miles of empty land.

Colley Bowman spoke to no one in particular when he said: "If they're over there, we'd ought to see 'em soon."

Mather nodded non-committally, and sharpened his scanning.

Where they encountered a set of ruts, the mark of a road, Mather pulled up, squinted in all directions, and dryly said: "Colson's home place is about a mile or so northwesterly."

Taciturn Fred Harper bobbed his head in response.

As they continued on the trail, Mather grumbled that someone had driven cattle over the tracks. He hauled to a stop before the others at the sound of someone with a bull-bass voice hailing them.

The rider was alone, distant, and big enough to cast as much of a shadow as his mount made.

Mather rested both hands atop his saddle horn as he said: "It'll be Crow."

They waited until the large man on his twelve-hundred-pound saddle animal loped the last dozen or so yards, then Mather raised his right arm, palm forward.

The approaching horseman did not return the salute. When he reined up, he looked at each of them in turn and settled for Mather. "Mather, you know better'n to trespass."

Mather explained about the missing horses.

The large Colson ran a gloved hand up one side of his unshaven face as he said: "Ain't no Jessup horses over here. If there was, we'd chouse 'em back."

Mather pointed at the ground. "Right here is where we tracked 'em. The sign's under all them cattle tracks."

Crow's very dark eyes pinched up into a humorless smile. "Well, now, I didn't know you could read sign under where cattle been. Mather, you head on back where you come from. We got enough to do gettin' ready for the gather. Mather?"

"What?"

"With Old Joe gone you won't have no Indians ridin' for you, will you?"

Mather's face had dark color. "We might."

"Who're them two? They work for you?"

"Yep."

"Good. Then you won't need no tomahawks, will you?"

Mather didn't answer. He reined around and led off back the way they had come.

After a ways, Joe eased up. "He's got no

call to drive cattle from west to east where those tracks went."

The corners of Mather's mouth pulled down as he replied: "He'd have reason if he wanted to wipe out horse sign, boy."

They loped steadily to get back to the yard before sunset. Neither of the new hirelings said a word until the Lazy J rooftops were in sight, then Colley spoke. "Not a real friendly cuss, is he?"

Joe answered, Mather having pulled ahead out of hearing distance. "His name's Crow Colson. He runs Big C cattle over an awful lot of land. His land abuts our line north to south for three miles, plumb all the way to the northerly upland timber country."

"Indian?"

"Part I guess. That's what folks say anyway. He looks it more'n his wife or his kids."

"Cranky, is he?"

Joe grinned. "Where'd you ever get such a notion?"

The discussion ended in the yard where each man went to care for his saddle animal. Mather said nothing, heading directly to his log house. Inside, he dug among his gatherings until he found what he'd been looking for. He swung the shell belt around his middle, lifted out the holstered Colt, jammed it back, lifted it out again, repeating this draw several times. Next he went to hunt for his hidden bottle of popskull. He hadn't been so angry in years. He'd never liked Crow Colson. Old Joe hadn't liked him. If a man thought about it for long, he'd be hard pressed to name anyone who liked any of the Colson clan.

Inside the house, May listened to Joe's recital of the meeting with Crow Colson. He reminded her that the new hands had ridden out two days in a row. The only thing they had encountered was two bucks up near where the game trails came out of the uplands.

Little more was said then or at suppertime. May might have encouraged conversation on the subject, but when she looked across the table, Mather was staring straight at her. She changed the subject.

Readying for a gather commonly stirred up stock people. It was an event of concern months before the actual rounding up was undertaken. Mather was getting anxious. Under certain circumstances Old Joe had reacted the same way.

After the meal Mather caught Joe out behind the barn. "Boy, if that 'possum-bellied 'breed son-of-a-bitch didn't have somethin' to do with the loss of them horses, I'll buy you a new hat."

Joe smiled. "They wasn't the best horses, Bart."

"I know that, damn it." Mather cocked his head. "It's the idea of the thing. I got a feelin', boy. There'll be other things happening."

Joe did not argue, and, after Mather had gone over to his house, Joe rolled and lighted a cigarette. He, too, had a hunch, but on a full gut he wasn't inclined to seek problems he wasn't convinced needed worrying over.

A week later, May livened up, which she always did the closer it got to gathering time. She waited until after supper one night to catch Joe before he left the house to do the evening chores.

She wanted to ride the mare that had been a wedding present on the drive. Joe considered, studying the floor before saying: "Ma, she's too old. Remember, I told you she's shedding her grinders. I'm not sure she'd make it through. I could pick out an animal to replace her."

May's expression changed. "One time. Last time. We take along a pouch of oats or barley."

Joe was going out the following day with Bart. He needed his sleep, so he kissed her cheek, said — "We'll see." — and left her sitting in the parlor. There were times when May said something or did something that troubled him. Bart called it "their ghost talk."

He was late at the barn the following morning. Bart said nothing; that was his way when he was annoyed; his eyes did what his mouth was supposed to do.

They were a mile out, heading east, when Mather leaned and said: "I told Colley and Fred to go see if the bulls was wallowin' in the mud at the pond."

Joe leaned, straightened, and pointed far ahead.

Sunrise was still coming, but Mather saw them, too. He growled: "What the devil? They don't know north from east, boy."

Joe angled in the direction of a *bosque* of old-growth oaks. Mather said nothing until they were sheltered, then he reined up, watching the distant horsemen. "You got a feeling, boy?" he asked gruffly.

"Somethin' like that."

"You want to shag 'em?"

"No, just set a spell. That's open country dang' near to town."

Mather cheeked a cud. "Goin' to town in the middle of the week."

Joe did not say a word for a while, then he

jutted his jaw. "I sort of wondered, Bart."

"They're goin' to meet him, boy."

Joe neither moved nor spoke until the pair of hired Jessup riders veered to intercept the solitary rider, then all he said was: "I'm not surprised. That there's Crow, isn't it?"

Mather was too annoyed to reply until he was ready. "It's Crow. Boy, they'll have an excuse."

After the distant meeting was finished and the large man astride the large horse turned back the way he had come, Mather spoke again. "Thinkin' on it, boy, I don't expect I'll say anything to 'em."

Joe nodded agreement without speaking. They picked up where they had veered off and rode until Joe raised an arm. "Ma?"

Mather squinted. "Now what in hell's she doin' up there?"

The gunshot sounded sharp, the sound a carbine would make. They watched as May went off the horse like a pinwheel, both arms outspread.

Mather exploded — "Son-of-a-bitch!" — and hooked his drowsing-along saddle animal. It reacted as though a hot iron had touched it. Mather went up the slope like it was pure flat land and was off his horse in one bound. Joe couldn't keep up.

There was blood enough. Mather got

May onto her back with his right arm, lifting her into a sitting position. Her breathing was coming in spasmodic jerks. Mather leaned back to look at his hand. It was coated in red. He looked at Joe. "You stay with her. I'll go get the wagon. Boy, don't make no target of yourself. I'll get back soon as I can."

As Mather went back down the slope, setting a beeline for home, Joe unsaddled his horse. He then used the saddle to prop up May. Balanced on one knee, he scanned the area. Whoever the bushwhacker had been, he'd been a fair distance off. May made a sound. Joe hiked the saddle so that it pushed her a trifle forward. May spoke to him.

"You see him, Joe?"

"No. Bart's gone for the light rig. You hurtin', Ma?"

"No . . . some. One leg. . . . Who was he?"

Joe shook his head. "We was headin' out . . . easterly a spell . . . saw you go off like a bundle of rags."

"Joe? He be down in that deep place."

He showed her his smile. "We'll do some scoutin' tomorrow. Meantime, we got to stop that bleedin'."

She fainted which made it easier for him. The bullet was barely visible in the setting of old leather May kept draped around her hips. Joe hooked the leather on both sides as May regained consciousness. He looked at her as he said: "It'll hurt, Ma."

"Pull, Joe."

He did, the slug that was folded into the leather and driven into her flesh pulled out. The moment it came loose, Joe said: "Gawd a'mighty!"

Seeming to have improved immediately, May held out her hand, indicating she wanted to examine the slug. Joe gave it to her. She brought it up to her face, turned it around and over, then handed it back to her son. She was repositioning herself, when someone calling from a distance caught and held both her and Joe's attention.

It was Mather in the buggy. They watched as Bart, crouched forward in the seat, approached. They both held their breath when the buggy struck a boulder. It rose off the ground on one side, dropped back, and settled. Joe shook his head. One of the easiest things to do on this earth was to drive a light top buggy too fast. Mather hit the binders and came up the slope like he was tied to a log.

It was one hell of a chore, but they got May into the rig. She didn't make a sound, but her jaw muscles pumped like a machine. It wasn't much easier getting her into bed, once they got home. Mather brought the kitchen bottle, helped her take a drink, took the bottle back. After they were sure she was comfortable, Mather said he'd go to town and fetch back the sawbones, a real white-skin medicine man by the name of Barry Leger.

May was adamant in her response. "No! I go up there."

Mather rolled his eyes. "You can't no more make that ride then I can fly. You hungry?"

"No."

Mather's jaw muscles quivered. May spoke through clenched teeth. "I make it. Up there an' back."

"Over my dead body you can make it. Joe? You know how to make tea?"

"No," Joe lied.

"Well, then . . . just set here with her."

After Mather was gone, May reached for Joe's fingers and held on. "You know milk-weed?"

He nodded.

"Go find some. Bring it here to me. *Go!*"

The moment he was gone, May shifted over until she could get a purchase and, after a bit of a struggle, pulled herself to a sitting position, then slid her legs down the side of the bed until she was standing. She waited until the strange sensation in her leg and hip subsided before attempting to put weight on the injured side of her body. Getting to the porch was difficult, but not impossible making use of the walls and furniture for support along the way. Beads of sweat poured down her face as she passed through the parlor and out to the porch. The pain became excruciating as she descended the porch steps. The distance to the barn had never seemed great, but it did now as May stood gripping a porch post. She loosened her grip gradually and let go. Each time she put weight on her injured side, she let out a gasp. A lightheadedness overwhelmed her, and she stopped, measured the remaining distance, and collapsed, not even midway to the barn.

That was where Joe found her. The trail of dark red droplets would have led him to her if he hadn't seen the crumpled form stretched out in the yard. Without ever having given a thought to her weight, Joe crouched to push both arms underneath so that he could lift her. He had to try three times before he could finally straighten up with her in his arms. He got as far as the steps, where he paused to breathe deeply and lean against the upright where May herself had rested before attempting to make it to the barn. Taking in a large gulp of air, Joe mounted one step, re-distributed the weight, and climbed the next two steps. He would not allow himself to stop on the porch, rather he kicked the door open and staggered through the house and into the bedroom with his mother.

Near collapse himself, Joe got his mother into the bed. He sat on the edge of the bed, his muscles trembling, his heart pumping. He considered the whisky bottle, dismissed it as a bad idea, and considered it a second time when he no longer had to gasp for air.

May stirred and made a guttural sound. Joe fussed with the blankets, trying to reassure her before he checked the wound again. He found the makeshift bandage he had put on the bullet hole soaked in blood, but he was comforted by the fact that the bullet had been removed. He moved the room's only chair over by the bed, sank down in it, wondering how long it would be before Bart returned with the medicine man.

May stirred again and mumbled: "I ride old mare."

Joe leaned out, resting his elbows on the bed so he could return her steady gaze. He said: "Soon. Not today." Then the annoyance surfaced. "What're you tryin' to do, kill yourself?"

Her smile was feeble but genuine. "You worry?"

"Yes, I worried. You like to scared the hell out of me."

"Bart?"

"He's not back yet." He studied her face, feeling badly for having gotten angry with her. "You want to go up there, Ma? You want to go up there with me? You know you can. That is . . . when you can ride."

Her smiled widened as Joe eased back into the chair. Her gaze should have told Joe enough, had he known more about reading expressions. She heaved slightly to get more comfortable, and laughed at him.

When she asked him to get the whisky bottle, he said: "You got to be plumb rational when Bart brings back the doctor."

Joe spent an hour at her side, watching her slip in and out of a restless sleep, before he realized he was starving. He made something to eat, put it on a platter, and returned to the bedroom, thinking he might share at least a part of it with his mother. May roused as he moved the chair with his foot, settled in, balancing the platter on his knees. She managed to prop herself up a little, regarded the platter, and then grasped one of his hands and squeezed it before she shook her head and spoke.

"Not hungry."

Joe nodded, ate only a small portion of the

food, having lost his appetite somewhere between the kitchen and the bedroom, and then took the platter back to the kitchen where he left it on the table. It was getting along toward chore time, but he wasn't sure he should leave May, so he sat, dozing, as the sun slipped lower.

He jerked awake at the sound of voices. It took him several seconds to identify the sounds of the hired hands, Bowman and Harper. Several minutes later he heard the sound of a buggy wheeling into the yard. He hoped it was Leger's fringe-top that was usually drawn by his overfed seal-brown horse.

Joe checked on May, who seemed to be resting more comfortably. As he made himself presentable, tucking in his shirt, Bart appeared at the bedroom doorway. He was accompanied by a bird-like man as gray as a badger, who peered owlishly from behind thick glasses.

Mather introduced Dr. Barry Leger before heading back outside where he spoke briefly with Bowman and Harper. Joe heard the porch door close, and waited for Mather's return. The old man, who appeared even older at the moment, told May the hired hands sent her their wishes for a fast recovery.

Anxious to get to work, Dr. Leger ordered Joe and Bart out of the room. Joe was always bothered by the fact that Leger was one of those individuals who did not quite meet a man's eyes, but rather tended to look slightly past people.

In the kitchen Joe fetched the whisky bottle and handed it to Mather, who looked like he could use it. With a nod of appreciation, Bart took it, tipped it, handed it back, and said: "Crow an' his boys was in town."

"Troublesome was they?"

"No. They was different for a change, hardly looked at me." He extended his hand toward the bottle. After another long pull, he asked: "How's she doin'?"

Joe did not mention May's attempt to leave nor the trouble he had had getting her back to the house. "She wants to go up yonder."

Mather made a face and gave his usual response. "They're like that." He started to raise the bottle to his lips again, thought better of it, and handed it back to Joe. As they walked out onto the porch, Mather said: "On the way back I rode beside the buggy an' told the doc what happened. He talked like he'd tended wounds before. . . . Joe?"

In anticipation the younger man, whose thoughts had been elsewhere, said: "It'll be too dark directly, Bart. I'll go prowl around up there first thing in the morning. You want to come along?"

Mather nodded. They sat down on the porch bench.

It was nearly an hour later when Leger appeared in the doorway, where he paused to roll down his sleeves. He seemed to be waiting for Joe and Mather to invite him out. When he spoke, he addressed Mather. "It's a mean one, but I've seen worse. You got to feed her rare meat an' lots of it. She's lost considerable blood." He switched his attention to Joe. "Did you find anything up there where she got hit?"

Joe shook his head. "I'll go see in the morning. Doctor, what about poisoned blood? Pa used to tell me about poisoned blood."

Dr. Leger's fine features showed a thin smile. "Blood poisoning, lad. No sign . . . but there mightn't be for a few days. You watch her. If the wound swells an' gets red, let me know immediately." That seemed to be the end of it, and he nodded curtly at Joe in what appeared to be an obvious dismissal. As he headed down the steps, he turned and said: "Bart, walk to the barn with me."

Joe watched them cross the yard and frowned. He wasn't a little kid. He was eighteen. There wasn't anything the doc could tell Mather that Joe couldn't hear. *Damn it!* Joe cursed to himself, deciding in a split second that he best tend to the chores.

Colley Bowman was in the barn as Joe began searching the mangers for eggs. He didn't have a bowl or basket, so as usual his hat would have to do. As he dug through the straw, Bowman asked questions. Joe answered them, briefly. When he mentioned how May had been shot, where she had been when it happened, Colley said: "Me 'n' Fred was close by there earlier. Didn't see anyone."

"Bart and me'll go scoutin' in the morning," Joe told him. "You fellers find any sore-footed bulls or hung-up heifers?"

"Worst thing we saw lately was a skinny bitch wolf tryin' to drag off the afterbirth from where an old muley cow had a calf."

Without saying another word, Joe took his hatful of eggs to the kitchen where he left it sitting on the table. He crossed the room to the porch where he encountered Mather.

"I'll be getting some supper together. So, if you're hungry. . . . And you better sleep light tonight, boy," Mather suggested as an afterthought. "She might get out of her head or something."

Joe nodded, dismissed the suggestion, said only — "About sunup . . . tomorrow morning." — and went to the harness room to be alone briefly.

If Colley and Harper had been in the area, how could it be that they didn't hear a gunshot? Joe wondered. *And Colley had deliberately lied when he said they hadn't seen anyone. They had seen Colson.*

Mather surprised Joe, not to mention the new hands, when he put together a supper from leftovers that was as tasteful as those May made herself.

After cleaning up with everyone's help and before heading for his cabin, Mather told Bowman and Harper to go north the next day and begin pushing any cattle they'd find south toward the home place. He reminded them, unnecessarily, that right directly it would be time to make the annual roundup, and that, when the time was right to do the choosing, most of the critters should be at hand.

Mather entered the barn in the silence of the predawn where Joe was waiting, having already saddled the horse he intended to ride. The old man mumbled something about how the long ride to get the medicine man and back had tuckered him out; otherwise, he would have been waiting for Joe, instead of the boot being on the other foot, as it was this morning. Joe stood quietly, ready to ride.

They left the yard side by side, hunched inside drover's coats, talking only when it was necessary. During one of their limited word exchanges, they decided they would split up when they reached the place where May had been shot, to cover both sides of the hill.

Chapter Four

Whitmore!

Mather was on the far side of the hill when he whooped and hollered. Joe joined him. Mather led him to an arroyo, stopped, and pointed where the brilliant new day sunlight reflected off a shiny brass casing.

As Joe swung down, Mather spoke sharply: "Don't touch it, boy!" Then he also dismounted and led his horse to the shiny spent cartridge casing. Next he studied the ground around the area before looking up the slope and saying: "This is where he fired from."

They spent an hour making sense of the sign. Whoever the shooter had been had come from the north, from which direction he had a mile-long view of the range in all directions. Mather scowled. "Indian, boy? Look there . . . unshod horse tracks comin' south to this arroyo where he saw her goin' up to the topout."

Mather's agitation was transferred to Joe who didn't say anything but showed in his expression how upset he was.

Mather led his horse into shade and leaned there looking in a northerly direction. "Indian watched her as he come southward. Joe . . . ?"

The younger man inclined his head. "Wouldn't be a tribesman, Bart. Unless maybe he didn't know it was May."

"He'd know, boy. He rode down here with her in plain sight."

Joe's stubborn streak surfaced. "It could be someone else. Someone skirtin' the uplands."

Mather got a cud settled before speaking again. "You're like her, boy. You don't want to believe what you see. We're the only folks who visit up yonder. Other range men keep clear of this territory."

"Bart, why would a tomahawk shoot her?"

The older man gazed in the direction of the densely timbered upland. "With Indians, boy, you can't never be sure."

Joe considered the position of the sun. "We couldn't make it up there 'n' back before real late."

Mather said no more. He snugged up his cinch, got astride, and turned back the way they had come.

The silence they had maintained was broken when Mather said: "Be better if she wasn't told what we found. It'd worry the hell out of her, an' right now she don't need that."

Joe agreed, slouching along until his companion grunted and raised his free arm.

"I told 'em to look for sore-footed bulls at the pond. What in hell are they doin' over there?"

Joe slackened a little. The distance was a tad far to make a positive identification, except that Joe knew the horse. Colley Bowman had taken a shine to the grulla gelding. Joe looked at Mather.

"They could see our tracks."

Mather said nothing, concentrating on the pair of distant men.

They changed course, headed for home on the opposite side of the hill where May had been shot and where Bowman and Harper were now pecking around like a pair of hungry coyotes. As long as they had the hill between them and the pair, they were safe, but a mile or so southward they would become visible.

Joe said: "There's other things, Bart."

The older man turned his face, saying nothing until the huge old shaggy cottonwoods in the yard were visible. He scowled and said: "I expect they'll have an excuse."

Having cared for their animals, Joe joined

Bart at his cabin until the pair of hirelings got back.

Mather said: "I'll brace 'em in the barn."

Joe responded curtly: "Leave it be for now."

Mather was already at the door when he responded. "They was pokin' around up where someone bushwhacked May! Boy, I never liked settin' on my hands. For all we know they could've come back . . . with May flat on her back at the house to finish the job."

That last remark brought Joe straight up. He brushed past at the door before Mather caught him. "Boy, we do this together."

Joe hesitated which provided Mather with the time to say: "You go around front, I'll come through from the back."

Out front someone called. Mather moved quickly, halted, and spoke without facing around. "It's the medicine man in his buggy . . . an' Emmet on horseback with him."

Joe proceeded through the doorway. Dr. Leger was dropping his tether weight over in front of the house and the local law man, Constable Forbes, was looping the reins of his saddle horse to the hitch rack out front of the house.

Joe and Mather waited until the men from town were on the porch then turned together to enter the barn from out back.

Mather swore a blue streak when he saw two horsemen loping toward the northeast. He turned toward Joe and shrugged. "Well, that's that. Best tend to our visitors."

Mather strode into the sight of Forbes, who sat on the porch. He hailed him. "Forbes!"

The constable shifted a little, recognized Mather, then turned his attention to the pair of riders growing increasingly smaller as they continued their riding.

Noting that the doc must already be inside, Mather reached the porch, excused himself, pushed past the large law man, and went inside. Not far behind Mather, Joe stopped on the porch, faced the constable, and started talking. He was still at it, when Mather appeared in the doorway to say: "She's all right, boy. But, if my figurin' is right, it was a close call."

The constable began asking Joe a series of questions. Mather went back into the house.

Fifteen minutes later Mather appeared again. This time he joined the law man and Joe on the porch and did not leave.

The constable had known Mather many years. He asked about May, and Mather repeated what Leger had told him in the sick room.

"She'll mend. He figures another couple of weeks an' she'll be up an' around."

Mather looked in Joe's direction. "Did you tell him what we figured?"

Joe nodded. "An' he told me somethin', Mather. Them two men you hired . . . they worked for Colson until a few weeks ago."

Mather looked at the large constable. "You know that for a fact, Emmet?"

The constable made a bleak smile as he answered. "I'm plumb certain, Bart."

Mather leaned back and swore: "Why that underhanded son-of-a-bitch." He glared at the constable. "That's why you come out today with the doctor?"

"Well, no, not exactly Bart." The big man held out a folded piece of paper. As Mather reached for it, he said: "What is it?"

The constable removed his hat to reveal a nearly hairless dome and mopped sweat off with a blue bandanna as he said: "It's an eviction notice, Bart."

The old man's outstretched hand froze twelve inches from the paper in Forbes's hand. Joe didn't think Mather was breathing.

The constable spoke again, still mopping his head. "It wasn't my idea, but you got to know it's my job to serve them papers."

Mather drew back his arm, staring at the constable. "Eviction notice? What's it for, Emmet?"

Forbes pocketed the damp bandanna. "It

gives notice to May that her . . . an' you an' the lad got thirty days to leave. You better look at it, Bart. Read it."

Mather finally took the paper, unfolded it, read slowly. After he had finished, he said: "Nicholson? Frank Nicholson, for Chris' sake?"

"He had it drawn up legal, Bart. Old Joe borrowed six thousand dollars, two years ago, put up his ranch as security, and never paid in a dime since Nicholson gave him the money."

"That's what that son-of-a-bitch says," Joe said, shaking his head. He took up the paper again, read it, and tipped back his hat. He returned the notice to the constable.

Taking it, Forbes turned to the young boy. "Joe, I don't know anythin' about your pa puttin' up the ranch for the money Nicholson gave him. All I can tell you is that the paper's plumb legal. I've served dozens just like it. Nicholson told me this mornin' that, when your pa borrowed the money, he'd had two bad years in a row."

His recovery slow, Mather left the two talking on the porch, heading into the house without a word. Too late, Joe realized he should have stopped Mather. May wasn't up to hearing what Mather had gone in to tell her.

The constable stood up, fished out his watch, opened it, consulted the little black spidery hand, closed it, re-pocketed it, and spoke without looking at Joe. "I got to get back." He held out the paper to Joe. When Joe made no move to take it, the big man said: "It won't bite, Joe. I got to tell you, I never in my life hated to do somethin' like servin' this paper. Your pa 'n' me was friends from 'way back."

Joe took the paper and told the constable about the time he and Mather had found the banker, Nicholson, trying to get May to sign something he'd brought from town with him.

Emmet Forbes stood a long moment without moving, then made a little shrug and left the porch.

Joe watched him free up his animal, mount, and ride slowly out of the yard. He went inside. He didn't find Mather in the bedroom as expected, but in the little room Old Joe had said was his office. Mather didn't notice him, so Joe went to the bedroom.

May was lying perfectly still, gazing out the only window in the room, as Leger went about tending her wound. She did not turn her face when she said: "Old Wisdom Maker was right."

Joe sat on the only chair. "Wisdom Maker, Ma?"

"He died when you young. He spokesman when I was my mother's baby." She showed a wan smile. "He said white men big thieves, big liars."

Mather appeared in the doorway, holding a pile of papers. He nodded at Joe but addressed May. "There's no such a paper here. I don't think Joe signed any such a paper, an', if he got six thousand dollars from that no-good Nicholson, I would have known. May . . . ?"

Her smile was fixed. "We go up there, Bart. Let thieves have it."

Mather jerked his head for Joe to follow him. They went out to the porch where Mather spoke, sounding tired. "Boy, it belongs to her an' to you. Frank Nicholson's not goin' to get away with this. Both your pa and me know of other things he's done. But this time he's not going to get away with it. I'll settle it."

Joe sat perched on the peeled log stringer that ran the full length of the porch, looking at the old man. "No," he said. "I'll do it. You swear to Emmet I wasn't off the place."

Mather showed a death's-head smile. "Boy, you don't know. . . ."

"I know enough. Look after her. I'll be back directly."

"No!" Mather slumped in a chair. "Let me go tell Jem Whitmore. In the meantime, boy, you stay here, and don't try anything stupid. I'll let Jem know it's a life 'n' death matter." As Mather rose to leave the porch, he said: "Take care of her, Joe. She's got to be fed 'n' all. You're all she's got."

"What about Bowman and Harper?"

The old man teetered on the topmost step as though he was trying to unclog his mind. "Well, we can kinda keep an eye on them, if they work for us, I guess." He started down off the porch. "Boy, don't you do anythin' you got no business tryin'."

Joe went back inside. He met Leger coming out, rolling down his sleeves, a worried look on his face. Joe asked the natural question. "Any heat 'n' swellin' yet?"

The bird-like medical practitioner looked Joe squarely in the face when he replied: "There's somethin', lad. Maybe just bein' sore. I won't be able to say for another few days yet. I left a blue bottle on the table. If she gets to grievin' too much, mix a tad of it with water an' get it down her. I'll be back in a few days. Boy, I'm sorry. It isn't right. Emmet said that at least five times on the ride out here. It's not right."

Joe agreed, shook hands, and waited until

the doctor was on his way before returning to May's room.

Her eyes were bright. Her face was flushed. Joe went to the kitchen, groped in the cupboard until he found the bottle, and held it up. It lacked a little of being empty. Upon his return, May laughed, wiped her eyes, and held out a hand. He watched. Years earlier he had sneaked one swallow of whisky. Since then he'd marveled how people could drink liquor in any kind of quantity. A swallow now and then to steel the nerves. But actually to look forward to drinking the stuff. But May liked it. For that matter so had Old Joe, and Bart seemed to need his daily dose. When Jem Whitmore told him liquor could ruin a person's liver, that's when he decided he would leave the stuff to others.

There was no denying that, in spite of the doctor's concern, May looked better and sounded better. She mentioned getting Bart to work the ground of her garden. She wanted to expand it next year. Joe nodded in agreement until she also said she would go up yonder. Her people saved seeds from every planting. At least that was her excuse.

Joe repeated his admonition about making the ride until she was plumb healed, and changed the subject by telling her Bart had gone to town to visit Jem. That made her smile vanish. She said when those two got together someone was in trouble.

Joe avoided that topic by talking again about the garden patch. He left when May had trouble keeping her eyes open.

Mather did not return until after dark, but before that time, when the sun was still up, Joe had another visitor. An Indian a few years older than Joe. They had been friends for years. Old Joe had called him C.L. Young Joe used the same designation. He was in the barn at the time, sorting horseshoes, and did not hear anything until C.L. appeared in the doorway. He was not smiling as he usually was.

Joe offered to take him to the house and feed him. Old Mather had a saying about Indians; they were born hungry and never got filled up. C.L. shook his head; he wasn't hungry, at least he said he wasn't. He also said: "They burn your big calf."

Joe considered his friend. To Indians branding was burning. Joe asked: "Who?"

C.L didn't know who they were. He had been hunting down along the low country and saw them rope and tie the big, long-yearling and brand it. With his hands he pantomimed how the branding had been done. He knelt, used a stiff finger in the dust

71

to draw a circle with two letters inside it, CC.

Joe's jaw muscles rippled. First the Jessup saddle stock, now a Jessup long-yearling. He hunkered next to C.L.

C.L. drew another mark, Jessup's brand, the Lazy J. He said: "This burn on your cow with big calf."

Joe sat back, looking steadily at the Indian. "I'll get a horse, and I want you to show me where. All right?"

C.L. unwound up to his full height with animal agility. He smiled and watched Joe rig out. They left out the barn's opening and loped without looking back, otherwise they would have seen Mather and another man enter the yard from the east.

C.L. didn't favor his horse. It was just natural. Life was cruel to Indians. They treated a horse no differently. It wasn't a matter of indifference; it was how their world turned.

Joe called for slack, and C.L. dropped to a spine-jolting trot. When they topped out above a broad spread of graze near a creek, C.L. pointed and put his mount straight down.

Daylight was fading, but there was enough sign to show where two booted men had roped, thrown, and tied the big calf, where they had gotten a tiny hot fire going and put the D ring into it. When it was ready, one of them would have hooked two green twigs through the D and squeezed the ends tightly. All the man had to do was take his cinched-up sizzling hot D and work the circle with two letters, CC, inside it.

C.L. could read sign well enough to mimic the entire process, then he stood up pointing toward the southwest. "Cow take big calf," he said, and Joe nodded. Her calf would have fought and bawled. The cow had pawed until her baby was free, then she had been led off in a dead run, tail over her back like a scorpion.

C.L. had to get back up yonder. Even then it would be dark before he reached the *rancheria*.

Joe rode home alone, slowly. He arrived at the ranch to find they had another visitor. The large, rawboned old man who had come with Mather was on the porch. He studied Joe's face and said: "Boy, nothin's that bad. Come up here and set."

Joe smiled at Jem Whitmore. He wasn't surprised to see him on the porch. Whitmore jerked his head. "Bart's in with May. I come out here. Boy, I could never abide men who'd shoot womenfolk."

"Did she tell you, Jem?"

"She told me." Jem propped his chair

back and looked at Joe. "It's botherin' you too much, boy. She'll recover."

Joe agreed and told Jem about the two unidentified men who had misbranded a Jessup long-yearling that C.L. had seen.

Whitmore grinned. "That's how the best ones do it. Big calf's mostly weaned. You don't gather for another couple months. By that time the cow's gone dry, and her an' the calf don't have anythin' to do with each other. During your gather you find a Colson-branded critter, cut it out, and drive it over onto Colson range. 'Cept it's your critter." Jem paused. "Boy, I wish your pa was here."

Joe nodded without speaking. Bart came out, and Jem related what Joe had just told him. Old Mather reddened, sank down on the porch bench, and spoke to his old friend. "How many, I wonder?"

"Enough, Bart. Ten, twenty, every late summer until you make a gather an' come up short."

Mather looked at Joe but addressed the other old man. "I'd like to ride over there 'n' hang that puss-gutted son-of-a-bitch."

Whitmore made a humorless smile. "An' the law'd hang you. Then where'd May an' the lad be?"

On the ride back from town Mather had

told Whitmore about the legal-looking eviction notice. Jem did not mention it now, for he wasn't sure whether Young Joe knew about it. But he did say: "You can hire one of them fee lawyers. I got a feelin' you're goin' to need one. Maybe one that can shoot straight."

Mather told Joe to go inside. "Tell May they're figurin' to steal us into the poor house."

After Joe had left the porch, Mather quietly asked: "How much, Jem?"

"A man can't charge an old partner. No charge, Bart, but don't expect a trap to spring tomorrow. It's got to be done when things is right."

Mather's wide mouth pulled wider in a wolfish smile. "I'd like to pay you, Jem."

"You insist?"

"Yes. An' May'd like to, too."

"All right. No money. You know that big ugly grulla horse?"

Mather nodded. "Take him."

"I can't do that. Grullas is mighty rare. How long would it take folks to figure out how I got that horse?"

"Well, how then?"

"After it's done. Maybe a month or so after. By then I expect folks'll believe I bought him, since during that time I'll men-

75

tion my interest in it. You do know that Colson is only one of your problems."

Mather stood up and shoved out a hand. "I do, but one less ain't gonna hurt us none. Good luck, Jem. Remember, Crow's got those two kids and plenty of riders."

Whitmore gripped the extended hand, released it, and was turning to depart, when he said: "Partner, we been close a long time. So, gawd-dammit, don't tell me how to do it!"

Chapter Five

A Loose Horse

As promised, Dr. Leger returned several days later to check on May. As soon as he stepped out of the room, she felt restless. Trying to distract herself, she stared out the window, noting that the locust trees were beginning to curl their leaves and even drop a few. She saw Bart in the yard, and she felt saddened that Joe was gone. She watched Bart hovering in the yard until he saw the doctor leave the house, heading for his buggy. She perked up as Bart crossed toward the house at the same time.

Leger greeted Mather with a solemn nod. "It looks like maybe she's went an' got somethin' like blood poisoning."

Mather nodded. "She goes out of her head now 'n' then. Is that a sign?"

The bird-like doctor readied his rig as he replied: "Trouble is, Bart, it don't have to be. There's other things." Leger turned to face Bart. "I've seen it enough times."

"Anythin' I can do?"

"Take that whisky bottle an' hide it. Make her eat even if you've got to sit on her to do it. I don't believe it's just a fever, but, if it is an' she wakes up rational one day, let me know." The doctor seemed to hesitate before continuing. "Bart, I didn't know she was a drinker."

"No reason for you to know, Doc. She don't go to town an', until recently, you had no call to come out here."

"How long, Bart?"

"Since Old Joe took to his bed. He was her life, you know. Don't worry. I'll wean her off, when she's better."

"The sooner the better," Leger replied.

When Joe came home, Mather told him of the doctor's visit and what they'd discussed.

Joe was swinging his saddle onto the pole where several other saddles rested, when he said: "I didn't know it kills folks."

"Well, boy, it can and it does. We got to wean her off it a little at a time. I know somethin' about tomahawks an' whisky."

After Joe had cleaned up, he headed for the kitchen where he went to work making supper. Ordinarily he would have first visited with May, but what Bart had told him was upsetting. He did, however, take a plate of supper to her when it was ready, inter-

78

rupting her sleep. She sat up, looking at him, and smiled. He sat in dogged silence while she ate. He did not tell her, nor had he told Mather, what he had encountered today a few miles northwest of the ranch: four big weaned calves with fresh scabs over fairly recent brands. The Circle CC brand.

The following afternoon Joe heard the gunshot, but it had been too distant to place its origin. Some time later, Joe watched Mather ride in, pushing a large Durham bull ahead. Something wasn't right. The bull didn't track straight. He studied the situation as Mather corralled the animal, then he went down through the barn where he found Mather attempting to examine the bull which didn't want to be examined. Joe walked over and climbed into the corral.

Mather turned as he said: "Shot. Come over here. You can't see where it went in real well" — he motioned — "come around on the other side."

Joe could see that where the bullet had exited there was blood and torn flesh. He got a few inches closer before Mather warned him back. "Leave him be, boy. He might get over it. The slug went plumb through and out."

Joe squatted, watching as the big bull

sought the trough to bury his muzzle. "Who did it, Bart?"

"I can guess, but they was gone before I found him. That one would've been gone, too, except that he didn't feel like runnin'." Mather retreated to the far poles and leaned there gazing balefully at the gut-shot bull. When Joe came up next to him, he said: "Sometimes they die, but sometimes they pull through. Boy, they're goin' to keep it up. I sure wish your pa was here. . . ."

"He could doctor it?"

Mather was staring at the ground when Joe left to care for his saddle animal. After that, Mather went to his house and stayed there.

Returning to the corral, Joe chummed the bull, until he could walk up to him. The animal didn't seem to be in that much pain. Joe fed him rolled barley. Now if he could just get May to eat.

Mather was awakening from a restless night of sleep, when he heard a horse enter the yard. By the time he had dressed, the horse he'd heard had left the yard and someone had hit the hanging iron that was used to summon folks to breakfast.

When he entered the house, he stopped stone still. May was hunched at the kitchen

80

table eating like a horse. She briefly looked up, smiled, and went back to her meal. He joined her, sitting down directly opposite, and looked around. May spoke around a mouthful. "Gone. Tell you he be back."

Mather got up, filled his platter at the stove, sat back down, and ate while his anger built up. "Where'd he go, May?"

"I don't know. C.L. come. They went off together." May raised her smiling face.

He watched her rise to clear the table, first retying the old bathrobe. She limped as she crossed the room, and Mather jumped up to help her carry the dishes. He said nothing while they worked, but when they'd finished, he asked which way Joe and C.L. had gone. Her answer was another of those smiles that meant whatever the recipient wanted them to mean.

Mather went outside and down to the barn. Out in the corral the big bull was lying down. He scarcely looked at Mather. He found the speckled-rump horse was gone, an animal Mather himself sometimes rode. Bart brought in the buckskin. He wasn't fast, they usually weren't, but they had bottom. A man could ride a buckskin hard all day and still he'd cake-walk all the way home. The difficulty would be in tracking Joe and C.L. on the two horses, one shod

81

and one shoeless. He spent almost a full hour discarding tracks and got a fair distance out before he found the sign he was looking for.

The tracks led almost due north with a slight bend westerly. Mather was satisfied about one thing — unless they changed course up yonder somewhere, they'd be in the arroyo country that bordered the timbered uplands.

He watered his horse at a creek, looped the reins, and, while gnawing off a corner of his plug and pouching it into his cheek, he studied the country where his hunt would only be successful providing the two were not down in one of the arroyos that had been made by rainfall run-off from the highlands over the centuries. As he freed up the reins, he resumed reading sign to the edge of a drop-off where he halted again, this time because he had heard something, or thought he'd heard something.

He tipped down into the arroyo and hunched up the far side where he definitely did hear something. It was a man's snarling voice. The words were indistinguishable, but the tone was definitely harsh. He climbed out of that swale, topped out, and was reining toward the next one when he heard a gunshot, close and unmistakable for anything other than what it was.

He swung to the ground, taking the Winchester with him, and started to lead the buckskin up the far side when he heard a horse coming in his direction. He quickly assessed the area. The only concealment was down the draw, too far for him to head the horse off in time. He pulled for his horse to follow. It balked, dug in all four hoofs, stretched its neck, and would not move. Mather had one arm to pull with. The other one was holding the carbine. He wanted to swear.

Suddenly a saddled animal burst out of the next arroyo, stirrups flying, reins whipping loose. Mather stole one good look, then jerked the buckskin clear. Now, the buckskin allowed itself to be led out of the way. The fleeing horse came down the far slope within a few feet of where Mather had been. It did not look left or right, but crossed the flat place in three bounds and went up the east side, stepped on one rein, tearing it, and hurled itself at the slope. Mather watched in wonder. The terrified horse did not slack off. One moment it was skylined on the eastern topout, the next moment it went plunging down the side, out of sight, the sound of its hoofs vanishing nearly as quickly.

Mather got beside the buckskin, stepped

in, and swung up. The horse was shaken by the experience. Mather progressed up the western slope with care. From the north, he heard someone cursing a blue streak. Near the topout, Mather dismounted, then led his mount with caution. He stopped when he could see what was ahead, then hunkered down, cocked the carbine, and inched his way to the top.

Down below were several horses. One was hobbled but trying to crow-hop back down the arroyo to the south. The other horses stood like carvings, watching two men who were crouched over a third man.

Mather snugged up his Winchester and called out. "Stand up you sons-a-bitches! No guns, just stand up!"

The two men obeyed, their backs to Mather, their hands raised shoulder-high.

Mather raised his squinted eye above the carbine barrel, then, when recognition set in, called out: "Joe, turn around, boy!" Joe turned. Mather made a low groan. "What in the hell . . . ?"

Joe said: "Mind that chaparral, Bart! The other one's hid in there."

As Mather shifted his weapon, a man arose from among the chaparral that reached waist-high. It was Bowman. Mather gestured with the carbine for him to move.

"Go get with the others. Leave the pistol behind."

Joe lowered his arms. With everyone in view now, Mather addressed Joe. "Now you gonna tell me what in the hell . . . ?" He stood up with the cocked Winchester pointed down into the arroyo from which emanated the strong smell of smoke.

Joe pointed in that direction. "The runnin' iron's near the fire. Our hired hands had just turned a misbranded critter loose, when me and C.L. come onto 'em."

Each of Joe's words seared into Mather's head. He said softly: "Bowman an' Harper, for Chris' sake!"

Joe nodded, retrieved his Colt, and holstered it. He walked toward Mather, muttering: "Almost in the same place that they worked over the other one not long back."

Mather's brow slowly gathered into a frown. The shock was wearing off. He looked at Colley Bowman. "He pays you to do this?"

The other range man answered. "Two dollars for every one. We split it."

Bowman snarled. "Shut up, Harper."

Mather glanced at C.L. on the ground, asking Joe: "What happened to him?"

Before Joe had a chance to answer, Mather had knelt down at the Indian's side. There was blood on his upper right arm and chest.

C.L. touched the wound with his left hand. "Bullet miss. Rock hit."

Mather thumbed back his hat and leaned closer. There was a rip where the bullet had grazed him. Mather told C.L. to roll over. C.L. obeyed. There were no other wounds.

Mather stood up and extended one hand. When the Indian gripped it, Mather reared, and C.L. was yanked upright.

He went over by the horses, removed a canteen, and splashed its contents on the wound until it showed only fresh blood and a lessening of it. That accomplished, C.L. grinned at Mather, walked without haste toward Frank Harper, and hit him under the ear with a very brown, very hard fist.

Harper was staggered, but he didn't go down.

Joe shook his head and addressed Bart. "C.L. was huntin' down low. He saw 'em doin' what they'd done the other time. They must've been ridin' through the arroyo, found a little band, cut out the oldest calf with its mama, run off the rest, and burnt the circle CC on the calf. Couple months it'll be healed and weaned off its mama. You heard him. Crow pays 'em two dollars for every one they work over."

Mather faced Colley Bowman, the one he

had liked when he'd hired them on in town.

Colley smiled. "Didn't see you comin'," he said to Joe.

Mather nodded. "I expect you didn't. You shoot the Indian?"

"No. Frank seen him sneakin' up an' shot. Missed him, hit a big rock, an' a chip off the rock downed the Indian."

Mather turned away. "Where's the critter?"

"Run off with an old cow," Joe said, and took three steps to face Frank Harper and poke him hard in the middle of the chest with a rigid finger. "You shot May," he said, making it a statement instead of a question.

Harper took a backward step before speaking. "Wasn't me, Joe."

Joe turned on Colley whose smile seemed to have curdled. Colley said: "He's lyin', Joe."

Mather resolved the issue. "Hang 'em both. I was ten years old when I helped my pappy hang a rustler."

Frank Harper, who had taken his share of abuse, blanched, looking at Mather, the one man among the three whom he believed would lynch a man. He said: "Mather, I'll make a trade with you."

Mather looked at Harper without speaking. His expression was set in iron.

Harper cleared his throat before speaking.

"We can point out every critter of yours we branded."

Mather asked: "How many?"

Harper looked at his partner who answered for him. "Twenty-six head."

That shocked even Mather. "Twenty-six? How long you boys been at it?"

"Since before we worked for you. We met Colson in town a couple months back, an' he made the offer."

Joe, who had been listening in silence said: "What about our horses, Harper?"

"We run 'em northwesterly onto the edge of Colson's range. I'm sure they're still up there."

"Did you put Colson's mark on 'em, too?"

Harper shook his head. "Crow said not to."

Mather hitched around to lean on his horse. His back and ribs were paining him.

Joe sidled over and quietly said: "Let's take 'em home with us and get Forbes to come out and listen to their story."

Mather scowled. He had very little respect for the law. "Is that how you want to handle it, boy?"

When Joe nodded, Mather said: "What about the tomahawk?"

"He'll be all right. He can ride up yonder an' get his hurt looked after."

"We'll be short a horse, Joe."

The younger man grinned. "I'm sure Bowman and Harper'll agree that walkin's good for the soul, Bart."

The old man laughed.

Chapter Six

A Trail

A man can walk a fair distance with three inch undershot heels. They put Frank Harper out front, and he did well enough until the weight of his spurs began to bother him. He abruptly dropped down, removed the spurs, rose, and resumed walking, all without saying a word.

Colley was riding for the time being. He commented: "Farther'n I figured he'd make it."

Mather growled — "You're next." — and tipped down his hat.

As soon as they reached the Lazy J, Harper and Bowman veered off, went down through the barn to the old stone trough, shed their boots, and put their feet into the water.

Mather went over to the house. May was rocking on the porch. She smiled at him. "Them same two?"

Mather nodded and sat beside her. "Same

two. Colson gives 'em two dollars for each calf. C.L. got hurt."

"Bad?"

"No. He left us up there. By now he'll be home. May?"

"What?"

"He was huntin', must have seen 'em scoutin', and then come here to warn Joe."

"I figured something like that." Her smile faded. "We owe him, Bart."

He pushed himself up, making some kind of relenting sound, left the porch, and was back in the barn before he cursed under his breath. By now Joe had the Colson riders tied to a snubbing post. Mather stopped beside him and said: "Keep 'em overnight, then, in the morning, one of us can ride to town and bring Forbes back."

Joe nodded. The prisoners said they were thirsty. Mather got a bucketful of water from the trough and held it high enough for Harper and his friend to tank up. Afterward Colley said: "Thanks. I'd admire a smoke."

Mather's face was expressionless as he built two smokes, lighted each one, and plugged one into Colley's mouth.

Joe left Mather with the rustlers, went back over to the house where May was making supper, sank down at the kitchen table, and gave her a full recital, to which

May responded by nodding, never once interrupting to ask questions. Joe had just finished when Mather entered the kitchen.

Joe went to check in the cupboard. May had fortified herself. There was no more than a smidgen left in the kitchen bottle. He mentioned he'd have to bring in another bottle from the storage shed.

May passed behind his chair, ducked low, and kissed his cheek.

After they had eaten, Mather and Joe fed the prisoners, but it was Joe who returned the platters to the kitchen. Mather said he'd bed the two down before he went to bed himself. So Joe went to May's bedroom to keep her company. An hour later, he went to his own room, figuring Mather had bedded down at his house. It was a reasonable supposition, but incorrect. Mather had tied Harper in one of the barn's stalls, thrown a blanket over him, and taken Bowman to his cabin where they'd talked half the night away. When their conversation was finished, Mather said: "Boy, I got a pair of Oregon boots."

Bowman looked at the man old enough to be his father and said: "I'll be here. Good night."

He wasn't. Before dawn Mather prowled the barn, where he had loosely tied Bowman, the corrals, and the yard. He discovered that a horse was gone along with a saddle, the one that had belonged to Old Joe. A bridle and a blanket were also found missing from among the equipment.

Mather sat in the brightening dawn, working his first cud of the day. When Joe came down from the house, he smiled, stood up, winked, and said: "There's only one left that needs feedin'."

Joe took breakfast to Frank Harper, cursing himself for having trusted Bart. When he told May the younger of the rustlers had taken a horse and left in the night on Old Joe's saddle she said: "Coup." Joe saddled up and headed for town.

Before Joe reached Cumberland, he saw a pair of riders watching him from a brushy *barranca,* but rode past as though they were invisible. On the ride back with the constable he mentioned being watched by a pair of horsemen. Forbes's only comment was: "Tell me what happened. All of it, Joe."

Joe was in no hurry. The farther they rode and the more he watched Forbes listening, the more he was reminded of Old Joe. The choice of words, the variety of profanity, even the mannerisms. As they were nearing the yard, Forbes said: "Two peas from the same pod, boy."

Forbes told Joe he would talk to him later, leaving Joe to look after their animals. The law man went around to Mather's house, where he listened to an onslaught of vituperation for almost a solid hour. His visit with May was short. The time spent with Frank Harper even briefer. When he'd heard enough, he handcuffed Harper, helped him mount a horse, and led him out of the yard, east, in the direction of Cumberland.

Forbes was a good law man, who'd been trying to balance right from wrong for many years. He'd also been making judgments based on what was his version of justice — not what was lawful. He was crowding his fifties. His wife had died three years back, and there were times, increasingly so of late, when he thought back to the good years they'd had.

On the ride to town with his prisoner he didn't say but ten words. He just listened. Forbes had always been a good listener, but he'd gotten better at it lately.

By the time they reached town, dusk was settling. Forbes was tired, dog-assed tired. He left the horses with the liveryman, took Harper to the jailhouse, lighted an overhead lamp, and sat his prisoner down on a bench opposite his desk. He began asking questions that Harper appeared to answer as truthfully as he was able. When he could barely stay awake, Forbes locked Harper in one of the cells, the cleaner of the *juzgado*'s two, and sat, dozing in a chair in the increasing gloom until someone rattling the roadway door roused him.

Crow Colson was one of those successful 'breeds that exuded confidence. He nodded curtly, dropped down on the wall bench, and wasted no time. "I'm missin' two of my riders, Harper and Bowman."

Forbes viewed the large man stolidly. "How do you know they're missin'?"

"Because they didn't show up last night."

"Was they supposed to?"

Colson snorted. "When it's time to eat, range men just naturally come home." The big, heavy man leaned forward. "I got a feelin' they run into trouble with Joe Jessup's crew."

Forbes shifted in the chair. Of late long horseback rides bothered him. He pushed forward and did not so much as blink when he said: "I got one of 'em in a cell, Crow."

"Where's the other one, Emmet?"

"Damned if I know."

"You went out today . . . ?"

"I did. Young Joe had a run in with two men runnin' your iron on a Jessup critter."

Colson continued to look at the constable. "They lynched the other one?"

"Not that I know of." Forbes shifted again. "Crow, what's your riders doin' over on Jessup land?"

Crow got up. Sitting or standing, he was formidable. "You find that other one or I'll undertake to do it myself" — he stopped at the door, adding — "and there'll be hell to pay."

When the door was slammed shut, Forbes sat for a few minutes wagging his head, then he doused the light, and, after a decent interval, he headed for home. He hadn't gotten as far as the harness works when he paused in a recessed doorway and looked back. His side of the road was empty, but the opposite side had a solitary individual shagging him. As he watched, Crow Colson emerged from the saloon, whispered something into the ear of the shagger, and went back inside the saloon.

Forbes stepped out from the doorway and neither increased nor decreased his stride toward the cottage he and his wife had bought a few months after Forbes had signed on as Cumberland's community law man.

At home he was just getting settled when the unmistakable sound of a gunshot brought him straight up in his bed. With a hearty curse he slid into his britches, his boots, and was flinging into his shirt when someone with the lungs of a bull buffalo yelled. He was halfway down the hallway, heading for the door, when his nearest neighbor began pounding on the door, yelling: "Emmet! Get up! There's been a shooting!"

Forbes brushed the neighbor aside as he left the house, attempting a one-handed job of whipping the gun belt around his middle. As he turned the corner and encountered a small crowd in front of the saloon, he handled them in the same way, shouldering them aside. He stopped when a man he did not recognize caught him by the sleeve and cried: "Murder, Constable! Pure an' simple murder."

Forbes jerked free roughly and stopped. The dead man was a half yard from the boardwalk in front of the saloon, face down where he had fallen.

An old man jostled his way closer and flipped the downed man onto his back.

Several onlookers audibly gasped. One sounded breathless when he said: "For Chris' sake, it's Crow Colson!"

Forbes stood still, staring down. Even in poor light he was easily recognizable. So was the wet stain on his shirt front. It wasn't more than a half hour earlier that he had been visited by the corpse.

The local saloon man, Rory Murphy, teetered on the edge of the plank walk gazing at the dead man as he said: "There won't be many tears shed over this one, Emmet."

The conjecture as to who shot him started even as one of Murphy's late night regulars said: "I'd better fetch Eric. Can't leave him lyin' in the roadway an' all."

The constable raised his head. "You stay right where you are. Whoever did it was real close. All of you just wait a bit. Anybody see it happen?"

No one said a word. The saloon proprietor looked at Forbes. "You know us all."

Forbes faced slowly around. For a fact he did know them all. But once again he asked who had seen the killing. As before no one said a word.

One man left the small crowd, heading southward in the direction of the town carpenter who was also the local undertaker.

Forbes was gruff. "None of you saw it?"

A few heads were shaking, but not a word was said. Finally a tousle-headed range man few of the others knew well stepped forward and said: "He was outside talkin' to someone. I saw that much. There was a lull. He was turning to come back inside when he got shot."

"From outside?" Forbes asked.

The man couldn't answer this question, nor could anyone else. In that moment of silence a running horse was audibly heard west of town. As the onlookers concentrated on the sound, someone said: "He's goin' straight westerly!"

Rory Murphy was straightening his bar apron, when the man at his right side suggested: "Jessup place. Sure as hell he's dustin' it for the Jessup place."

That added substance to the diminishing sound of a horse being ridden hard.

A youth about the same age as Joe Jessup rode in from the north. When men cleared the way for him to get closer, he jolted forward, halted abruptly, and called out: "Pa!"

Someone volunteered a buggy. By the time it was fit to be used, the crowd had noticeably decreased.

Forbes helped boost the inert, heavy man into the wagon bed. Only Rory and three or four others were still in place. Forbes spoke briefly to Robin Colson, the younger son of Crow, on horseback, who nodded and led off northward with the light rig following. Forbes allowed himself to be carried along with the others back into the saloon. He heard at least a dozen theorists put forth how the killing had occurred.

Of one thing he was certain — now all hell would bust loose, for the Colsons would not take Crow's killing lightly. Vengeance would be sought, and not just by Harland, the elder heir, and Robin, but other members of the brood, including some still living down in Indian Territory.

He heard something that bothered him. Old Bart Mather had been in town. The clerk at the emporium was supposed to have said he had helped him at the store.

Forbes went to the store after breakfast the following morning, and the clerk, a fox-faced, thin individual, denied he'd ever said such a thing.

Forbes returned to the street, thinking that it made no difference whether the remark had been made by the store man or not, it would spread if for no other reason than that there was a long standing feud between the Jessups and the Colsons.

Forbes told a friend that what had been building up toward a shooting war would now come to a head the first time Mather or Young Joe appeared in town and encountered a Colson. The idea caught on, especially after the town blacksmith related that two freighters in his shop had ended an argument by wagering money that Mather would kill any Colson he met in town. With that precedent established, there were other bets made which, over time, had the effect of dividing Cumberland's wagering inhabitants into separate factions.

Forbes rode out to the Jessup place and had a long powwow with both Joe and Mather. Afterward, on the ride back, he had reason to feel as outraged as he'd felt on the ride out. Mather had made it plain that the killing of Crow Colson didn't make any difference and that any Colson he ran into would be in danger, in or out of town.

Next Forbes visited the Colson place where Harland met him in the doorway in a fierce mood. He had heard the rumor that Mather had been in town the evening Crow had been shot. His intention was to hunt Mather down and kill him, and he made no secret of it to the constable.

In town, at the general store, Forbes was stocking up on smoking tobacco when the clerk again vehemently denied starting the rumor about Bart.

Forbes smiled sourly, took his purchases over to the jailhouse, put all but one sack in a drawer, and tucked that remaining sack in a shirt pocket. He was building a smoke when Harland walked in, nodded once, and went to sit on the wall bench. Regarding the constable from an expressionless face, he said: "You know my cousin Gunn from down in the Territory?"

Forbes was lighting up when he nodded his head. He knew the Colson clan was extensive on both sides, Indian and white.

"He's comin', Mister Forbes. You've likely seen him. He comes up when we're ready to make a drive. Big feller, mostly Indian. Reservation policeman."

Forbes exhaled, looked steadily at the large, pulpy man, and said: "Are you tellin' me this to make me fret?"

Harland's round face with its thick features showed a hint of a sardonic smile. "We talked, Mister Forbes. We decided you might not be able to find the murderin' son-of-a-bitch. Gunn's the best they got down yonder for ferretin' out murderers. You an' him ought to work good together."

Forbes removed the quirley before he spoke. "That's decent of you folks, Harland, but I don't need a helper."

"Well, he's comin' anyway." Harland rose, pulled on a pair of doeskin roping gloves as he went to the door. Gripping the latch, he said: "You better find Crow's murderer, Mister Forbes."

After the door closed, Forbes went to the little barred window that allowed a decent view to the roadway and watched Harland Colson enter the general store. He built another smoke and lighted it. He knew something about reservation policemen, and he had no intention of permitting one of them to undertake the hunting of the man who had killed Crow Colson.

Later, up at the stage company's corral, he was invited into the office of the yard boss, Sam Blaise, a dark, hefty, unmarried individual with whom Forbes had struck up a friendship when he had first arrived in the Cumberland country.

Sam Blaise closed the door, motioned for the constable to sit. After Forbes sat down, the yard boss went to stand behind a littered table, saying: "Got somethin' that maybe don't mean anythin'." He paused. "But the night Crow Colson got killed, I was workin' late, and I heard the gunshot real clear." The yard boss leaned forward, picked something off his desk, and held it out for Forbes to take, which he did. The object was a spent .30-.30 caliber Winchester casing where the firing pin hadn't struck plumb center. Ideally, a rifle fired when it hit where it was supposed to strike, half on the bead of the bullet, half on the firing pin.

As Forbes was examining the casing, Sam Blaise spoke again: "I found it in the alley

. . . where my pole fence borders it. I can show you the exact spot." Blaise was eyeing the constable as he said: "Smell it."

Forbes did, looking at Blaise the entire time. "Any ideas, Sam?"

"No. But my Mex yardman said he saw someone come up the alley when he went out to pee. Said he couldn't make out much except that he was a limping feller and was carryin' a carbine."

Forbes stood up and pocketed the casing. "You don't mind?" he asked.

Blaise shook his head. "Figured to look you up an' give it to you. Forbes, he was one hell of a sharpshooter. From where he shot, a man could see the front of the saloon real good. But it's still a fair distance, an' it was dark." Blaise went over to open the door for his visitor. "How did he know Colson would walk outside?"

Forbes was passing outside when he smiled at his old friend. "I got no idea. Do me a favor, Sam . . . don't say anything."

"I won't. Emmet, let me know, all right?"

Forbes slapped Blaise lightly on the shoulder. He walked the full distance to the jailhouse, feeling better than he'd felt an hour or so earlier. He took his seat behind the desk to spend some time thinking.

The brass casing couldn't be incriminating by itself unless he could locate someone who owned a saddle gun with an off-center firing pin, and it might not mean anything even then. It was likely there was more than one rifle with a firing pin that struck off center. It also stuck in his mind that, if the rifle with the off-center firing pin belonged to the killer of Crow Colson, sure as hell was hot he wouldn't have ejected the casing where he had stood. The only time a person might do that was if he was too green to know the casing would be found, or unless he habitually levered up for a second shot. If Forbes were a greenhorn, he would go around town asking to see carbines. But he was many years past being that green. Nevertheless, the casing was all he had. Maybe the Mexican yardman could recall more than he had said. He decided to give it a try.

Forbes was preparing to head for the corral yard, when a rickety old man named Ben Bryan came into the jail, showed an uncertain smile, and went to the wall bench where he eased down seemingly surprised that he had made it.

Ben Bryan had a small fix-it shop where he repaired guns, honed knives, worked over tools, and was a regular at the saloon. He shifted around on the bench until he was comfortable. When he spoke, it was in a fading kind of faltering tone of voice. "About that feller that got himself shot. Crow Colson. . . ."

Forbes smiled. He was hopeful. Bryan's little shop was next door and north of the saloon. "Care for a drink, Ben?"

"Wouldn't mind at all."

Forbes dug out his private bottle, handed it over, and took it back when the old man had swallowed three times and cleared his throat to resume speaking.

Now, in a stronger voice, he said: "I think I might have shot him."

Chapter Seven

Dead-ends

They went up to the fix-it shop where Ben Bryan fussed with a coal-oil lamp until he had it lighted. He went behind the counter and fished around in the shelves and looked relieved when he found what he sought. It was an old wartime six-shooter with a barrel almost as long as a man's forearm. As he handed it to the constable, he said: "That there's my invention, Constable."

Forbes was holding the old gun respectfully. "What's that thing on the barrel, Ben?"

"Well, I been workin' on that there for years. Sometimes it works, sometimes it don't. Here, let me show you." Forbes handed Bryan the gun. The old-timer held the gun and strained, gasping, before the last three or four inches of the barrel came off. Bryan held it up looking sheepish. "It's an invention. You thread it on . . . like this. Now then, fire it, Constable."

Forbes put the old weapon carefully on the counter. "What happens?"

"Let me show you." Ben faced away in the direction of two cracker sacks half full of sand, and fired. One sack spewed its graying, flour-like contents. The sound was something between an empty bucket being dropped and what happens when a man kicks a punky log.

Bryan's forehead wrinkled. "Didn't do it, the son-of-a-bitch."

"What's it supposed to do?"

"Nothing. Hardly any sound at all. Like I told you, sometimes it works, other times it don't. It's not supposed to hardly make a sound." Ben Bryan grinned with embarrassment. "If that feller who shot President Lincoln had had my gun an' there wasn't no report after he fired, he would've likely got away, scotfree. Constable, I was testin' it the same time Colson got killed. That time it worked perfect."

Forbes picked up the gun, examined it more closely, and asked a question. "Which way were you aimin', Ben?"

"Well, toward the sacks."

"That'd be the wrong direction, Ben."

Bryan took back his old hogleg, looking crestfallen. "That's the hell of it, Mister Forbes. But imagine if my bullet had hit

Colson. I'd have 'em kickin' in my door to buy the idea."

Forbes had to down two-fingers of pop-skull before he could get away from the dingy little shop, but he wasn't disappointed. On his way home he imagined that someday someone would perfect Bryan's silent-shooting pistol.

He was still thinking of it the following morning when he arrived at the eatery later than usual. He sat down next to Frank Nicholson who asked about the Crow Colson killing.

Forbes shared with others in the Cumberland territory a deserved respect for the banker, so he listened to Nicholson's explanation about how the Jessups were going to lose their ranch because of a defaulted loan. Nicholson wasn't pompous, not quite, but he skirted mighty close to it.

The only topic on which they conversed of interest to Forbes was the killing of Crow Colson. He did not share any information beyond mentioning where the killer had waited in the west side alley, a remark that brought Frank Nicholson straight up at the counter. The banker seemed at least surprised, or maybe shocked, and said: "In the alley behind the corral yard! You don't say!"

The morning was passing quickly so

Forbes got some food at the café and took it over to his prisoner.

But Harper was gone. When Forbes reflected, he remembered that the keys to the cell door had been carelessly tossed atop his desk. He stood near the cell door and cursed. It had always been his custom to lock up from the outside when he left the jailhouse for any length of time. He hadn't had a prisoner in a long time and had forgotten to do so. Not that he would particularly miss Harper, but his escape would cause no end of disparaging comments.

Forbes went down to the livery barn. Upon checking, the proprietor said he wasn't missing any animal. Next the constable visited the corral yard where he found Sam Blaise profanely indignant over a missing saddle-broke mule. None of Sam's yardmen knew anything about the missing mule.

Forbes was as discreet as he could be as he continued to search for information. When he learned that two generally penniless teenagers had been spending money at the emporium, he tracked them down and got some interesting answers to the questions he posed. Harper had gotten the attention of the boys through the cell window and had offered them fifteen dollars if they'd steal a mount for him. They had complied, and Harper had paid them. They told Forbes the last they had seen of his prisoner was on the corral yard mule as he loped north out of town.

While mules had value and worthiness, using one to escape from town was not the best or fastest way to run for it. Forbes got his horse and left town by the west side alley, eventually veering east toward the coach road, and then north. Luckily a man didn't have to be a top-notch tracker to sift through roadway tracks for sign of a mule. Compared to a horseshoe, a mule's shoe is narrow and sometimes shorter. The only time he encountered a difficulty was when he encountered a four-mule hitch, otherwise, he was able to lope parallel to the single marks of a ridden mule.

He was worrying about ever closing the distance when he saw two riders. Before he was able to make a distinction between a ridden mule and a ridden horse, he neared the turn-off that led from the main road to the Colson ranch headquarters. In fact, he could just about make out the Colson buildings nestled in their setting of old trees.

Forbes figured the mule tracks would veer off from the main road, and he indifferently shifted his attention between watching the road and the dusty turn-off. Then he slackened to a stop. Two sets of shod horse tracks turned off in the direction of those distant buildings. The mule tracks continued northward. There wasn't even any scuffed sign where the pair of riders had paused to palaver with the man on muleback.

Forbes knew this country. The territory northward, on both sides of the coach road, was Colson cattle country as far as a man could see. Years back, a homesteader had filed on one hundred and sixty acres, and the Colsons had shot him up and burned what little he had built. So once again a man could ride for more miles than he could count and not see another set of buildings other than those owned by the Colsons.

Forbes rode ahead, watching the roadbed. He only left the road once, and that was when one of Sam Blaise's stages came forward in a dusty gallop.

The whip waved, eased his binders to a slower gait, and yelled: "Lookin' for a feller on a mule?"

Forbes yelled back. "Yeah. How far ahead?"

"Couple miles. Talkin' to some folks in a wagon."

Forbes eased over into an easy lope and held to it until he saw a wagon off the road in the distance with several people around it, along with a long-legged, long-eared animal wearing a saddle. He picked up the gait a little. He knew in open country he was as visible as the people with the wagon were to him. He yanked loose the tie-down thong over his holstered Colt, then placed the six-gun in his lap, uncocked but ready.

One of the people ahead flung around, vaulted onto the mule, and lit out up the road.

Forbes's mount was an old friend. He wouldn't risk chest foundering his horse to overtake one no good miserable son-of-a-bitch up ahead. Still, he was gaining, even though the mule was doing his best. Within another mile or so the race would end.

Forbes aimed high and fired twice. What happened next was totally unexpected, yet it explained something about the stolen mule, for it lunged ahead until it had the bit in its mouth, then it ducked its head and began bucking. Not just colty bucking, but genuine angry big mule bucking, left and right bucking. The rider lost his hat, then one stirrup, then both reins at which point he went off, both arms wide like a bird.

Forbes slackened to a walk, got close to the man struggling to get up, and aimed his six-gun.

Harper stood up, but unsteadily.

Forbes ordered: "Shed your gun!"

Harper made a helpless gesture, faced around, and called back: "Got no gun!"

"Go catch your mule. Bring him back. You try somethin' clever, an' I'll blow your head off. *Now get the mule!*"

The mule was busy picking grass as Harper came up to him. He allowed himself to be caught and led back.

As Harper tied up, Forbes snapped: "Shed those spurs!"

Harper followed orders. The mule permitted himself to be mounted, cocking his head as Harper climbed on. Apparently he wasn't the only mule that did not like spurs.

Forbes held the left side rein as they turned back.

At the wagon a man with coal black hair was waiting at the roadside.

Forbes asked: "You robbed 'em?"

"A little."

"Toss it to the feller, all of it, or I'll help them hang you from their wagon tongue."

Forbes heard the man with the coal black hair mutter something, and he caught some kind of thick accent. This made Forbes even angrier, and he growled at Harper: "Drop it. Everything you took an' more. *Drop it!*"

Harper emptied his pockets.

Forbes glared. "Turn the pockets inside out!"

The black-headed man scrambled about in the dust, talking fast as he worked at gathering what came out of Harper's pockets.

Satisfied, Forbes bobbed his head. He and his prisoner continued southward with the wagon man's strangely accented gratitude audible for a fair distance. They were within sight of Cumberland before Forbes said: "Where'd you think you were goin'?"

Harper was dirty and bruised. He spat his reply. "I'd've likely made it but for that damned mule."

Forbes let that pass. It wasn't important anyway. When they were on the edge of town he asked another question. "Colson pay you to kill May Jessup?"

Harper looked sullenly at the constable. "What difference would it make, what with him dead."

Disgusted, Forbes left the animals with the liveryman and herded his prisoner back to the jailhouse. This time, after locking Harper in the cell, he pocketed the key. He was turning away when Harper said: "You got no decent charge to hold me on."

Forbes grinned, said — "Good night." — and hadn't gotten ten feet when Harper spoke again. "When you goin' to feed me?"

This time the constable neither stopped nor answered.

Well before dawn the following morning Emmet Forbes took food and coffee to his prisoner. He had to stomp the bottoms of his boots to waken him. Forbes kicked at the cell's solitary piece of furniture other than the bed — a three legged stool near the door — and sat down to roll a smoke and wait.

Harper ate everything in sight, used a sleeve to wipe his face, finally saying: "Constable, I been thinkin'. . . ."

Forbes nodded, got up, scooped up the platter, and said: "I'll guess. You got a cache full of money, an', if I'll turn you loose. . . ." His voice trailed off as he locked the cell door from the outside.

Harper glared but tried again. "I got no cache, an', if I did, I wouldn't. . . . Listen, I'll make you a trade. You want to know who shot that Indian woman. It wasn't me."

Forbes looked past the steel slats. "Colley Bowman?"

"Nope, it wasn't him."

Forbes looked stonily at Harper. "There was only the two of you when she got shot. If it wasn't you or Colley Bowman. . . . ?"

"You want to trade, Constable?"

"I don't think so."

Back in the jailhouse office Forbes sat down and leaned back, a rising anger overcoming him. Maybe he should have told Harper he'd done his share of tracking. Harper was almost as stupid as old Ben Bryan who thought he had shot off his new-fangled gun, killing Crow Colson. Ben had fired from his roadway shop. The bullet that killed Colson had hit him in the back, not the front.

Forbes left town at sunup, rode all the way to the Jessup place before the folks out there had even finished breakfast. He accepted a cup of coffee from Mather, who advised him that Joe was in with May and that she was running another fever.

Forbes emptied the cup, put it aside, and followed Mather out to the porch. Mather offered him his plug, got a refusal, and gnawed off a cud for himself. Forbes sat down, looking out across Jessup land as far as he could see.

Mather said: "The Colsons ready for war?"

Forbes's reply was noncommittal. "Not that I know of."

"They should be. You got any idea who shot Crow?"

"No, I thought you might have."

Mather's face came around. "Why would

117

I know anythin' about it?"

"Was you in town?"

"No! Did somebody tell you I was?"

"No, I just wondered. He was shot from the alley behind the corral yard. That'd be in the direction someone from out here would come."

Mather shifted the cud, expectorated, and said: "I wouldn't have back-shot that son-of-a-bitch."

Forbes allowed the silence to go on for a spell before speaking again. "You 'n' Joe got reason, Bart."

The old man snorted. "Half the folks in the territory got reason to do that an' you know it."

"Where was Joe a couple of nights back?"

"In bed, as far as I know."

Forbes changed the subject. "You'll start gatherin' directly won't you?"

Mather frowned. "Directly I expect. What's that got to do with whoever shot Crow?"

"Nothing. Seems to me it's about your time of year to be bringin' 'em in."

Mather glared. "You rode all the way out here to ask questions that you know the answers to? Forbes, if you want me to, I'll help you run that ambusher down. I done that an' other things like it for a livin' for more years than you are old."

Forbes grinned and stood up. "You're not that old, Bart."

Mather interpreted Forbes's rising to mean he was readying to leave and so stood up himself.

Forbes said: "I'd like to see May."

Mather's gaze narrowed. "Come along, Emmet. If I didn't know better, I'd say you'd spent some time with Sam Blaise."

"Why would you think that?"

"Because since you been here, you haven't said much that made any sense. An' that don't make sense, neither."

Joe pushed himself out of the chair when the two entered the room. He nodded without smiling, and Forbes nodded back as he moved closer to bedside. May smiled up at him. Her eyes were bright, and her color was high. Forbes took her hand.

She squeezed his hand and said: "You could maybe bring doctor with you."

Forbes freed his hand. "You look pretty good to me, May."

"No! Thirsty, sweat. . . . You send him?"

"As soon as I get back an' find him."

Joe jerked his head, indicating it was time for Forbes to leave. They went through the parlor to the porch where Joe said: "It comes on her an' goes. She's healin' well, but she takes these fever spells."

Forbes gave Joe a light slap on the shoulder. "I'll send out the sawbones, if I got to search hell's half acre to find him."

Joe accompanied the constable to the barn. While Forbes was rigging out, Joe said: "I don't think it's the gun shot, Forbes."

They walked together outside the barn where Forbes said: "What else could it be, then? She's always seemed to me to be healthy as a bull."

Joe said: "Find him an' send him out . . . fast. I'd take it as a favor."

Forbes left the yard with the sun almost directly overhead. He made good time, considering the distance, and, after leaving his animal with the liveryman, he began his manhunt.

Dr. Leger was busy splinting the arm of a lad who had climbed a tree and fallen. Forbes whispered the reason for his needing him and waited outside until the doctor was ready to make the drive in his top buggy.

When Leger came out, he asked Forbes what it was exactly that was bothering May. Forbes explained to the best of his ability. Then he watched the buggy go lurching in the direction of the Jessup place.

Chapter Eight

"You Stay!"

When Dr. Leger reached the yard, Joe was waiting for him, pacing back and forth on the porch. No sooner had he stepped down from his buggy than Joe was at his side, ushering him into the house. May's fever had broken shortly after Forbes had departed, he was told by Joe.

May had made her own diagnosis. Whether it was good or bad, whether it was serious or not, where others argued, May smiled. Barry Leger returned May's smile as he opened his satchel and bent over her, saying: "Let's have a look-see at that wound." It took several minutes for the doctor to uncover the wound. Then: "May, it's healing. It was torn open pretty bad, but it's mending. So you've got to stay in bed . . . stay off your feet. If you keep busting it open, it'll never heal."

May's black gaze reflected the pain she felt as the Leger worked at cleaning the wound, sprinkling it with disinfectant powder that smelled like something dead.

When he was done with his ministrations, he pulled the chair around, and sat down. He said: "May, I don't know all that's been botherin' you, but, I can tell you, if you don't stop frettin', we're goin' to keep you abed until next spring. You've got to let Joe or Bart do things for you. Are you listenin' to me, May?"

Her reply showed how much she had been listening. "Who shot Crow?"

Leger rolled his eyes and picked up his satchel. "You'll have to take that up with Constable Forbes. I'm a doctor." He closed the door gently behind him and went in search of Bart. When he couldn't find him, he had to settle for Joe who was in the smithy taking the warp out of a buggy wheel.

Joe damped down the forge, sat on the anvil, and looked eye to eye with Leger. "She gets up in the night," Joe said. "That's none of my business, so I go back to sleep."

"Boy," Leger said, "you and Bart got to fix it so's she don't have to leave the bed."

"How, Doc?"

"Damned if I know. Ask Bart. I got to get back to town."

The smithy shed, like most structures of its

kind, had three walls, none in front. Joe continued to sit on the anvil while he watched the top buggy leave the yard, wheel to the right, and hold steadily to its eastbound course.

Some time later Joe rigged his horse and rode out, looking for Mather. From inside the house, May watched him leave through the partly opened front door.

Joe was a good sign reader, something else his pa had taught him. But, this day, Joe couldn't find Mather. The places where the old man ordinarily rode, almost invariably with some kind of shade nearby, had no sign of anyone having ridden past in days. Whenever he came across fresh tracks, he would follow them, but none turned out to be Bart's trail.

He was thirsty, as was his horse, so Joe went off course in the direction of a piddling little warm water creek known as Old Camp Creek. Like most watercourses Old Camp Creek was in the bottom of a swale with creek willows for two thirds of its full length. There were game trails and cattle trails going down into the swale on both sides of the creek and an abundance of readable tracks of both wild and domestic animals. Joe didn't bother to read sign; he rode directly by the shortest route. It led him around a side hill, joined with an even older more commonly used trail, and debouched where the side hill began to slope off and the north-south trail picked up. There Joe found sign. There was also a fair-size scattering of trees, mostly creek willows, although farther out one could see oaks — white oaks and black oaks.

He instinctively looked ahead and to both sides. He even checked to the north where the side hill sloped higher in that direction. Although he failed to look southward, his horse did, and he began veering slightly in that direction. There was no trail or fresh shod-horse sign in the dust. Joe irritably corrected the route. His horse obeyed. It was a matter of indifference to the animal whether he went north or south as long as they got home by feeding time. So the horse plodded along on a loose rein, until, all in a moment, he suddenly jammed to a stiff-legged halt, his head jerking up with a snort. Joe had no time to yank loose his tie-down or draw his gun. The animal scent Joe's horse had detected moments earlier came out of the thick creek willows, head, whithers, and shoulders emerging, looking as round-eyed and startled as Joe and his mount were.

Now, with an opportunity, Joe still didn't

reach for the tie-down. He had recognized the horse, and would have recognized it even without the bloody-hand insignia on the left shoulder and the forelock braided into a warlock.

He called: "C.L, what'n hell you doin' this far out?"

The lithe buck pushed clear of a clump of willows. "You alone?" he asked.

"Yeah. Why?"

"Get down. Come with me?"

Joe dismounted but remained beside his horse. "What is it?"

"Come! Follow me!"

Joe looped his reins and followed the Indian. It was a fair hike up, heading northward, staying at creek side all the way. When C.L threw out a rigid arm, Joe heard a man say: "All right, when you're ready."

A few more steps and Joe saw a large man mounting a horse. He watched as the man raised his right arm in a high salute and burst over into a lope. Joe almost spoke, but C.L., as if reading his mind, signaled for silence. Joe crept forward a few steps. It became easier to see a second man, also massively built but not as tall, turn a horse and mount, ducking low as he worked his way toward open country on the creek's west side. Joe crept forward to get a better view, as the man ducked and twisted in the saddle to avoid thickets. The rider turned to his left. At that instant Joe had no difficulty recognizing him, screwed up face or not. It was Bart.

Joe held his breath, not knowing what to do. He could not go back the way he had come without being detected, nor he could ride ahead and brace Mather. But for the old man's sake, he decided to backtrack quickly, so he nodded a farewell to C.L. Running light-footed and carefully, he remained stooped until he got to his horse. Then he rode hell-bent for home.

The distance was considerable and the day was waning, but he made good time. He cared for the horse and scrubbed up before heading for the main house. He was sitting in the parlor when he heard a horse gallop in. It wasn't long before Mather's spurs echoed on the front steps and then the porch. He turned to go to May's bedroom when she appeared soundlessly in the kitchen doorway, smiling.

"I go," she said conspiratorially and disappeared in the direction of her bedroom.

At the same time Mather stomped into the front room, grunted a hasty greeting, and headed for the kitchen. When Joe entered the room, Mather was at the water bucket, drinking dipperful after dipperful. He looked up at Joe and said: "Didn't find a single damned sore-footed damned critter. Not a blessed one."

Joe spoke to the back of the old man. "They're out there. Come next spring a third of the cows will come up dry. Bart?"

"Yes."

"Can you go look in on May? I got a feelin' she gets up an' around a lot more than we know."

After Mather left the kitchen, Joe hunted down the kitchen bottle. He found the recently replaced bottle half empty. He tipped it back and swallowed twice. He had to suppress a coughing fit while replacing the bottle. He could hear Mather and May laughing in the back of the house. He put together an unappetizing supper which he and Mather ate in the kitchen together, May having said she was tired and not very hungry. Joe tried to start up a conversation, relaying that Doc Leger had insisted May needed to keep to her bed.

That drew a sly look from Mather who said nothing while he pretended to eat, pushing the food around on his plate with his fork. All he finally said was that he'd try to find some critters tomorrow and that they'd have to find men to replace Harper and Bowman, at the least, before beginning the gather.

Joe, mindful of what had happened the last time Mather had gone to Cumberland alone, said he wouldn't mind riding along.

Mather didn't answer. He didn't have to. Anyone knowing the old man recognized that narrow eyed, locked jaw expression that said plainly: "Don't even try it."

Joe kept his face lowered as he filled his mouth and vigorously chewed.

May called out. Mather, now busy eating, ignored it, so Joe went. As he entered the room, May held out one hand that was obviously holding something. Joe walked over to the bed.

May said: "For you. Take it!"

As Joe took the object, Mather appeared in the doorway. Not moving an inch, Mather hissed: "Gawd-damned Indians. Like shadows they are. Skulkin' around an' not gettin' seen." He walked to bedside, next to Joe.

Joe held up what May had placed in his hand. Mather made a rattling sigh. "C.L.! Damn him, anyway. Why didn't he give you that thing when we were up at the *ranchería?*"

May looked at Joe, smiling softly as she said: "She make you good woman."

Mather leaned in close to Joe's face, whispering: "We got enough trouble. Now the Indians are buyin' in. Boy, did you encourage her?"

Still not having said a word, Joe reddened as he carefully tucked the small beaded object into his shirt pocket and looked straight into Mather's face. "I never promised her anythin'. She just upped and took it for granted."

May fixed Bart with her obsidian black gaze and did not smile. "He ready. She fine for him. She Blue Barrel granddaughter. It fixed long ago, Bart."

The old-timer responded gruffly: "It's not right, May."

"It right. Old Joe say many time it right. Bart, you know he say Donna right for boy!"

At this Mather stormed out of the room. The mother and son heard the porch door slam shut.

May's smile came back, a tad more radiant.

Joe said: "What am I supposed to do?"

"Go up yonder. Make long sing. I teach you." May paused, her smile dimming slightly. "You want this, Young Joe?"

His gaze went to the small window through which someone had probably passed the totem, then back to her face. May was a handsome woman. Once she had been a beautiful girl. He smiled.

May brightened. "Good. I teach you."

"But not tomorrow. I'm goin' to town with Bart to find a couple men for the gather."

"Day after. You come here, by me, day after tomorrow."

Joe kissed her cheek and went to the yard. He found Mather at the barn. Mather kept his back to Joe until he finished what he was doing, then he faced around.

"Did you look at her wound?"

Joe was shocked. "No. That's between her 'n' the doctor."

"Sit down, boy."

Joe obeyed, sitting on the empty nail keg.

Mather grinned, got a fresh chew pouched, expectorated once, and said: "You don't need to go to town with me in the morning."

Joe's expression was wooden. "Two're better'n one, Bart."

"There won't be no trouble, boy."

Joe's retort was bone dry. "No. Not if there aren't any Colson folks in town. Can I ask something, Bart?"

"What?"

"Who did you meet out at Cow Camp Creek?"

Mather's jaw stopped working. His stare

at Joe was unwavering. "What're you talkin' about?"

"Bart, I saw you. I saw somebody with you . . . but not his face."

Mather went slowly in his explanation. "It was one of those new fellers who ride for the Colsons. He was scoutin' along the lower timber country for Colson strays."

Joe squirmed. Wooden kegs did not make for the most comfortable seating. He stood up and said: "C.L. was snoopin' around, too."

Mather heaved a sigh. The topic had been changed. "I told your pa, boy. I told him a dozen times you shouldn't be too friendly with those tomahawks."

Exasperated, Joe said: "I'll ride with you tomorrow."

"No!" Mather protested. "You heard what that medicine man said, boy. Someone's got to mind May. She's movin' around too much, an' it's not good for her. She'll rip open that wound. You mind the place. I'll be just fine."

Joe nodded. "Like the last time?"

Mather ended the discussion by abruptly turning and heading for his cabin.

Joe watched until Mather was out of sight, then he removed his hat and proceeded to the stalls to hunt for eggs. While groping about in the straw, Joe considered that Bart was most likely right about May. For a fact she was up and about whenever left alone. And doing what? Who knew? Once Joe had a hatful of eggs, he dropped them off in the kitchen, and headed for bed.

By dawn light Mather had done it again. Having been neglectful of his chores, Joe was busy at them when he noticed Mather's saddle was gone. He violated the old man's privacy by going to his shack. Inside, he found that the carbine boot that usually hung from a set of buckhorns was gone, along with the Winchester that had been in the boot.

While leaving the cabin, Joe did something he rarely did, he cussed a blue streak. He worked his anger out, and, once the chores were completed, he looked in on May. May asked about Bart. Joe's answer was dourly given. "Rode to town to hire a couple riders."

May smiled. "Maybe better'n last time."

"Yeah. Ma, was it C.L. who brought the totem?" She nodded, so he said: "You didn't tell him we was goin' to commence gatherin', did you?"

"Told him. Your pa did that. He liked their help."

Joe said — "Son-of-a-bitch!" — and May's

smile disappeared. Anything else she might have been willing to share was forgotten. Joe stamped out of the house.

He clumped to the trough to duck his head and clear his brain. The gut-shot bull was on the other side, also drinking. He raised a dripping snout, staring at Joe. He had been tracking a little better the last few days, but he still flinched if he turned. This time he did not turn; his face remained about a foot from the water.

Joe drank, straightened up, and said: "How d'you feel, you ugly big hunk of wolf bait?"

The bull took two backward steps, dropped his head low, and made a deep, throaty sound almost like a growl.

Joe turned back toward the barn, saying: "You won't be tryin' to find young heifers for a while."

He brought forth a tall, leggy bay horse with a skimpy mane and tail, cross-tied him, and went to work saddling and bridling. It was cool in the barn, cool and fragrant. Years back, when he would climb to the loft to cry, May would always find him, hold him close, and croon a Paiute song to him. Today there was no song, and he did not see her in the shadows out front until she spoke.

"Joe! You stay!"

He looked over the saddle seat at her. She wasn't smiling, and she was using a knobby cane Old Joe had used near the end of his life.

Joe didn't speak. He couldn't think of what to say.

She came inside where the shadows made her look larger and darker. "Son, you listen. It already happened. Whatever it was. It already happened. Joe, your father tell me once, long time ago . . . Bart fastest best shot he ever seen. Joe, you stay with May. Very sick now."

He stood with the tag end of the latigo in his hand, looking at her and still not knowing what to say. She repeated her words. Joe unlooped the latigo, lifted off the saddle, and upended it on the ground. May came up to the horse, used one hand to un-buckle the throatlatch, slipped off the bridle, and faced him. Then, with slight dif-ficulty, she turned back. She got as far as the doorless opening before she stopped to look back. Feeling somewhat ashamed, Joe joined her.

As they crossed very slowly toward the house together, he said: "There's trouble coming, Ma. I had ought to be there with Bart." He helped her up the steps and held the door for her to enter first and spoke again. "You'll be bleedin', Ma. Set down. I'll get us somethin' to eat."

She smiled, sat in Old Joe's rocking chair with Old Joe's knobby stick between her knees. "Men don't cook. You no better."

Joe paused in the kitchen doorway. "I don't know how to make them blueberry cakes."

May hoisted herself out of the chair. "I show you," she said, and pushed past him into the kitchen. Joe followed her. As she worked, she talked. She was trying to keep his mind occupied, and he knew it. To the north, a bitch coyote sat back and sounded. He went to the window, but he could not see her.

May sat down on one of the kitchen chairs, telling Joe to eat. She mentioned the girl, explained about the feather token. She made him laugh as he ate.

They were sitting on the porch, the sun blood red and sinking, as a wagon appeared over the hill heading toward the Lazy J. The same thought came to them at the same time — *Bart had ridden to town; he hadn't taken a wheeled rig.*

May remained in her chair, expressionless, while Joe went to the porch railing and leaned out. It was a light wagon owned by somebody in town; Joe had seen it there many times. Squinting, Joe could now make out that a man on horseback was on the off side. It seemed from that distance that neither the mounted man nor the one driving the wagon was talking. Overcome by curiosity, Joe left the porch and stood clear of the steps until the horseman saw him and raised an arm. Joe didn't return the salute.

May said — "He don't go to log house. He stay in this house." — making Joe even more curious because he still hadn't identified the men.

The horseman loped ahead, and pulled up shy of Joe by a few feet. Immediately Joe recognized Jem Whitmore. He addressed Joe, unaware that May was sitting on the porch: "We tied him off as best we could."

At this point May stood up and used her stick to prop open the door as the dray wagon made a wide circle of a turn, hauling to a stop close to the porch steps. The driver, who it turned out was Barry Leger, got out, handed Joe his little satchel, and went around to let down the tailgate.

Whitmore tied up nearby, seeing May for the first time as he studied the house. Now he spoke to her. "May, didn't see you there when I come in. So where do you want him?"

May gestured toward the open doorway.

Whitmore joined Dr. Leger at the back of the wagon. Belly wedged against the open tailgate, he began pulling gently at a bundle of blankets that contained Bart. "Doc, stand clear," he said, as he jumped up into the wagon.

Mather's unsteady, feeble voice instructed: "Jem, mind that second step. It's loose."

Whitmore maneuvered Mather to the edge of the tailgate, jumped out, and then lifted him out of the wagon, blanket and all. Joe, who had felt paralyzed through the whole process, moved in beside the two. "Is he bad off, Jem? What happened?"

Whitmore answered almost scornfully. "Him? Hurt bad? Boy, I've known him to be hurt worse an' not even stop cussing." He climbed the steps.

May pushed back to provide room for Jem. "Joe's room," she told him as he brushed past, twisting sideways to clear the doorjamb. She then called: "Joe! Get the bear grease!"

Whitmore carried Mather to Joe's room, easing him down gently onto the bed. The doctor followed them while Joe went to find the bear grease. Leger looked at May, shaking his head with disgust having discovered her out of bed. "Woman, what did I tell you? Dumb damned Indian." As Leger shuffled through his medicine bag, he snapped at Whitmore: "Get rid of that stinking blanket!" Joe arrived just in time to have the doctor shout at him. "Boy, light a lamp. Light two, if you have them."

Confused, Joe watched as the doctor leaned over Mather. "I told you," Leger said to his patient who seemed lost among the blankets that still covered him, "didn't I? We made it, didn't we?"

Mather replied through clenched teeth. "Damned old pill pusher, it's wearin' off."

"All right. Boy, get a cup of water and bring that satchel over to me. Bart, I'm going to give you enough medicine this time to help you sleep through the night."

Mather's arm raised up as he mumbled: "May?"

"Here, Bart."

"Fetch the bottle from the kitchen," he said.

As May turned, the doctor caught her by the arm. "No!" he said to her, and then to Mather: "No whisky. Do you hear me, Bart?"

"You scrawny old rack of bones. What is it?"

"Maybe later. In the meantime, you got to get cleaned up. Hot water."

May responded before any of the others. "Joe, we make water hot."

Leger shot May a look and said: "You should be in bed." He paused, sighing. "Just don't carry anything heavy, May," he added, knowing it was useless to try and stop her from doing what she wanted.

As May neared the door, Mather managed to raise his head and his voice. "May! No female woman's going to give me no bath!"

Chapter Nine

A Long Night

Doc Leger had to get back to town. Outside, by his rig, he handed Joe a small bottle. "You douse her with this . . . same goes for Bart."

Joe took the bottle, paying little attention to it. "How bad's Bart hurt?"

"Not bad . . . except a man his age hurts harder an' longer than a feller your age."

"What happened?"

"He was at the saloon lookin' for riders to hire, an' some dark 'breed-lookin' feller half his age knocked him down and put the boots to him before the others could haul him off. He'll be all right . . . give him time." Leger settled onto the wagon seat before adding: "May looks better. But she's limpin' bad, boy. You better make her stay in bed. That medicine ought to keep them both quiet for a day or two. Get Bart cleaned up before he falls asleep."

Joe nodded as the medicine man wheeled

around and headed out of the yard. *Keep May in bed? Get Mather cleaned up,* Joe thought to himself. *Now there's a couple of tall orders.* He headed back inside, where he found May tending to the water that was heating up. She smiled as he passed through the room to look in on Bart.

Mather glared when Joe appeared in the doorway. "What's she doin'? No damned female woman gives me no all-over bath."

Joe pulled a side chair to the foot of the bed. "You should've waited, Bart."

"Why? So's that son-of-a-bitch could overhaul us both?" Mather pulled up to a sitting position, resting his back against the bed's headboard. "I could use a drink," he stated, a smirk crossing his face. "You'll find a bottle in my house at the bottom of the wood box."

May slipped soundlessly into the room. Mather gripped the blankets as he said: "You ain't givin' me no bath. I'm fine just as I am. Give me a day or two an' I'll be good as new. Joe, you tell her!"

May came to bedside and brought out her hand that had been hidden behind her back. It held a full bottle of whisky. "Big medicine," she said.

Now where in tarnation did she get that? Joe thought to himself.

Mather grabbed the bottle with both hands, pulled the stopper out with his teeth, and drank deeply. He bawled like a bull steer, tears streaming from his eyes, and handed back the bottle.

Knowing it was a little late, Joe said: "Doc don't want him to have any, May."

She left the room as soundlessly as she'd entered.

Mather watched her and then scowled. "She's limpin' worse, boy."

Joe ignored that remark to ask a question. "Which one mauled you, Bart?"

"That Colson from the reservation. Gunn. Darker'n most of the others. Mean fella."

"What got him going?"

"Didn't need a reason, boy. I've seen him on an' off over the years. He's comes up to help the Colsons during gathering." Mather's eyes closed momentarily. When his eyes snapped open, he smiled at Joe and said: "I recall that when your pa was younger, he could whip a passel of them Colsons. One time he put Crow down in the middle of the road, right in front of the saloon. Whupped him until he couldn't get up."

At this point Whitmore entered the bedroom. It was a fair-size room, but he made it seem smaller.

Mather said: "What took you so long?"

The big man wagged his head. "I didn't know you was in town. Didn't know nothin' till I heard about the fight."

May stepped through the doorway. "Water hot," she said. "Joe, you help." As he walked toward her, she asked: "Doctor give you blue bottle?"

Joe nodded, then the two left the room, leaving the pair of old men alone.

When Joe brought the pan of water into the room, Whitmore took command. He sent Joe out of the room, and gently bathed Mather, something he himself could not recall ever having done inside a house. Men like Whitmore and Mather rarely bathed in wintertime; they generally used creeks when the weather was temperate.

After Joe gave May a dose of the medicine that Leger had left behind, she went to her bedroom, saying she was tired. Whitmore, having finished washing Bart, found a couple of Indian blankets and rolled up in them like a cocoon in the same room with Mather. Joe bedded down in the front room. Lately May had cost him sleep. Now with another one bedded down Joe expected additional interruptions.

Joe fell into a heavy sleep. So heavy that it took several minutes before he realized that someone was yanking at him, at his blankets. Slowly he made out May's bulky silhouette. She was in an agitated condition, and she hit him twice with her cane. He looked around; it was as dark as the inside of a boot. As his mind cleared, he realized that May was clipping off her words in the manner in which she had done years earlier when Old Joe had been teaching her English. "What in the . . . ?" he mumbled, groping for his britches and shirt as he tried to orient himself, finally recalling that he had gone to sleep in the parlor.

"Listen out window," she whispered.

Joe obeyed, approaching the window at the same time Whitmore appeared soundlessly in the doorway, cocked six-gun in his fist. He snarled at Joe: "Get down! You want to get killed? Get down 'n' stay down."

"There!" May rasped, using her stick as a pointer.

Joe, crouching beside the window now, risked a peek out and saw nothing. Whitmore slid in next to him and nudged him aside. With the moon shining in, Joe swore he could see Whitmore's ears perking up, listening. After a long moment, Whitmore muttered: "In the middle of the night for Chris' sake!"

Joe edged in closer, positioning himself next to Whitmore.

Whitmore yanked him by the shoulder. "You deef, boy?"

Then Joe heard it, too.

More dismayed than before, May cried: "They come here. They burn us out."

Whitmore turned even more gruff. "They're not comin' here," he stated, turning to face May. "Don't worry, May." Then he grabbed Joe's arm, saying: "Come with me. If you got a gun, fetch it."

Joe got his gun. As the two headed for the door, May stopped them. "Jem, what they want?" she said.

"You deef, too, May? Somebody's running off cattle. Know how to use that gun, boy?"

By the time they reached the barn and got rigged out, the sounds, like reverberations telegraphed in the ground rather than an actual sound that could be heard, had stopped. Whitmore stood with reins in one hand, facing north, rigid. He turned. "Be sunrise before we pick 'em up, boy. You want to try anyway?"

Joe nodded, even though he felt nervous about leaving May and Bart alone.

They left the yard in a fast walk, and were out of sight of the buildings before Whitmore signaled his horse into a lope, holding to it, except when he would halt, cock his head, and indicate their direction with an upraised arm. Then he let Joe come up even with him and leaned out of his saddle to comment: "They can't keep this up much longer . . . horses run, but cattle sort of stumble along."

Joe bobbed his head once, signifying his agreement, and they resumed traveling eastward. They held to that course as the faint shade of predawn gray emerged before them. It was at this promise of another day, that Joe's eyes caught something. He stood in his stirrups and shouted: "Jem!"

"I see 'em, boy," was the calm reply. "Slack off."

They continued their pursuit at a walk. They did not gain which meant the cattle were moving along at about the same gait. Joe strained to see the riders among the herd but failed.

Whitmore turned toward Joe, and in the beginning of light he looked thirty years younger. The old man said — "Hold up, boy." — and reined to a halt, sitting straight up and gazing to the north. Not until he pointed did Joe see a lame critter that had stopped, head down, in a thicket. Whitmore led off.

At sight of men on horseback the lame animal started to break out the far side. Both riders eased around and met the critter head on. It was two-thirds in view.

"Face her, boy. Don't let her bust loose," Whitmore warned, as he worked his way toward the thicket. He rode, leaning far to one side. The moment no one was blocking the animal in front, it went hobbling away.

Whitmore was sitting with slack reins as Joe approached and said: "We can drive it back."

Jem's answer was curt. "No need, boy. It's a steer, an' it's wearin' Colson's mark."

Joe watched the disabled animal stumble toward the northeast. "It happens every year," he said. "Colson strays on our range."

Whitmore eased forward and leaned back, getting resettled, and said: "It don't make sense, boy, drivin' cattle at night, an', besides. . . . Ah, never mind, we'll talk it over with Bart soon enough."

For now, Joe had to accept that, and nothing more was said between the two as they worked their way back home. Once there, they cared for their animals before trooping over to the main house, the sun being delivered above the horizon like the effort of a dog passing a peach seed.

May was in the kitchen, her hair straggly, her old bathrobe loosely cinched at the waist. Because they only nodded at her, she traipsed after them to the bedroom.

They found Mather up, washing in a large bowl of water May had brought him. He looked up, snorted, reached for a towel, and spoke through it. "Wolves again, Jem? I told Joe's pa years back we got to clean them outta the country."

Whitmore was patient. "Riders takin' cattle easterly."

Mather was shocked. "In the night? What the hell for?"

"Bart, they was Colson-marked."

"Strays . . . all right, but why at night?"

"Want me to guess? Because they wasn't Colson's long-yearlings. They was probably doin' what some big calves'll do . . . drift back where they was raised."

Mather held the towel in both hands, staring.

Whitmore continued: "You sure as hell knew they've been using running irons on Jessup cattle. You had to know that."

"Well, now 'n' then, I expect. Anyone can afford to lose a few head."

Whitmore yanked the chair around, dropped down on it, and glared. "A few head, you say! There was at least thirty critters in that bunch."

Mather reacted to his old friend's annoyance with his own variety of irritation. "An' tell me, just how do we prove anythin'?"

Jem relaxed before answering. "It can be done. Colson's not the first person to use a runnin' iron."

"Prove it? How?"

"Some two weeks back you caught two, didn't you? What'd you do with their runnin' iron?"

Mather looked toward Joe. "You got it, boy?"

"No, but I can find it where it got thrown when we was riding back," Joe answered, then looked at Jem.

Whitmore announced — "Let's get some breakfast first." — then he laughed as he added: "Hell, I could eat me a whole Colson steer."

"I'll go help May fix somethin'," Joe stated, when he didn't catch anybody else volunteering.

As soon as Joe had left the room, Whitmore lit into his old friend. "What's the matter with you? I'd've hung those two you caught. So would've Old Joe. So, how do you feel? Well enough to ride?"

The confused look on Mather's face as he sat down on the edge of the bed made Whitmore shoot up to his feet. "I'll go with the boy. You 'n' May stay home, swap groans."

Mather sat straight up and said: "I'll get dressed. Let Joe stay with May." He pushed forward and reached for the floor with both feet, but hung there unable to catch his breath. Then he sank back, cursing a blue streak.

"Bart," Whitmore began, feeling sorry for his long-time friend, "you let this get out of hand. They've just about put the Jessups out of business. We'll eat, head out, and be back directly."

When May brought Bart a plateful of scrambled eggs to eat a half hour later, he snarled at her: "Where did they go?" He glared when she didn't respond. "Ah, never mind that. Help me get up."

May put the platter down on the chair and said: "No! You stay there! You get hungry. Eat this."

Mather was too weak to get up, and he shouted — "May!" — when she left the room, closing the door behind her. "Damn," he muttered as he settled back into the bed. "Damn that woman."

Pausing once to catch her breath on the way to the porch, May had barely situated herself in the rocking chair when she saw a pair of riders. Even from this distance she could see that one was massive. Realizing they weren't headed in, she sat back. Her hip, which had been healing well enough, was no longer doing so, and every move caused her pain. The cane helped but little.

She drifted off, Joe having given her a healthy dose of the medicine from the doctor before leaving. She was still sitting there when a solitary rider appeared from the direction of Cumberland. As he approached, she recognized him. His name was Percy Sullivan, and he had been friends with Old Joe for years. He was both a cattle buyer and an agent for the railroad company. He also sold land for the railroad. May was truly surprised. Sullivan hadn't come by since her husband's funeral. She pushed herself up with the help of the cane as soon as he signaled his arrival by raising an arm upon entering the yard. May waved back.

As he approached the steps, after tying up his horse, he removed his hat, beating it against his leg, making the dust fly. "What you doin' with that cane, May? You been sick?"

She smiled. "Got shot."

Sullivan stopped. After a speechless moment he said: "Shot? How . . . ?"

She explained, and after that she brought him up to date on everything else that had gone wrong recently.

As May talked, Sullivan sat in squinty-eyed silence. When she had finished, Sullivan nodded and said: "All right if I go see Bart?"

May actually laughed. "You go. Plenty cranky. In Joe's room." She remained on the porch when Sullivan went inside.

On his way through the house Sullivan observed the tidiness maintained by May in spite of her injury. At the door he paused, steeling himself against Mather's temper. Before the door was even cracked open several inches, he was bombarded with Mather's anger.

"Help me with these gawd-damned britches!"

Sullivan considered Mather a moment, then moved toward the bed. "Get your dang' carcass back into that bed before I do it for you!" he commanded.

Although Sullivan could tell Mather was poised to argue, he didn't. Meekly settling himself back under the blankets, Mather said: "I expect May told you 'bout the goings on around here."

Sullivan eyed the chair but remained standing. "She did. Bart, sure as God made green apples, them Colsons are tryin' to do in the lot of you."

Mather was sarcastic. "How'd you ever

figure that? Percy, where you been the last year or so?"

Sullivan pulled out the chair before speaking. "That don't matter. The constable in town told me Jem come out this way."

"He an' the lad'll be back directly."

"Who's behind it, Bart? I heard in town Crow Colson got himself killed."

"He did. Shot in the back in the middle of the road out front of the saloon. Jem was supposed to get him, but never got the chance. Jem thinks it's one of his own clan likely done it."

"Where's Jem?"

"I just told you . . . him 'n' Young Joe'll be back directly."

Percy Sullivan rubbed his hands together and leaned forward. "You stay in that bed. I'm hungry, and I smell something good cookin' in the kitchen. I'll be right back. You hungry?"

Mather growled — " 'Tain't!" — and turned his back.

"Now you stay in there, you hear me?" Sullivan reiterated as he left the room. He found May in the kitchen, turning some sputtering bacon in a fry pan on the cook stove. Pulling out a chair, he returned May's smile.

They talked as May cooked and Sullivan ate.

★ ★ ★

It was the early evening hour, and Sullivan, having cared for his horse, had joined May on the porch. They were enjoying each other's company in spite of the silence, or maybe because of it, when Joe and Whitmore returned.

The greeting of old friends was rough and hearty. They took care of the horses and were seated, talking on the porch, when Joe handed Sullivan the running iron he and Jem had found that day and had stashed by the steps before sitting down.

Sullivan took it, hefted it with both hands while examining it. When he spoke, he addressed Whitmore. "Someone's runnin' iron?"

As Whitmore replied, he looked in May's direction. "A Colson runnin' iron, Percy." He turned his attention to Joe, saying: "I bet you're as hungry as me, boy. Why don't you help May put something together."

Joe stood up, nodding as he helped May to her feet. "Ma, just tell me what we got, I'll cook while you keep me company."

Whitmore pushed out his long, muscular legs, staring at his boots as he told Percy Sullivan what he knew and what he suspected. Sullivan listened, turning the running iron in his hands as he looked steadily at Jem. "Percy, Old Joe's gone, May got herself bushwhacked, and Bart's . . . well, Bart's old. That leaves me 'n' the boy. Them Colsons is a *coyote* bunch. My guess is that, what with the Jessups being taken down in one way or another. . . . Percy, you know them Colsons. They. . . . Ah, hell, for Chris' sakes we're plumb short-handed around here. And when the Colsons make their big move, which they're bound to do, they'll put the Jessup outfit out of business. They'll wear down the Jessup cattle. They've already stole the string of Jessup usin' horses, an', now, with just the lad here left. . . . Well, if they get rid of him 'n' move in, they'll get title some way an' own half the damned countryside."

"But Crow's dead?"

"Crow is dead, but Harland's no kid any more, and Robin ain't much better. They're mean, chips off the old block. His cousin, Gunn, from the reservation's here, an' he's got hired riders."

Sullivan was scratching the back of his neck as he said: "Jem, I heard how Crow was shot . . . in the back."

"No, damn your mangy old hide, I didn't do it!" he shouted, pausing for an instant. "But I got a notion who did. I wasn't even in Cumberland. If I remember correctly that's the day I went up to. . . ."

"Jem," Sullivan interrupted, "you know, some folks in town think you done it."

Jem exploded. "Sons-of-bitches! All of 'em. They never get anythin' straight, so they make things up. Partner, my word I didn't shoot Crow, but whoever he was that done it, did a good turn for everyone."

"Who do you figure, Jem?"

Joe brought an end to the discussion by appearing on the porch with two small glasses filled to the brim with popskull. "Food's on the table," he announced, handing the glasses to the two men, and then returned to the kitchen.

Sullivan downed the whisky, stood up, and, while looking north as far as the eye could see, said: "Chore time, Jem. I got to look after my horse. Him and me been partners a long time."

When Whitmore failed to come in and eat, Joe went to fetch him. When he saw Sullivan leaving the yard, he asked Jem: "Where's he goin'?"

Whitmore, who had closed his eyes for what he thought was merely a second, straightened in his chair and looked around, saying: "He never said nothin' to me about leavin'."

Motioning with his head, Joe observed the

distant rider, getting smaller, and said: "Goin' to town."

Whitmore said nothing. Clearly Sullivan was headed in the direction of Cumberland.

May appeared now on the porch, and, just as she was getting ready to sit, Bart groped his way to the doorway, saw the distant rider, and growled: "Did you run him off, Jem?"

"Back to bed," May said, as she tried to shoo Bart back into the house with the tip of her cane.

But Mather wouldn't leave, he just kept squinting and clinging to the doorjamb.

Addressing Joe, Whitmore said: "Boy, look around and see if you can find that runnin' iron."

Joe searched the porch and came up empty. "I'll try the barn," he said, stepping off the porch.

In the meantime, May managed to pry Mather's grip free of the door, turn him, and herd him back inside.

"Didn't find it, didya?" Whitmore said as Joe approached the porch, again empty-handed.

Joe shook his head.

Scowling and speaking to no one in particular, Whitmore said: "Now what'd he expect to do with that runnin' iron?"

Looking to be in pain herself, May announced: "Bart hurtin' bad."

At this Whitmore left the porch. May exchanged a meaningful look with Joe, and started to rock. When she spoke again, the subject had nothing to do with the missing rustler's branding iron.

"Son, you go up yonder. Bring C.L. back."

Joe gazed at May. "Why?"

"We hire no riders for gather. You go. You pay them beef to help gather."

"May, there was bad feelin' about that, an' you know it."

"Joe, they not going to let us hire nobody. Look at Bart, when he try." She recognized the look that clouded Joe's face whenever he was uncertain, and added: "Up there you give feather bundle back to Donna."

May was successful. Joe patted May's arm and kissed her forehead before heading in the direction of the barn. She intended to watch her boy ride out, but before Joe had even reached the barn, Mather let go a bellow of urgency. She took a deep breath, readying herself for the pain that would inevitably pierce through her hip, got up, and went back into the house.

Mather demanded to know what was going on. "First, Sullivan leaves . . . now what?"

"Joe. He go north."

Mather half sat up. "You sent him to fetch tomahawks back to help with the gather?"

May nodded, waiting for the outburst she was certain would come.

Instead, Mather was quiet a long time. Eventually he spoke. "All right. Your husband did it. Nobody liked the idea. But I was there . . . he told them his Indians come along or he'd turn 'em loose to stampede the cattle all the way to Mexico. May, for an Indian you're pretty *coyote*."

"You like shot?"

Mather's grin was wide. "You're one of them mind readers. There's nothin' I'd like better than a little whisky just about now."

"I go."

Mather eased back down, sighed, and swiveled his head until he could see far out through the room's one small window, and whispered: "I'll be a son-of-a-bitch. Tomahawks. For sixty years now I wouldn't give 'em the time of day, an' she come up with knowin' what Old Joe would've done. Old Joe knew what he was doin' when he took 'em along. They never stole no Jessup beef. He worked 'em an' paid 'em in meat."

When May came through the door, Mather held out a scrawny arm, took the glass, dropped its contents down in one swallow, and snorted like that bull out in the corral. He felt content as he watched May take back his glass, refill it, and tip back her head, downing the whisky just as he had done. But she didn't snort, she just smiled.

Chapter Ten

Old Jem

Constable Emmet Forbes had just blown out the hanging lantern in the jailhouse office when Percy Sullivan walked in.

Forbes, standing behind his desk, said: "Percy?"

Without answering, Sullivan crossed to the desk and dropped the CC iron on it while Forbes relit the lantern.

"Runnin' iron, Percy?"

"Colson was usin' it on Jessup cattle."

The law man sat down with a sigh. There'd be no poker session at the saloon for him this evening. "Why would Colson rustle cattle? He owns about as many as anyone in the state."

Sullivan made a dour half grin. "Not because he needs 'em, but because if he can take over enough Jessup cattle, May and Young Joe'll have to give up. You want me to tell you how the Colsons would make out if the Jessups give up and they got their range?"

Forbes laboriously built a smoke and lighted it before answering. "Percy . . . can you prove what you just said? The Colsons are more'n likely richer'n the Jessups."

Sitting on the wall bench, Sullivan considered his scuffed boots. "Forbes, there's folks that never get enough. With Crow gone, his boys and other kin'll pick up where he left off. Think about it. How'd you like a territory of nothin' but Colsons?"

Considering the unevenly burning tip of his cigarette, the constable responded: "Percy, you're imagination is runnin' away with you."

"Is that a fact?" Sullivan leaned forward, propping his elbows on his knees. "I been gone a while. There was bad blood back then. Them Colsons is just naturally ornery. You know that's a fact. How else can a man figure it, Forbes? Think on it. I'll be up at the saloon."

After Sullivan departed, Forbes studied the CC iron. For a fact, it was the favorite rustler tool, and this one showed clear evidence of having been in many fires. Puzzled, he placed the running iron against the wall beneath his gun rack, and went to the café where he enjoyed a tasty stew. He ordered the same for his prisoner, Harper, and, while it was being readied, he sat and pondered some more on the running iron. When he returned to the jailhouse, Forbes handed over the food and said: "That partner of yours . . . Colley something-or-other . . . where is he?"

"Bowman, his name is Bowman. And how would I know? Last time I seen him that old buzzard at the Jessup place was taking him away."

Even more confused now, Forbes snapped: "You're lyin'."

Fred Harper shook his head. He couldn't speak around a mouthful of stew.

"I got a runnin' iron, there, in my office, Harper. Now tell me you 'n' your partner didn't use one to run Colson's mark on Jessup critters."

"I'll tell you nothin'," Harper replied slowly, smiling.

His anger getting the best of him, Forbes jumped up from the stool, drew his gun, and walked toward Harper. "I can't shoot you, but I can make you see stars. Tell me what I want to know . . . now!"

"All right, all right," Harper groaned, surprisingly cowed by the old constable. "Crow paid us two dollars for every Jessup slick we run his mark on."

"Just you and Bowman?"

"No. Anyone Colson hired on to ride for him. Now you're goin' to ask how many. I could only guess. Over a two, three year period, maybe two, three hundred. Always slick long-yearlings that Jessup hadn't brought in for markin'."

Forbes sank down on the cell's stool. He was doing schoolboy arithmetic. He scowled at Harper, got up, and collected the stew container and utensils. Back at his desk, he dug out a stub of a pencil and a scrap of paper and worked for a good half hour. When he was done, he leaned back. "For Chris' sake. Two, maybe three, years of whittlin' away at the Jessup herd." He pocketed the scrap of paper, locked up the jail, and went home, where all he could think as he prepared for bed was: *How could that have happened for any length of time without the Jessups at least wondering?*

The following morning he was the café's first customer. He was also the liveryman's first visitor. He declined the offer of help in rigging out his horse and left, headed west, through the back alley from the barn. The ride to the Jessup place always seemed long to Forbes, but this time he wasn't bothered by the distance as he was preoccupied by the information he had been given by Harper.

When he arrived, he found May and Mather on the porch. Both were bundled in blankets. After tying up his horse near the

164

barn, he proceeded to the house. The pair welcomed the constable with a wary minimum of warmth.

"Where's Joe?" he asked after a moment of silence.

May answered: "He rode out with Jem."

Forbes inclined his head. "With Jem? Let me ask you something, Bart. Over the past few years have you had many miscarried cows?"

Mather pulled the blanket up higher around his neck. "Well, can't say, Forbes. We just run 'em through an' get it over with. When you got as many cattle as we got. . . ."

Seeing he wasn't going to get anywhere, the constable asked: "Jem been stayin' out here lately?"

"Last day or two. Percy bring in that runnin' iron, did he? Well, seems Jem 'n' Joe come onto some fellers a few nights back drivin' Colsons' drifters back home." Mather flicked a glance at May who was wearing a gentle smile as she followed the conversation.

Forbes pushed his legs out, crossed them at the ankles, and gazed off into the horizon, expressionless and withdrawn.

Mather fidgeted. It had been May who had wrapped him in a blanket and insisted they sit on the porch in the sunshine. He was feeling better, but he just couldn't get his energy back up.

May's words broke the silence. "Colsons rustle. Old Joe told me that before he die."

Mather sat forward and said: "Forbes, do *you* think they been raidin' us?"

Forbes nodded slowly without speaking. He was watching two distant riders approach from the north. May noticed them, too, even though she was a little disappointed. She had hoped Joe would bring back the girl with him.

Forbes sat for several minutes, then announced: "I got a little ridin' to do, folks. If that's Jem and Joe, tell 'em I couldn't wait." At the bottom step he turned to look at the man and the woman, gave his head a gentle little wag, and then walked on in the direction of the barn.

Mather addressed May: "You make any sense of all that?"

She did. "Perry give him runnin' iron. He come to us to know how we lose cattle. He go now an' scout up Colson. Make count."

Mather snorted. "How can anyone count all the Colson beef?"

"No beef, Bart, cows. Colson have more calves to sell off at end of drive than he do cows. . . ."

Mather slowly turned his head. Although

166

he had intended to speak, he did not. Joe hailed the two porch sitters. So, silently, they watched as the new arrivals forked feed to their mounts and dealt with their outfits.

When Whitmore reached the porch, he was scowling. "Was that the constable? We waved, but he just kept on ridin'."

"It was him," Mather confirmed. "Percy showed him that runnin' iron sure as I'm settin' here."

When Joe came up on the porch, he squatted next to May. She reached over and pinched the back of his hand. "She don't come with you?"

Joe reddened, cleared his throat, and shook his head.

May spoke again. "She not up yonder? This season hunt for berries?"

Joe still did not speak, but he bobbed his head.

Mather and Whitmore talked at some length. Whitmore listened as Mather repeated May's supposition about the constable's plan.

"Him, alone?" Jem said, shaking his head. "Partner, not countin' hired hands, there's at least five, six of them Colsons. Mostly young, too. An' young rattlers is just as poisonous as old ones."

Whitmore looked past Mather to Joe, who

sat quietly next to May. He raised his voice slightly. "Boy! You up to some more ridin'?"

Joe'd had enough saddlebacking, but he nodded his assent; after all, he needed to get away from May before she weaseled it out of him that he hadn't gone up yonder.

May snapped at Whitmore. "Joe need feedin' up. His pa say a man can't work on empty gut."

Whitmore had the answer to that. "Me, too, May. I ain't eaten, neither."

May rose, threw off the old blanket, gave Whitmore an unfriendly look, and headed for the door. "I make. You eat!" she said, and disappeared inside the house.

Mather winked at Joe. "He'p her, boy. She's limpin' worse'n ever."

Joe went inside, and Mather faced the large man. "Jem, you 'n' me is too old."

Jem's answer dripped with disapproval. "Too old? What's got into you? You give up, Bart, an' you'll end up in a wagon loaded with furniture goin' down the road."

Mather felt for the pocket that wasn't there and cursed. He needed a chew. His friend fished out a gnawed plug and handed it over. Mather worried off a hunk and, handing it back, said: "I never saw you chew."

Whitmore irritable mood lingered. "You

168

never seen me naked in a creek, neither. So what? I'll take the lad, we'll find Forbes, an', if there's trouble, we can likely even things up a mite."

Mather savored the cud by shifting it from one side of his face to the other side. He said: "See you nikked? Why'n hell would anyone want to see you nikked? There's just more of you'n there is to other folks. If you wait a day or so, I'll ride over there with you."

Whitmore snorted. "You think Forbes's goin' to be ridin' to Colson range for two days?"

"Jem, you get that boy hurt, May'll slit your pouch an' pull your leg through it."

Whitmore did something he very rarely did. He slapped Mather on the arm as he said: "I give you my word, he won't get hurt. Now I'm goin' in there an' get fed."

Once Mather was alone on the porch and certain the others were all occupied in the kitchen, he stood up, gripped the blanket tightly around himself, and slowly made his way to his room.

Inside, Whitmore ate enough for two men, praising the meal until May glowed. He savored a cup of coffee while Joe helped May clean up, then he took Joe outside with him. There was no one on the porch.

Whitmore jerked his head, led off in the direction of the barn, and said: "Joe, get your carbine. I'll have the horses ready. And, whatever you do, don't let May see you."

Whitmore dearly wanted to take the grulla, but satisfied himself with talking to it while readying his second choice and waiting for Joe. It didn't take long for the youth to retrieve the booted Winchester, and soon they were on their way, heading northwest so as not to be seen from the house.

When they were well out of sight, they changed course, heading due north, near enough to the heavily forested foothills to be invisible from the south as well. Whitmore clearly had a destination. Joe was surprised at how well Whitmore knew the territory, considering he didn't own a horse. When Whitmore turned up a narrow dusty trail where timber grew thickly on both sides, Joe noted that his whole body seemed to relax.

The sun was directly overhead by the time Joe was led to a prone plinth of petrified wood. Whitmore dismounted and went out on the age-old, rock-like platform and hunkered down. Joe did the same. The view was endless; it was possible to take in the limitless miles of Colson range.

Whitmore raised a massive arm. "Them

trees southerly a ways? That's the Colson headquarters."

Joe nodded. He'd been in that distant yard many times. "Must be rest time. I don't see no one outside."

Jem chuckled. "Their kind never sleep. They'll be down there, boy. I've lived hereabouts so long I pretty well know their habits. Look easterly, there."

Joe saw and asked: "That'd be them critters we saw 'em drive off in the dark?"

Although he figured they were the same ones, Whitmore did not reply; instead, he led Joe back to the horses. When they were astride, they rode north for a while, then cut straight westward. By the time they found a place to descend, the sun was close enough to be teetering on the farthest rim of the world.

Now they were in territory that hadn't been logged off. It was like riding a snake's path — weave this way, then that way. In some places they were barely able to avoid colliding with huge old trees. When they began sloping downward, Whitmore announced — "Creek ahead." — and unerringly led the way to it. They stopped briefly to let their horses take their fill, then rode the last distance to the wide valley that separated two high, thickly timbered slopes.

Joe figured they would turn down the cleft, and he was right. Suddenly they encountered three bears — two snarling and tumbling, the other, a sow bear in heat, nipping wild growth as her suitors battled. She was patient, unconcerned as to which of the two would win out and follow her to a secret place to consummate courtship. After a number of fierce snarls, one of the two bears broke loose and fled, a long-yearling with a deathly fear of man scent, probably.

Whitmore reined up, waiting and watching much like the she-bear. Finally the sow sidled up to her new mate, nuzzled and licked him, and then went ambling off, occasionally glancing over her shoulder to be sure the boar bear was following. He was.

Whitmore moved out. Joe continued to watch the bears. He couldn't figure it out. "All three had to have picked up man scent," he said to Jem, "but only the young one ran." Jem grinned but said nothing. There were plenty of things Joe would have to learn on his own.

They came out of the deep, long cañon into what seemed to be miles of graze and browse country. Joe raised an arm, and Whitmore nodded. Neither spoke as they maneuvered so they would come out above the band of young cattle. Joe felt exposed since there were no trees except on the farthest curve of country, miles away in all directions. He mentioned this to Whitmore, whose response was a smile followed by: "We'll see 'em as quick as they see us, boy. You worry too much."

When Whitmore was satisfied they had traveled far enough north, he changed course and continued to ride until several of the cattle threw up their heads, then he changed course again, and the wary animals went back to cropping graze. He halted, shaded his face, and strained to see the animals clearly. "Too far yet," he said, and rode ahead. The second time he stopped, he'd no more than begun looking, when Joe blurted out: "There's one . . . looks like a heifer. She's got our mark! The one with the blazed face and the bob tail."

Smiling, Whitmore said: "Well, hell, boy . . . you satisfied?"

Joe nodded and snugged up his reins. His companion stopped before he could move.

"No! Back the way we come. We can't chance drivin' that bunch."

For a brief moment, Joe was unwilling to turn back, but Whitmore was already moving in the direction of the long cañon out of which they had ridden. Joe followed, riding sideways until he could no longer separate the mis-marked animal from her companions. Then he rode to catch up.

Back in the timber, dusk arrived a long hour before it would shadow the open country. There were parts of the uplands where daylight never shone through the iron-stiff topouts. They rode for what Joe thought had to be ten miles before Whitmore hauled to a stop near a piddling little creek, swung off, and went to work removing his outfit. Saddle sore, Joe willingly emulated his companion. Whitmore carelessly tossed one of his bedroll blankets to Joe, hobbled the horses, and went to the creek to drink, wash, and soak his feet which made it necessary for Joe to go upstream a piece before drinking.

When Joe returned to the makeshift camp, Whitmore handed him a tin. Joe studied it, realizing it was sardines. He made a face, for he had never liked those little fishes inside the flat tins, and they certainly weren't a meal. Still, a man could carry three days' supply in his shirt or pants pocket. Whitmore even drank the oil.

They didn't make a fire; they didn't need one, although the night was chilly. They rolled cocoon-like into their blankets and slept. Joe, being young, got along well enough with four hours sleep. He was surprised, upon waking, to find Jem already rigging out. They had breakfast — another flat tin.

Whitmore was a man of instinct. When they made it back as far as the pinnacle, where the petrified log was, he handed Joe his reins, went gingerly out, and stood as straight as a pole, studying the land below. Back at his horse, digging for something in his saddlebag, he said: "There's three of 'em. They're studyin' the tracks where we rode out of the timber onto the meadow." Then he turned his horse once, swung astraddle, and led off without another word.

Joe could tell Whitmore was thinking hard on something, but he was afraid to say anything. Just as Joe was about to try making small talk, Jem turned in his saddle and said: "Boy, can you find your way back from here?"

Joe nodded.

"OK," he said, pointing ahead. "You keep goin' the way we come. I'll cut off to the west, here, an' give 'em somethin' to puzzle over."

Joe watched his companion ride off through the timber, suddenly feeling very small. He waited a moment, straining to hear the sound of horse hoofs, and, when he heard none, settled his saddle gun across his lap, and continued following their earlier tracks. Three times he left the trail, stopping to listen. Not until the last time did he actually hear something, a sound like a steel horseshoe striking a rock. He eased ahead a little faster. If someone were following him and Jem, they had made pretty good time and had to be riding a tough range horse. Scanning the land ahead, he saw one place that was flat and clear enough for Joe to lope a fair distance. As soon as he kicked his horse into action, he didn't waste time stopping to listen again.

Soon enough he found himself in the gloom of what seemed a perpetual forest. Joe thought his mount was beginning to drag his hind hoofs a little. He knew the horse had a right to show tiredness. But he still had a considerable distance to cover, and what he didn't want was his animal to give out.

Far behind him he heard a shout. The distance was encouraging. He reined back to an easy walk. He speculated about that shout. It wasn't reasonable, he told himself, for someone following him to make a sound that would carry. Yet, he'd heard someone, something. He continued on.

Dusk settled deeper as always happened in heavily timbered country. He wondered about Jem. And he wasn't comforted by the thought that as good a mountaineer as Whitmore undoubtedly was, there was also someone, somewhere, who was just as good or maybe even a tad better.

Chapter Eleven

Toward Tomorrow

Dusk trailed off into night by the time Joe began recognizing landmarks. Wondering if Whitmore had been successful in sidetracking their pursuers, he eased up a little, as he rode around a sump spring that was one of Bart's private places. He had learned years back that everyone needed a private place to think about things that were bothering him. His horse picked up the scent of home and lengthened his stride a little. In less than an hour he'd be at the Lazy J.

Joe was just entering the yard, heading for the barn, when he heard a distant gunshot. He stopped, swung off his horse, and waited. There was no second gunshot. Cautiously, nonetheless, he led the horse into the barn, off saddled it, and put it into a stall. Before leaving the barn, he forked the manger full of feed.

The night was silent now. The house looked at peace. He shrugged and went in search of May and Bart. He had barely got inside the house when Mather, fully clothed and dozing in a parlor chair, snapped wide awake, stared, rubbed his eyes, and said: "Where's Jem?"

May appeared from the kitchen, leaning heavily on her cane. Joe told them everything. Asked if they'd heard the gunshot. Neither one responded, but then Mather jockeyed himself up to his feet and left the parlor.

May called after him. "You wait. He come. *Bart!*" She hobbled out of the room, following him onto the porch.

Joe was in the kitchen, eating with one hand and stuffing food into his pockets with the other. He could hear May and Bart arguing. Then, from the hallway, she called to Joe.

"You stay! You hear me, Son. *You stay!*"

Before he could pass through the kitchen, a voice sounded from out in the night.

"Boy? May? Bart? Lend me a hand!"

There was no mistaking that voice — it was Whitmore. Joe hurried from the house, fisting his sidearm. As he strode off the porch, May and Bart brought up the rear.

The bull-like voice called again, coming from the direction of the yard near the barn. "Hurry up, damn it!"

Running now, Joe came up to Jem and his horse. He saw immediately that Jem had brought company. A man was tied across the back of Jem's horse, his legs dangling in front of Joe's face. Joe looked questioningly at Jem in the dark.

Whitmore shook his head as he said: "It's Harland. He come over my sign. I sneaked up on him where he'd stopped. Put up quite a fight, he did."

"He is dead, Jem?" came from May who stood nearby now, panting from the exertion of the walk from the house to the barn.

"I expect not. I clipped him a good one . . . but 'tweren't enough to kill him," Whitmore explained, scratching his head. He continued: "His damned horse run off. He's pretty heavy to be carried double on a tired animal." Whitmore indicated he needed Joe's help in hoisting Harland off the horse. "We best get him inside, and, if you could take care of the horse, boy, I'd 'preciate it."

Once they got Harland Colson down on the ground, Bart, who since his arrival on the scene had gone to and from the trough, threw a pail of water on him. Joe jumped back as the water splashed against the ground. The prisoner groaned, his shoulders shifting in a kind of rolling motion. Whitmore squatted down beside him and punched his six-gun barrel into Colson's soft parts, triggering another groan in response.

Jem fished for a hideout weapon and found a Derringer boot gun of large caliber. He handed it to Joe, saying: "They'll be lookin' for him."

Joe grunted in agreement as he watched Harland's eyes flutter open.

Jem smiled and said: "Look's like maybe we can get us some answers now."

Colson sputtered — "What the hell?" — as he came fully back to consciousness, sitting up and pushing Whitmore aside.

Whitmore pushed the gun into the slight roll of fat that hung over the waistband of Colson's pants. "Eh-eh, don't get jumpy, Colson. We just want to talk to you. Y'understand?"

Colson nodded, rubbing his head.

"First off," Whitmore said, "you can tell us where Gunn, that big 'breed cousin of yours, is."

"Back yonder somewhere," was the response.

Harland and Bart exchanged a hostile stare. The two were pretty much the same size. The difference was that Colson ran to fat, whereas Mather was bones, sinew, and muscle.

Leaning forward and feeling the back of his head, Harland asked: "What d'ya hit me with, Whitmore?"

"A dead fall scantling," he responded flatly, rising to his feet. "Let's go inside the house," he added. "Let's move, Colson!" he ordered, kicking at Harland's boot. "Give him a hand, Joe," he added.

Joe complied, but reluctantly. With three of them incapacitated in some way or another, the quintet crossed the yard slowly.

Inside, May got a lamp lighted in the parlor. Joe brought a straight-back chair from the kitchen. He could tell May was in a sour mood and ready to light into Harland, so he placed himself in the chair between the two when he sat down.

Whitmore, who had gone to the kitchen, returned to the parlor, a small glass of whisky in his hand. He handed it to Harland Colson, who downed it gratefully, muttering — "Thanks." — nearly inaudibly.

Angry at the idea of wasting whisky on a Colson, Mather stated: "I say we hang the son-of-a-bitch from the barn balk. That's how Old Joe did it, when we caught a rustler."

May countermanded Mather's suggestion. "Talk first . . . then hang."

The whisky had had a fortifying effect on

Colson, and he snorted derisively: "They'll be riding in here any minute."

Realizing the logic of what Harland had just said, Joe walked to the front window and stood with his back to the others. Visibility was far from adequate, but it was good enough to see a fair distance to the north. At the moment there were no riders in sight.

Mather leaned forward on the settee where he had seated himself and asked: "How many's out there, Harland?" When Colson didn't answer, Mather got up and crossed the room. He repeated his question, his face now inches from Colson's.

"Enough, you old. . . ."

The slap was loud and distinct. "I said," Mather paused, moving in even closer, "how many, you mangy bastard?"

"Not includin' me," Harland began, looking reluctant, "there'd be five."

Jem interjected: "That bein' the case, Bart, we'd best hang him now. High . . . so's they can see him when they come into the yard."

"Wait," May shouted, positioning her cane in between her legs to steady herself when she leaned forward. "How many our beef you steal?"

Harland showed contempt when he turned to meet the woman's black gaze. "I don't know what you're talkin' about. Why would us Colsons bother with your rib-thin cattle?"

Mather shook his head and laughed. "I guess you don't know that we found the runnin' iron or that Colley Bowman talked. Oh, yeah, he talked a lot to me before I give him ten dollars and told him to run for it an' never come back."

Whitmore and May stared at Mather, who continued on, ignoring the shocked looks on their faces. "As far as I was concerned, he was just a damned stupid man being used by your pa and Fred Harper. So, I give him a second chance in exchange for some information."

Harland sneered. "You're old enough to know better'n to believe a hired hand, Mather. They lie even when the truth would fit better."

May rapped her cane on the floor, repeating her question: "How many Jessup head you steal?"

Colson shifted position, looked around the room before letting his eyes settle on May. "I got no idea," was his reply.

May glared back in response, muttering something incomprehensible. Old Joe would have understood, but no one among this group in the parlor did.

At the window, Joe, ignoring the conversation going on in the room, was focused on the dark in the distance. Now he was certain, and he announced: "Someone. . . ."

Whitmore managed to cross the room to his side in three steps. "Too many for the Colsons!" he exclaimed. He peered into the black, cursing the dimness of the moon. "Indians! By gawd, boy, them's Indians."

Uncertain now that he had seen anything, Joe strained his eyes, gazing out. "Where, Jem?" he asked.

"Boy, you sure don't have your pa's eyes. Look real hard. Plain as day, comin' in from the north. Look hard, boy."

Joe rubbed his eyes, then gradually tracked to the north. As his eyes adjusted, not straining this time, he saw something.

At the word Indians, May had made her way over to the window.

"You see 'em?" Jem asked her.

May barely inclined her head. "I see someone . . . by shoeing shed. But not Indian."

Vindicated, Whitmore expanded: "Good thing we're inside, an' they're outside."

May looked back into the room. "Burn us to ash, maybe."

As May moved away from the window, Joe, finding himself scared and confused, asked: "So, who's out there? Is it Indians or not?"

From the settee, Mather threw in: "If they're fired up, it don't matter none. Why don't you let 'em know we're on to them, Joe?"

Joe sidled to the door, cracked it, took a long rest with one hand, and fired. There was no acknowledgement of the shot for a period of almost three seconds then, suddenly, the crack of a response came from the area of the barn. As Joe jumped back away from the door, he saw May put a whisky bottle back in the sideboard on the far wall. There was no time for a remonstration now.

A gravelly voice called out to the house: "You got Harland in there?"

Taking charge, Whitmore called back: "Yeah, we got him. He's settin' in here with the Queen of England."

That note of sarcasm brought a series of gunshots aimed at the house and its inhabitants, of which only one came from the direction of the barn and the shoeing shed.

Mather still sat on the couch, but now he had a revolver in his hand aimed steadily at Harland Colson. "You boys best figure on what we plan to do," he stated.

Before Joe or Whitmore could respond, a volley of shots thundered outside the house, well outside the yard. Instinctively Joe knew something was happening, but he couldn't say what. May was the one who understood, and she shot up to her feet, yelling at the top of her voice: "No enemies! No shoot! Listen!"

Joe perked up his ears to the echoing silence that always follows a deafening noise. On the settee, Mather fidgeted as he made a startling discovery: he could not hear as well as he had been able just a few days earlier. It came as such a shock he almost forgot what was happening.

Now the sound of riders nearing the yard could be discerned. Suddenly an order was snapped from somewhere out near the barn: "Somebody's comin'! Clear out now!"

May was shifting her weight to the cane as she limped toward the door, a smile widening across her face as she said to no one in particular: "I told you. I told you."

At the window Whitmore himself was laughing, shouting: "Look it! Look it. There goes all four of 'em. Hey, Harland, you wanna see your family's tail ends?"

Mather smiled. Harland did not.

At the door now, May threw it wide open. Joe and Jem scurried next to her, one on each side. Joe thought he saw his friend, C.L., among the dozen or so of the up yonder people filtering into the yard. All were armed as they scattered to places that provided the best cover. Some of the older ones had tami-axes in their belts.

Whitmore looked at Joe. "How'd they know to get down here?"

May spoke. "People know. They watch. They know. Always got to know. Everybody hate Indians. They got to not let no one sneak up on 'em."

Whitmore shook his head and muttered: "What a hell of a way to have to live."

One of the younger men on horseback danced into the center of the yard and, rearing back his horse, broke into a celebratory yell. In answer a different call came from another of the up yonder people

At this May smiled. "The wolf call," she said, sounding pleased.

A smile broke across Whitmore's face, and May understood perfectly, even if it wasn't in her native language that he spoke, when he said: "It is good to have friends."

Joe stepped through the doorway and let out his own whooping call. Several seconds of silence followed after which someone — a woman — called from her hiding place.

Then May stepped forward. A lilting sound emanated from her throat, filling the air with an other-worldliness for a passing moment. She did it again. After the second time she moved ahead and descended the porch steps, limping out into the yard.

An old voice sounded in greeting to May's approach. It broke off unsteadily.

Standing next to Joe, Whitmore, recognizing Red Buffalo's voice, said: "I'll be damned."

From the east a considerable distance, an echo of gunfire rode the wind back in the direction of the house.

At this, May laughed, shifted the cane stick to her left hand, and looked around for Joe.

Mather's gruff voice sounded from inside the house: "Can we eat now? I'm starving."

May teetered between returning to the house and remaining in the yard. Her eyes took in the yard, finally lingering questionably on Joe. When she spoke, it was in English and loud enough for all in the yard to hear: "Time to fill bellies!" She gimped over to the porch where she raised her cane high and swung it in a circular motion.

Understanding, Joe and Jem smiled at each other. They were not that many steps behind May as she proceeded to the house. She went inside, but the two men stood on the porch and watched the up yonder people emerge from their places of hiding in the dark. The first of the group to make it up on the porch was an old man. Older than Mather. He exchanged a hand grip with Joe and Jem and went inside. A few others followed. The volume of the noise increased significantly from inside the house.

"From the sounds of the goin's-on in there, I'd say some of May's guests must've taken a short-cut by going through the window," Jem said to Joe, elbowing him in the ribs. "I think I'll join them."

"I'll wait out here for a while," Joe responded.

He didn't have to wait long. The girl appeared in smoked tans at the bottom of the steps. She paused, her eyes looking down, and then was joined by an old woman, who said something in a guttural tone to her. As Donna came up the steps, she glanced at Joe before entering the house. He thought he saw the beginnings of a smile.

As the two women entered the house, Mather came out through the doorway. He sought the chair Old Joe had built for May and eased himself down. "Harland's gone," was all he said.

Chapter Twelve

Soldiers

The day after the Jessup Yard War, as it came to be known in after years, Constable Emmet Forbes rode out to the Lazy J. He'd heard about the stand-off between the Jessups and the Colsons from at least five sources in less than an hour's time this morning. Several members of the Colson clan had shown up in his office furious over the fact that Harland was being held captive by the Jessups.

"He ain't turned up yet, Forbes!" Robin Colson, the taller of the two shouted. "Now, what are you going to do about it? We got run out, trying to get him back. Those Jessups got them damn' holdout Indians backing them. A whole passel of them descended on the house. We barely got out with our lives."

"I'm checking on it," Forbes assured the two men. "I'm headin' out there, right away. Now, you get on home. Send me word the minute Harland gets back. I'm on my way,"

191

he reiterated, snatching up his gun belt and his hat. "Right now . . . see, I'm going." He stopped in briefly at the café, downed two cups of coffee, and headed out.

Forbes found Mather and Whitmore busy in the barn when he rode into the yard. It was Mather who voluntarily took care of his animal, and, therefore, he was still at the barn when Forbes sat down in the chair in May's bedroom. Forbes removed his hat as he studied May who was cocooned inside a number of blankets, only her face showing.

On the ride from Cumberland, Forbes had decided he would look around for signs of Harland then talk to May first, figuring Mather and Whitmore would keep him for hours with their recitals of the events. As it was, he found no sign of Harland, and by the time he got around to the men folk he'd already learned what he had wanted to from May's unembellished recollections. Harland had left shortly after the others. She did not mention the holdouts.

"What scared 'em off?" Forbes asked.

"Horses," May answered.

After questioning May, he spoke with Whitmore, and his version matched with May's, although it was more detailed, just as it meshed with Mather's. Harland had been let go. As for the Colsons being chased off by Indians. " 'Tweren't no Indians," both Jem and Mather had explained. "It was them horses we lost some time back . . . they found their way home and came charging in. Them Colsons were just jumpy. When they heard them horses galloping in, they let their imaginations run wild. There weren't no riders on those horses."

Forbes was satisfied, and he was readying himself to ride over to the Colson place, although he didn't relish that idea. He'd never liked Crow and had always avoided his sons, whom he had assessed as overweight bullies. Heading toward the barn, his plans to leave were abandoned when he espied Joe approaching the yard with a girl at his side. He glanced toward the house and saw that May was now up, dressed, and stationed in her favorite rocker.

"Hungry?" May called out to the constable as her eyes remained fixed on her son and his companion.

"As a horse," Forbes called back, his stomach growling at the mention of food, not having had time to down a breakfast earlier that morning at Nettie's café before heading out.

Donna went inside to help May with the preparations as soon as she and Joe had off saddled the horses. She had avoided looking directly at the law man, although he saw her sidewise glance as she passed him on the way to the house.

The meal was satisfying, and it gave Forbes the opportunity to question Joe casually concerning the events of the stand off. Clearly Joe had not worked out his story in advance with the others for, when Joe mentioned the Indians, Mather shot him a harsh glare.

The up yonder people's existence was one of those open secrets. Most folks in Cumberland either knew from personal experience or from others whose judgment they trusted that there were Indian hideouts up in the mountain's high timberlands. Those that weren't certain speculated on the subject, convinced of the natural ability of Indians to remain invisible. This in spite of the Army's firm contention that all renegades had been rounded up and placed on reservations.

Every citizen in Cumberland knew of May, knew Old Joe had taken the Indian woman to wife. It was assumed she had family that they visited. It was also common knowledge that Old Joe had used Indians when he needed riders during roundup time. Not that anybody was happy about that. In fact, it made the locals nervous and edgy, especially if the Indians got pushy. But nothing really bad had ever occurred during roundup, so everyone let it pass. Even a few others had hired a few young bucks now and then. Recent thinking had been that it was ancient history anyway, what with Old Joe dead now.

Besides Old Joe, the territory had its share of other squawmen, non-Indians marrying up with Indians. In part, the Indian problem was one of those that resolved itself — what the Army hadn't handled would be taken care of through assimilation.

Consequently, Forbes did not pursue the mention of Indians. He knew they were up there, but the chain of mountains was extensive and local upsets rarely had anything to do with the hideouts.

Foregoing the trip to the Colsons for another day, Forbes got back to town at dusk full as a tick and wondering what his next step should be. He knew the holdouts had been involved, but he also knew not a one of the Colsons would have stopped short of murder to get back Harland. Therefore, for the time being, he planned to sit back. He busied himself in the office after seeing to Harper's dinner and checking over the town. He was sitting at his desk, going over some long neglected paperwork, when

Robin Colson burst into the jail, announcing that Harland still hadn't shown up.

"I've been out to the Jessups, Robin. Harland's not there. They told me they let him go soon after you boys pulled out."

"They're lying!" Robin roared. "Now I wanna know what you're going to do about it, Forbes? Or do I have to find help elsewhere?"

Forbes stood up in an effort to calm down the raging Colson. "Listen, Robin, I. . . ."

Colson didn't give him a chance to finish. "Forget it, Forbes, you're in on this with those damn' Jessups and them holdouts. We don't need your help," he said, turning, and slammed out the door.

Two days later, when Forbes was at Cumberland's general store picking up his mail early in the morning, he glanced out the window and froze. A blue uniformed officer and a squad of enlisted soldiers rode past at a walk, heading for the livery barn. As the constable stepped outside, he heard a townsman standing nearby say: "Now what the hell?" Forbes strode out to the middle of the roadway, keeping his eye on the soldiers as he crossed over to the jailhouse to wait.

It wasn't much of a wait. The soldiers had

only to turn over their animals to the liveryman for care and walk a brief distance north to the jailhouse.

Forbes was not the mayor of Cumberland, that distinction belonged to the overweight proprietor of the general store. Last year the local blacksmith had been the elected mayor.

When the soldiers entered the jailhouse, the officer removed his dragoon gloves, folded them under his garrison belt, and introduced himself, extending his right hand across the desk toward Forbes.

"Captain Berthold, Sheriff. Up at Fort Laramie we got word of a range war, or some kind of a shooting matter down here involving Indians."

Forbes motioned toward the wall bench. The enlisted men sat, but Captain Berthold remained standing. He was an imposing individual. A tad over six feet, well put together with steady blue eyes and a handclasp Forbes wouldn't forget for some time, his hand still pulsating from the officer's firm grip.

"It was over some days back, Captain," he responded.

Berthold assumed the stance of a man who had been through this process before, standing in front of Forbes's desk, expressionless. After having taken the measure of the constable, he said: "What we heard was that a rancher was attacked by some hideout Indians."

Forbes arose. "Have a seat, Captain."

The officer remained standing, ignoring Forbes's invitation. "Is that true, Sheriff?"

"I'm the constable, not a sheriff," Forbes corrected, then continued. "There was a squabble some days back. Far as I know, it's over."

The officer's gaze lingered on Forbes. "Constable, last night we bedded down up-country, near the ranch of some folks named Colson. They're missing one of their men. They claim he was killed by Indians."

It occurred to Forbes slowly that the captain was using an old Army ploy. With Forbes sitting, the officer could look down at him. Irritation began to build up in him.

"The man you're talkin' about," he told the officer, "was named Harland . . . Harland Colson. Far as I know he's just missing."

"And you went after the bushwhacker, Constable?"

Forbes colored slightly. "I told you Harland's *missing*. You found a corpse I ain't heard about, Captain?"

The officer shifted his weight and hooked both thumbs in his garrison belt. "Well, no, Constable. But I am here to find out if folks got trouble with Indians."

One of the enlisted men on the wall bench had built a cigarette. When he lighted it, Forbes coughed, cleared his throat, and glared at the soldier who went right on smoking.

Berthold said: "Constable, we'll have to ask questions of folks hereabouts. These Indians . . . where are they?"

Forbes avoided a direct answer by saying: "The day when the Army ran things ended years back. If you want to talk to folks, I'll be going with you."

Captain Berthold stood in silence, looking at the constable. He jerked his head, and, when the enlisted men arose, he got as far as the door before speaking again. "The Army still runs things." As the last soldier passed through the door, he added: "Constable, don't interfere or you won't have a job."

Stewing, Forbes sat at his desk for a time before jackknifing up to his full height and heading for the door. He stepped out, locked the jailhouse door, and surveyed the town. The soldiers were over at the general store, buying supplies, so Forbes angled over to the far side plank walk and entered the harness shop where he took a position behind the skimpy front window. He watched as the soldiers left the store and walked south.

The harness maker paused at his cutting table to say: "Looks like the Army's in town, Constable."

Forbes nodded and left the shop, following the path of the soldiers. He saw them cross over to the café. When he was assured they were busy for the time being, he went to the livery barn, saddled and bridled his horse, and left the barn by the west side alley. He resented having to make the ride again, but someone had to do it.

By the time he reached the Jessup place, the sun was well on its way toward the highest westerly peaks, row after row of them for more miles than he could see, mostly Jessup country. The yard was empty. A corralled bull lowed, and someone in the barn swore at him.

Forbes bypassed the barn and was tying up out front of the house when he was hailed from the barn.

Joe leaned aside a hayfork and crossed briskly from the barn. He was in a good mood. Where they met at the hitch rack, he said: "Bart and Jem are out startin' the gather."

As Forbes acknowledged this, May appeared on the porch, smiling widely. She offered him a cup of coffee. The constable accepted, slapped Joe lightly on the shoulder, and went up the steps. May held the door for him.

Forbes went to the kitchen table, as May poured his coffee at the stove. He had barely sat down before she began her recitation.

When May stopped talking, he said: "There's soldiers in town, May."

He had seen her reaction before when mention of the Army was made. It looked even stormier this time.

She leaned aside her cane, sat opposite him, and spoke without smiling. "Who sent for 'em?"

Forbes shrugged. To him it mattered less who had gotten word to the Army about Indian holdouts than it did that soldiers had arrived.

When he delayed an answer, May spoke again, defensively this time. "Damned Colsons. Nothin' Army can do. Old Joe told me many times. Jessup land goes to far side of them mountains."

Forbes had heard this before. In fact, Old Joe had told him one afternoon, during a poker session at the saloon in town, that he'd once hired surveyors to establish his property limits. Even Old Joe had been surprised when they had told him how much northerly country belonged to him. But

Forbes knew from the past that, when the Army was after someone, it was not concerned with who owned what. He didn't mention this to May; it had nothing to do with his reason for making the visit.

He said: "May, your people ought to be warned."

Grimacing as she gripped her stick, she rose from the table, went to the porch, and called Joe.

He came from the barn in long strides. One look at his mother's face prompted immediate concern.

"Inside," was all she said.

At the kitchen table Forbes repeated what he had told May. He was not surprised at Joe's response.

"I'll pass the word." He jumped up from the table and headed out the door.

May smiled, calling: "She will be waiting." She turned her attention back to Forbes.

He asked: "Where will they go? They been up there longer'n I can remember."

"How many Army?" May asked in response.

When Forbes said one officer and four enlisted men, she snorted. Forbes shook his head. "There'll be others. This here is most likely a scoutin' party." He emptied his cup and stood up. "I'll do what I can," he told her, and left the house.

From the barn he could see a solitary horseman off in the distance. He thought to himself that Old Joe would be proud. Forbes rigged out, threw a wave to May on the porch, and set a course for Cumberland.

His thoughts were troubled on the journey. As far as he knew, the Army hadn't been in the Cumberland territory since about the time General Grant became President.

Cumberland was quiet when he got back; the roadway was empty. The plank walks on both sides of the road were empty. He rode the distance to the livery barn without seeing a single person.

The liveryman, normally a quiet, unruffled individual, was immediately at the side of Forbes's horse. "Them soldiers scairt hell out of folks, Constable."

Forbes nodded, said — "Take good care of my horse." — and hurried to the jailhouse, where he found the pompous banker, Frank Nicholson, waiting. Forbes nodded, let the banker enter first, walked in after, tossed aside his hat, and said: "Well . . . ?"

The paunchy individual, wearing a necktie and matching coat and britches, huffed: "Well? Is that all you got to say? There's talk around town a full company of soldiers is on the way an' there's goin' to be trouble. A wheeled gun is what they're saying. Forbes, I hid away the bank's money, bonds, and whatnot. I been sayin' for years we'd ought to have drove them danged tomahawks out of the territory."

Forbes said: "Have you talked with Berthold, the officer?"

Nicholson had. "He was askin' around about hideout Indians."

"An' you told him about May's tribesmen?"

"It's common knowledge, Constable."

That was true enough.

"Forbes, Barney Holden told me he favored makin' up a big posse to ride up there an' scatter 'em to the four winds."

Forbes sat like a carving, looking steadily at the banker.

Breaking out in a sweat, Nicholson said: "Folks say you 'n' the Jessups been helpin' them hideouts. You know Old Joe used 'em to make his gather an' took some of 'em along on the drive."

Forbes leaned back. "So have others," he commented dryly. The previous Cumberland law man had warned him that eventually there'd be trouble. As he sat there considering Nicholson, the money man, he had an idea that, when trouble came, he was looking straight into the face of one of whom would be its staunchest supporters.

He assured Nicholson things were under control, ushered him out, and headed for the café to get Harper his dinner. He listened quietly to Harper's verbal abuse about the lousy conditions of the jailhouse. That accomplished, he decided he needed a drink and headed for the saloon. When he passed through the spindle doors, the conversation that had been in progress abruptly died away.

Barney Holden was in the bar and with a mildly flushed face. When he saw the law man, he stated in a somewhat slurred voice: "I volunteer." He ran a limp sleeve over his mouth. "It's time, Forbes. In fact, it's past time."

Forbes ignored the small glass placed in front of him. "It's time for what, Barney?"

"Rousting them damned tomahawks out of the mountains."

"Why now?"

"They're thievin' bastards, for one thing. Why an Indian'll steal an axe outta your hands in mid-air."

A dissenting voice came from the direction of the poker tables when Percy Sullivan spoke up. "The days of them liftin' hair an' us ambushin' their women and children are over. If you don't believe me, go down south. Those folks have been witness to brutality or know folks who have. For years their opinion concerning Indians held to a conviction that the only good one was a dead one. But, nowadays, folks down there mostly leave 'em alone."

By now almost totally red in the face, Holden stated: "Maybe there. But not up here. Folks don't sleep easy. You mark my words, they'll be coming in the night."

"That's horse manure," responded Sullivan.

Forbes listened to Holden with mild surprise, determining that the man was definitely on his way to being drunk. When the subject of Indians was brought up, a person could never be sure where an individual's feelings lay.

Forbes downed his drink and returned to the roadway. Two soldiers were turning in at the livery barn. He went to the café, ordered a steak, and pondered the events of the day. He nursed a cup of coffee while Nettie watched him from over the counter. He was grateful for her silence and tipped her well on his way out. As he headed for the jailhouse, he cursed under his breath when he saw Berthold and one soldier sitting on the bench outside, legs stretched out.

When they saw him coming, they stood

up at attention. As he stepped up onto the plank walk, Forbes nodded. He unlocked and shoved open the door, letting the two uniformed men enter ahead of him.

The captain mopped off sweat and heaved an audible sigh as he sank down on the wall bench. The enlisted man beside him, a sergeant according to the stripes on his sleeves, was large, pale-eyed, and red-faced. His name was Mallory. It could have been any Irish name. The sergeant was expressionless as though he anticipated something disagreeable, when his commanding officer said: "Constable, I been listenin' to some mighty interestin' stories. There's Indians all right . . . up in the hills. And those Jessup folks've been protectin' them."

Forbes went to work concentrating on building a smoke. After lighting up, he quietly said: "Is that against the law?"

The officer seemed to read hostility into the constable's question. He answered with his own ire rising. "Depends, Constable. Let's say the Indians stole someone's horses."

"Whose horses, Captain?"

"Jessup's horses. They run 'em off in the night. One of the Colson lads took me and the sergeant up north a ways and showed us the animals. We went down to the Jessup place and talked to that old Indian woman Jessup married. She confirmed it. Her boy and another feller found the horses far enough north to be near the hideouts' country."

Forbes gazed steadily at the soldier through trickling smoke before saying: "I'm surprised you didn't arrest May." The captain bristled, but Forbes continued. "You say Colson took you where those horses were?"

"Yes. We only just got back."

"Captain, how'd Colson know where the horses were?"

The officer reddened. "Are you implyin' . . . ?"

"I'm not implyin' nothin'. I just asked a question. There's an awful lot of country out yonder. How would the Colsons know where those stolen horses were?"

The officer shrugged. "That doesn't have anythin' to do with the horses being stolen, an' up where the Colsons said there's a *ranchería*."

Forbes stubbed out his smoke. "You know, I'm beginnin' to wonder who sent for the Army an' why they did it."

"Meanin' what, Constable?"

"Meanin' that those stolen horses was taken in the night."

"Jessup's horses?"

Forbes nodded. "None other. Now, Captain, if it's true what folks told you about the

Jessups mixin' with the Indians . . . ? How much do you know about Indians? 'Cuz, if you knew anything, Indians don't never steal from friends."

The sergeant had been quiet as long as he could. He reached inside his tunic to scratch as he said: "Constable, are you sayin' those Colsons had this all figured out before they sent for us?"

Forbes smiled for the first time. *So it was the Colsons who sent for the Army,* he thought to himself. "That's close, Sergeant. Did the Colsons tell you what makes them think Harland is dead?"

Neither soldier answered. Berthold stood up, said — "Thanks for taking time to talk to us, Constable." — nodded at the sergeant, and led the way out.

They crossed to the other side of the roadway before Mallory spoke. "I told you we'd ought to do more talkin' around before you wrote up north for a support detachment."

The captain's voice grated when he said: "I said I wrote the report. I didn't say I'd sent it."

Chapter Thirteen

A Night Ride to Remember

Mather and Whitmore were sharing a bottle in Mather's log house. The hanging lantern cast a pathetic light. It wasn't full night yet and wouldn't be for several hours.

Whitmore said: "What'll we do about that 'breed son-of-a-bitch?"

Mather refilled a small glass with a steady hand when he answered: "We catch him an' take him out a ways 'n' bury him."

Whitmore considered his old friend's flushed face. "Things have heated up too much for that, partner."

"They'd never find him. There's others I helped Old Joe bury an'. . . ."

Whitmore cut his friend off with a slashing motion with one arm. "There's trouble comin', Bart. They put the Jessups damned near out of business, an' someone helped *us* by putting a couple of Colsons down 'n' out."

Mather stoppered the bottle and put it

aside. "It's been years comin', Jem. I been closer to it than you have. Crow wanted Jessup range for years, and he come close a couple of times but never this close. We're mighty crippled up like you said, but I still got some fight in me. Jem, I owe May and Young Joe . . . hell, I owe Old Joe. You stay here 'n' mind things. I'm goin' to ride northward a spell, turn east, an' be waitin' when they appear in the yard come sunup."

Whitmore glared, reached for the bottle, pulled out the stopper with his teeth, and took a hefty swallow. "Bart, you'd do better by *not* riding out of the yard. No, I think you should stay here, and I'll ride over there."

Mather took back the bottle and put it on the floor beside his bench. "How 'bout we both go. We can do it an' get back here before folks is stirrin'."

Whitmore leaned on the table. If they were going to do it, there wasn't time to argue. He bobbed his head. "Let's go. When you give out, I'll hide you an' pick you up on the way back."

"I'll do the same for you," Bart snapped.

With dusk's shadows beginning to form, Joe left the house to tackle the chores. He was less than halfway to the barn when he heard Mather's unmistakably grating voice.

"How come you to hitch that saddle boot on the left side?"

"Because I've always carried it that way," came Whitmore's response.

"Are you left-handed?"

"No, you damned old screwt. I'm right-handed. This way I got room to maneuver."

Joe changed the direction of his path, angling down the south side of the barn and turning in along the rear wall. He crept soundlessly to the barn opening at the back of the building.

He could hear Whitmore scolding again. "You can't make this ride, you old screwt. You're too banged up an' old for. . . ."

"Shut up an' quit wastin' time. You got any idea how long a ride is ahead of us . . . an' back!"

Joe stood aghast as they broke a cardinal rule. Instead of leading their mounts outside before mounting, they both got astride inside the barn. Joe jumped clear, his heart pounding, as the two old men emerged through the rear barn opening. As it was, Whitmore's horse shied as he cleared the opening and got cursed for doing it.

Mather couldn't resist. "Maybe we'd best get you one of the older horses."

Whitmore remained silent, reined sharply northward, and broke another horseman's rule. Instead of warming out his mount, he kicked his horse into a lope and kept at it as they disappeared out of earshot.

Joe went directly to Mather's house, saw the naked wall pegs where the booted Winchester usually hung, walked to the doorway, and strained to hear. The settling evening was as quiet as the inside of a jug. At the main house the kitchen light was burning. Joe could only guess that Mather and Whitmore had gone north to find those stolen Jessup horses. His conclusion was wrong, but the direction was right. It didn't take him long to make the decision to go after the two. He considered telling May his plans, but he knew she'd refuse to sanction such a crazy idea and fighting her would waste more time.

He went after a horse, rigged it out in the barn, and let his anger get the best of him, mounting in the barn and boosting the horse into a lope the second he was outside. He didn't slack off until he could make out a solid wall of forest dead ahead, then he slowed enough to listen. All was quiet. He continued riding on, pausing only now and then. Then finally he heard something — two riders up ahead, eastbound.

Joe changed course. He was south of the two, a fair distance. He knew that when they eventually broke clear of the timber, he would be able to see them. He paused at a creek, dismounted so his animal could drink. It was at this spot that it occurred to him that, if there was trouble, it just might be the Winchester kind and he had no carbine, just a six-gun. That worried him.

Back in the saddle, Joe heard a horse squall and a gun explode to the north. After that the only sound was of a very angry man cursing and fighting a terrified horse. Smiling to himself, Joe guessed the old men had ridden afoul of a bear or a cougar. It required no more for a horse to scent either of those meat-eating predators to frighten it out of its wits. Joe's own mount had either picked up a faint scent or had been frightened by the commotion for it was staying up in the bit and moving hesitantly. When the horse had calmed enough, Joe reined in the direction of the sounds. His horse obeyed but bobbed its head and snorted. Joe positioned his gun in his lap.

There was clear country ahead. Joe recognized it as the big meadow he had seen while scouting with Jem. He could see two horsemen plainly visible in the moonlight, riding in a belly-down run. He stopped at the last fringe of trees to watch. The riders were angling to the south as they traveled eastward. Joe waited until it was difficult to see the two men, then, keeping within the fringe of trees, he paralleled the two horsemen.

Over the next hour Joe realized that, if they continued on their present course, they were going to pass the Colson buildings. Joe halted one more time. The riders were changing course, still in the direction of the Colson place but maintaining a fair distance to the west. The idea that gradually began to firm up in Joe's mind was something he had not considered before. *Those two old men were purposefully heading for the Colson place!*

He was partly right. Through the dark distance he watched one of the horsemen grind down to a halt. The other slowed, turned around, dismounted, and led his horse back to where his companion was bent over on his mount.

Joe pushed barely clear of the last fringe of trees and dismounted to watch. They were close enough to the Colson spread for Joe to be able to make out a scattered assortment of ranch buildings, although trees interfered with a good sighting.

Joe dared not ride out across the open country, and it bothered him to be unable to get closer. In the blackness he was unable to distinguish Bart from Jem, their horses blocking a clear view. Still, he could guess what they were up to, and he became agitated as he pondered whether it was more advisable to stay out of sight or move in to help.

The man afoot mounted, and the two continued on their way at a dead walk. Joe followed, the dark stands of trees shielding him from detection.

When they came within rifle range of the Colson buildings, the riders separated. Joe positioned himself near a spit of trees that grew south of the main timber. From this vantage he could finally distinguish the two men from each other. The man closest to Joe was Mather. He was not only shorter than Whitmore, but he was riding with his left hand supporting his upper weight on the saddle swells. He lost sight of Whitmore among the trees planted in the yard by several generations of Colsons.

Joe told himself Jem would have to be on his own as the distance between himself and Bart continued to close. Bart was leaning, intently looking in the direction of the buildings. He never once looked over his shoulder. He had no reason to. This was the last distance to be covered. He concentrated ahead, not behind.

A dog barked. Almost simultaneously a

horse nickered south of Joe's position, then several horses made a racket on the far side of the spit of Joe's timber. He stiffened, turned his head, and thought he saw horses rushing south out through the timber. He wasn't certain until a pale horse, darker than a buckskin but lighter than a palomino, broke through in a scattered rush toward the open country.

Joe's view was brief and interrupted by the large trees, but the animals were making for the eastside grassland. His mount fidgeted, tossed its head, and was ready to nicker, but Joe's hand on the reins kept it still. When it seemed the last of the loose stock was clearing the trees, Joe reined in their direction. He knew it was gamble, that anyone close could distinguish a mounted man from loose stock, but he chanced it. He maneuvered in with the back group, mingling among them, bent far over as he rode. The animals around him did not notice; they were intent on following the free running animals ahead. Once they were out in the open, they began to scatter a little. Joe scattered with them, in the direction of timber.

By now the barking dog was having a fit, but, thus far, there had been no response from the house in the form of a light, movement, or voices.

In the open Joe had the scent of dust in his face. The free-running animals were following a large, jug-headed bay. Joe knew that animal. It was the only ridgling the Jessups owned, and true to his kind he had established his leadership. No horse took the lead from him or tried to veer off sideways to tempt the other animals to break away with him.

As Joe looked around for Bart or Jem, a second dog joined in with the yelps of the first dog, this one with a higher, more excited way of barking. Moving hesitantly, Joe was soon able to make out the buildings, which meant he was probably within carbine range. A light firmed up from a wavering wick at the house. It had to be getting along toward sunrise. People with morning chores to take care of would be stirring.

The abrupt dazzling brilliance of a gunshot from the direction of the porch made Joe flinch. Someone with a scratchy voice yelled. What the words were, Joe could not make out. Then another gunshot erupted, this time fired from a gun slanted skyward, the kind of shot fired to divert stampeding horses. The animals in front of Joe didn't scatter, but they were heading more to the east than the south, the direction of the buildings. Joe was tempted to fire back but restrained himself. Perhaps the person on the porch was just trying to divert the loose stock.

Another gunshot blasted the air. The muzzle blast had come from the direction Joe had last seen Bart. Although there was no shooting in response, the yelling increased and seemed to be coming from a direction other than just the house. Joe guessed the well house or the bunkhouse, now that he was closer to the Colson outbuildings.

Next someone made a challenging shout and fired twice in rapid succession with a Winchester. Edging forward with the loose stock, Joe was able to make out shadowy figures on the porch, their backs to the house. Although he was tempted, he held off firing back. As the horses around him began a random scatter, Joe doubled over as far as possible, let go two shots in the direction of the unsteady shadows on the porch, and then reined hard northward.

A return shot was fired from the porch. Then someone let go with what had to have been a buffalo rifle. The slug came close enough for Joe instinctively to flinch and rein hard away. If it had been one of those heavy old rifles bored for buffalo, its shooter would require time to reload. They were single-shot weapons.

Without warning a horse cut diagonally in front of Joe, and he had only seconds to try to rein clear. The collision was more a jolt than a bump. The horse in front went down to its knees, recovered almost instantly, and sprang ahead in a floundering rush. Joe's mount was knocked off cadence, but bounced ahead. When its hoofs hit the ground, it was running belly down. It changed leads, which loosened Joe in the saddle, but did not change stride.

The pace of the horse nearly jarred Joe's six-gun loose from his hand. Instinctively tightening his grip, he stayed with the horse, gun arm raised for the next shot. The firing pin fell, but nothing happened. Joe cocked and squeezed off two more times, each time with the same result. His handgun was fired out. He jammed the weapon down into its holster and concentrated on traveling due north and holding to his pace.

His horse was going up and down but not coming down as far ahead. He eased up on the reins just as he passed several large stumps. As the horse slowed, he caught sight of a man off to the left. He swerved the horse to circle around, expecting a bullet to enter his body any second. He stroked the head of his horse as he neared the man who stood wide-legged and ramming charges into the side of a Winchester carbine. It was at that moment that he recognized Bart.

Mather's mouth fell open, the very picture of an individual startled half out of his wits. He took one step forward, his right leg folding, and went down without a sound.

Joe jumped ahead, caught the old man with both arms, and grunted as he strained to get Mather upright. The old man was round-eyed. He made a wheezing sound. "Where'd you come from?" He stood on his own now.

Joe was slow answering. "I trailed you two old idiots. Except I've lost sight of Jem. Did you see him?" He pulled out his Colt and began to reload it.

Instead of a verbal answer, Bart stumbled and waved his arm, a look of panic washing over his face.

Joe grabbed him under the arms and eased him over to a shaggy old pine tree. Propped limply against the base of the tree, Bart struggled to catch his breath while the dizziness passed. When he was somewhat recovered, he repeated: "Boy, where'd you come from?"

Joe heard a horse approaching, dropped into a crouch, and twisted. The horse went past, heading west. Joe straightened up slowly, leathered his sidearm for the second time, and sank to one knee. "Bart, where's Jem?"

"Last I seen he was going easterly toward the road." He groped in his various pockets until he found his tobacco. He gnawed off a fresh cud and looked in the direction of the buildings.

Joe said: "Jem's not over there. Do you think you can ride?"

"Lost my damned horse, boy. Jem'll be along directly."

Joe was rising as he said: "Stay here. You hear me? Don't move from here. I'll find your horse." Joe stooped down and looked directly into Mather's face. "Bart, you understand? They'll be comin' . . . boilin' up here like a nest of bees. Give me your gun."

Joe took the weapon, reloaded it from his shell belt, and handed it back. "Don't move from here. I got to find that horse."

Mather nodded. Even with limited visibility Joe could see the old man's face. His gaze seemed clearer. He even forced a lopsided little grin.

The farther out he scouted the more difficult it was to see or hear an animal. Once he heard a man's shout, but it was a long way off. After an interval it was answered, this time from the direction of the stage road.

Although he didn't find Mather's horse,

he did find one. It was the old pelter his pa had given his ma close to sixteen or more years earlier. It was standing, head hanging, tuckered out in a small stumped-over clearing and did not so much as raise its head as Joe pulled his trouser belt loose and chummed his way over to the old horse. He was barely noticed. He led the horse back, and, although it stumbled a couple of times, it came along willingly enough.

Joe found Bart standing beside the pine tree. When he recognized the led horse, he groaned. "Her? Boy, I can walk faster'n she can run."

Joe turned the animal and offered an arm. "Get up there an' shut up!"

Mather's jaw was clenched the entire time he was mounting.

Joe fashioned a squaw bridle out of his belt, shoved the buckle end into Mather's hand, and said: "Set there. I'll get mine."

Neither Mather nor the old mare had moved when Joe returned, astride. He jerked his head without speaking and led off in the distant direction of the spit of trees he'd used as shelter.

Mather was silent until they were in the big timber, heading south, then he said: "What about Jem?"

Joe's reply was curt. "He's on his own. My

guess is there isn't a Colson been born who can find him in the dark if he don't want to be found."

"He's maybe hurt, boy."

"For what you two idiots figured to do he deserves to be hurt. What'n hell did you think you were goin' to do?"

"Smoke 'em out an' have it out with 'em once 'n' for all. Joe, this damned feud's been goin' on since your pa brought you home, an' that's long enough. Besides, I got a personal grudge."

"Bart . . . oh, hell, forget it! Keep that old mare movin'. Sure as hell is hot they'll be after us."

Mather snorted. "Can't run us down in the dark, boy. In a damned forest."

"If I had some money, I'd bet you on that. They don't have to read sign. They'll know as well as I did who came after 'em . . . an' why. Bart?"

"What?"

"You know how many Colsons is up here? The two of you was goin' to settle with the whole passel of 'em? May'll be walkin' a hole in the floor with all three of us bein' gone."

"She won't do no such thing. May never worried none about Old Joe . . . and she had plenty of reason. She's not that way, boy. In fact, she's just the opposite."

"What're you talkin' about?"

Mather snorted derisively again. "You're dumber'n I thought you was. Who do you think shot Crow between them corral yard slats from the alley in town?"

Joe halted his horse in mid-stride, twisted, and looked back at Bart, a look of total disbelief on his face. He didn't make a sound. He didn't have to.

"Boy, your pa would have figured it out in ten minutes. You never noticed that since that evenin' her limp's been worse? You didn't figure anythin' when the Doc come out and re-patched her hip? Boy, I rode in. You don't even remember that, do you? I found the spot where she shot from. There was some drops of blood an' moccasin marks in the dirt. Forbes's blinder than a bat . . . thank, God. Me, I been readin' signs in dust since before you was born. She rode this same old mare, boy. She hid out until she had a sightin', an' then she shot that miserable son-of-a-bitch."

Joe said: "I don't believe it. I'm askin' her when we get back."

"You'll do no such a thing. Now, let's pick up the gait. I figure they'll not be too far back."

Chapter Fourteen

Riders!

Mather had been wrong about May. It was true that in the past she hadn't worried about Old Joe, but this night she could not shake off the troubled thoughts she was having about Young Joe. So she had made up her mind and gone out to the barn. Now she was sitting outside the barn door with her injured leg shoved straight out. She'd managed to cross-tie a horse. The bridle and saddle were on the ground next to her. It was as far as she had gotten them in an effort to saddle up and hunt for Joe when her leg gave out.

May watched as a sickly gray streak formed in the eastern sky. As she stared, she heard the sound of riders. She struggled to stand up, but to no avail. The minutes passed, and, as the riders approached the yard, she recognized the posture of her son. A sigh of relief passed through her. She resolved to say nothing, but, when she saw the animal Mather was riding, she lit into him

226

with a tangle of cuss words in three languages.

Joe cussed under his breath at the site of May, then glanced at Bart, wondering how long he was going to have to play nursemaid to these two characters? Joe led the horse with Bart up to the house, where he helped him dismount and get settled in the chair in the parlor. Next Joe checked on May, found nothing broken, and just about carried her to the settee in the parlor where she could stretch out her leg. He told them to shut up and stay put while he dealt with the horses and the gear. Mather wouldn't even look at May.

The horses tended to, Joe returned to the house and got a fire started in the hearth, got the wood stove burning in the kitchen, and put the coffee pot on to fight off the chill of the morning. He returned to the parlor to find that May had wandered off to bed while Mather sat awake, in pain. Feeling sorry for him in spite of everything, Joe got the whisky bottle and poured Bart a stiffener in a small glass. He set the bottle on the floor next to him and walked over to the fireplace, where he stood with his back to the heat, regarding the old man.

"Well, Bart?"

"What?"

"Why'd you make that up about her shootin' Crow Colson?"

"I didn't make nothin' up. Boy, you can't be around folks as long as I've been around her. After she went through her mourning, she'd feed that old pelter twice a day. She was up to somethin'. For a while I figured she did that so's the old horse'd be stout enough to carry her up yonder. I thought she wanted to go back to . . . up yonder. I missed it by a country mile. For a fact, she rode the old horse into town. She left after sunset. In the mornin' I grained it. It had been rode, boy. Its back was still sweaty."

"You tracked her?"

Mather snorted. "In the dark! No. But that mornin' she couldn't leave her bed. You remember that. It was the same day we heard Crow'd been shot in the back. I rode to town. She left sign. Drops of blood, boy. You 'n' me slept through it."

"Forbes?"

"Boy, the constable couldn't read sign if he made it hisself." Mather straightened up, saying: "We better get to bed."

As Mather rose, having trouble steadying himself, he looked straight at Joe. "Never said any of this to you, an' you should never repeat a word of it. You owe her that, boy. She done what she thought was right, what her people think is right. She blamed Crow for everything, including your pa's death. Now, lend me a hand, boy." As Mather grabbed for the arm of the settee for support, he added: "Not as long as she lives. Not as long as you live."

When Mather awakened, it was fully light outside. Inside, there was a troublesome aroma coming from the kitchen.

He worked himself to the edge of the bed. Sleeping even for such a short length of time had caused his every muscle to tighten up. He eased himself up to a standing position and headed for the kitchen.

He nearly jumped out of his skin, when Whitmore stepped back from the stove and said: "It's about time. I figured you was dead."

"For Chris' sakes, Jem, ya tryin' to give me a heart attack?"

Chuckling, Whitmore put a cup of black coffee on the table for Mather as he sat down. As he curled both hands around the cup, he asked: "What happened to you? I thought they might've got hold of you."

"Well, as a matter of fact they did. Two of 'em. Big boys, but young. I leaped out at 'em, took 'em down, an' knocked 'em senseless. They was over near the stage road. It was darker'n hell."

"Was it now? How'd you know you was near the road?"

Whitmore turned. "I heard a coach comin'. Didn't know what become of my horse, so I stopped the coach, borrowed off a horse, and headed for home. May don't look very chipper."

Mather sampled the coffee, which was as bitter as Original Sin and pushed the cup away as a platter of fried meat and sourdough bread was slid in front of him.

The food tasted better. Midway through Mather looked up. "Ya seen Joe?"

"Doin' the chores. That bull's been faunchin' an' bellerin'."

Mather did not interrupt his eating to comment. If the bull was pawing and bellowing, he was ready to go back to doing what he was supposed to do, finding some bulling cows.

Joe came in, slamming the front door behind him — something Old Joe had lit into him about often enough when he was alive for him to know better.

Figuring the door slamming had meant something, Mather and Whitmore waited with anticipation for Joe's entry through the doorway.

"Indians up yonder," he said, stomping into the kitchen and heading for the coffee pot, "across the big meadow in the trees, actin' like they want to palaver but don't want to come out into the open to do it." He poured a cup of coffee and downed it in one swallow.

Mather struggled up to his feet in the amount of time it took for Whitmore to close the stove's damper and head for the parlor. Joe was right behind him.

Mather squawked at them to wait.

Whitmore was standing in the open doorway, peering to the north. He did not seem to have heard. Joe was next to him.

Mather caught Joe by the shoulder and pushed him aside. He told Jem he and the boy would go palaver.

For once there was no argument.

Outside, Joe veered toward the barn, but Mather growled at him: "We'll walk, boy!"

They walked, but slightly less than midway the old man's legs began to falter. The Indians remained out of sight, but the two knew that meant nothing, that they were out there, watching, as still and silent as trees.

Joe steadied Bart, but they only managed a few more steps before Bart's legs folded under him. Without a word Joe hoisted up the old man and got him back on his feet. Braced against Joe, he tried a couple of steps, then shook his head. "Can't do it, boy."

Joe looked in the direction of the house and then out into the distance. *Hell of a situation,* he thought to himself. He looked back toward the house. Except for the bull nothing seemed to be stirring. *Where the hell is Jem?* he wondered. He shifted his shoulder and arm to better distribute Mather's weight. Mather hung limply, silently, concentrating on his breathing.

"I guess they're going to have to come to us," he said to himself as much as Bart. No sooner had the words emptied from his mouth than a mounted Indian emerged from the timber, riding toward them at a dead walk.

Slowly the Indian became recognizable. Joe sucked down a big breath and expelled it. It wasn't a buck, but a female. Not only that, it was Donna. His heart missed an occasional beat as he watched her approach.

His breathing back under control with the few moments of rest, Mather assured Joe: "Won't be no trouble, boy, otherwise they'd never send a woman."

Like May, Donna was Pawnee. Paiutes had captured her mother, and she had eventually found her way to the fugitive *rancheria,* along with her young daughter, as had so many others, by moccasin telegraph.

As she stopped in front of Joe and Mather, Donna smiled shyly.

Joe did not smile back, but merely said: "Are the people moving? If so, they're goin' in the wrong direction . . . they got enemies south of here thick as the hair on a dog's back."

"Not moving. Come to help." She gestured to the east. "Soldiers coming. Posse men with them."

"Comin' here?"

She nodded and fixed her gaze on Mather. "Coming here. Reach here when the sun is up there" — she pointed — "high up there."

With the news, Mather's legs seemed to gain strength. He added two inches in height as he pushed himself away from Joe. He addressed the pretty girl. "You sure? They could be comin' in this direction . . . but maybe not right here."

She smiled slightly. "Coming here!" Her horse threw up its head.

Bart and Joe responded by surveying the area in all directions. All was quiet. The horse had caught movement at the house and was now staring at the yard.

Joe asked how many, and the girl held up both hands, fingers extended. She did that twice.

Mather muffled a curse. "Can't be," he told Joe, who kept thinking the girl had to be wrong. He addressed Donna: "Young lady, why'd your people come down here?"

The reply was given simply. "To help fight." She returned her attention to Joe. "You come back with me. Warriors need spokesman."

Mather spoke gruffly. "You stay here, boy. Soldiers see you ridin' with hideouts. . . ." Mather made a throat-slashing gesture with one hand.

Joe had one hard fact on his mind. If soldiers were coming, and if they saw armed buck Indians. . . .

Joe walked up to the side of Donna's horse and, reaching up, touched her hand. "Tell 'em to keep out of sight. We don't know that the soldiers are comin' to make war."

She looked at him with a doubting expression. "If soldiers make war. . . . Joe, we have men of war. We will fight, too."

Mather made his snorting sound before speaking. "Young lady, you're likely right, but until we know for a fact, you tell them to be invisible unless shootin' starts."

Joe nodded, reached for her hand again, squeezed her fingers, and then loosened his grip.

Donna grasped his fingers a moment longer before letting go. She said: "My people are ready. We worked all yesterday and last night striking camp. They're ready to run far and hide after they fight."

Mather wagged his head. "Not until there's shootin'. You tell 'em that."

Joe slowly turned Donna's horse and lightly tapped the horse's rump. It started back the way it had come. The single rein of Donna's war bridle hung slack as she rode off.

Despite the seriousness of the situation Mather made a quiet comment. "Prettier'n a speckled bird for a fact. Help me walk back, boy."

Joe supported him, moving at a quarter of the pace that was his habit. He looked back once to see Donna raise her arm in a shy wave, and Joe returned the salute,

Jem was waiting on the porch. May was in the parlor, unable to gather enough energy to go any farther.

"Let's step inside," Mather suggested as he made his way up the porch steps with Joe's assistance.

Whitmore followed Joe into the parlor where Joe tossed his hat aside, got Mather settled in Old Joe's leather chair, and told his listeners what the gist and the result of the palaver had been. The up yonder people would remain invisible, unless there was gunfire.

May instructed Whitmore to station himself at the window.

When he announced — "Can't see a danged thing. Nothing's moving." — May wasn't satisfied.

"Scouts, Jem," she stated emphatically. "Always soldiers have scouts."

Uncomfortable and in pain, Mather was short and disagreeable when he spoke. "May, Indians got scouts out, too. Soldiers won't find 'em unless they want to be found. Now, not to change the subject, but, Joe, I'd sure admire a pull on a bottle, boy."

May surprised them, by scrambling up to her feet, limping to the kitchen, and bringing Mather the bottle.

"Thank ya kindly, May. Now go set down. You want that bleedin' to start again?" Ignoring his own advice, Mather pushed up off the chair, the strain of the effort showing in his face. He limped to the porch where he collapsed into May's rocker.

Whitmore disappeared into the kitchen. When he heard May grunting, he appeared in the doorway, pointing with a large stiff finger. "You set still," he told her. "All's I'm getting is a dipper of water."

May eased sheepishly back down, looked at Joe, and shook her head. "In this place too many chiefs."

Whitmore returned to the parlor with a glass full of diluted tan whisky that he handed to May. "I'm hungry. How 'bout you two?"

They nodded their assent.

"Food coming up," Jem said jovially. "Can't face a herd of soldiers on an empty stomach."

May sampled the water glass's contents and winked at Joe. "Your pa say many times Indian got no business with this." She held up the glass, smiled, and tipped back her head. Swallowing slowly, she smiled at Joe and called out. "Bart, they come yet?"

"No. Well, there's dust easterly. Relax, May, they'll be along."

Her face was gaining color and her eyes brightening. She lowered her voice in Joe's direction. "He no see good. Long time now."

Joe went to stand in the doorway as Mather looked around. "I heard that, boy. I can see good as an eagle. As good as any danged Siwash Indian ever borned."

Joe raised an arm. "Is that your dust, Bart?"

The old man twisted from the waist up and strained for almost a full minute before saying: "That's it, boy."

Joe nodded with no expression. There was no dust in the direction he had pointed.

Some fifteen minutes later, Whitmore returned to the parlor eating from a platter. "Your plate's on the table, Joe," he said. He sat down beside May, spooned up a piece of warmed-over meat, and held it before her. She snapped at it like a mud turtle. Then Jem took a bite. They shared the rest of the meal this way while, in the doorway, Joe stood, trying not to grin.

Mather called sharply. "Boy? You see 'em now? Look a little northerly and westerly."

Joe walked to the door, looked out, and quietly said: "It'll be them. I guess you can see good enough, Bart? Can you see some blue coats among 'em?"

Mather lied with no qualm of conscience. "I see 'em, boy."

Joe remained expressionless when he said: "Fifteen, maybe twenty of 'em. Blue coats, Bart?"

"At least. Hard to make decent count with them others movin' among 'em."

Joe considered the old man for a moment before turning to go back inside. "Holler when they're close, Bart."

"I'll do that, boy."

As Joe turned into the parlor, Whitmore

raised his eyes. In a much softer tone than was normal, he said: "Joe . . . did you really see 'em, lad?"

Joe shook his head and went toward the kitchen. He was getting hungry. Before disappearing beyond the doorway, he said: "Nothin', 'cept a couple of deer."

Jem stopped feeding May, staring into space. "I didn't think so."

"It's all right. He'll see 'em when he should."

As Joe sat eating at the table, Whitmore came into the kitchen to sluice off his totally empty plate. He grinned at Joe. "She liked to eaten it all. She fell asleep."

Whatever retort Joe might have given was spoiled by Mather's calling from the porch.

"They're comin'. Boy, come out here an' make a count. Looks like half a damned Army. There's a pair of scouts up north and down south. *Joe! Jem!*"

Whitmore hurried out to the porch while Joe finished eating. He rinsed down the food with a couple of gulps of water, and was then by Jem's side. As the trio watched the group approach off in the distance, May hobbled shakily out to the porch. Joe helped her ease into the chair next to the rocker.

"Why all the yelling?" she asked, sniffing at Bart who sat comfortably in her rocker.

"Look, Ma," Joe said, pointing in the direction of the riders.

Joe made a quick count of the blue coats. He made out one riding stirrup to stirrup with Forbes out front, and three or four more back with the local riders, who made up the posse.

Squinting, May abruptly said: "That medicine man."

Mather responded gruffly. "I'll be glad to see him. Boy, is that an officer up ahead with the constable?"

Joe didn't answer. He didn't know an officer from an enlisted man, but Jem did.

"It's an officer," he told Mather.

Chapter Fifteen

The Meeting

Big Jem Whitmore faced Mather with a bright anticipatory gaze and said: "You still seventy-three?"

Mather frowned, trying to see past the large man. "What's that got to do with anythin'?"

Jem raised his head and said loudly: "*Ozu we tawatas!*" He looked down at Mather and translated: "Men of war, you old screwt. Today we're goin' to be genuine bloody-hands!"

Mather fished forth his old hogleg Colt and settled it in his lap as he retorted: "You old fool!"

Whitmore's expression did not change. "It's a good day to die, Bart."

Mather leaned forward and narrowed his eyes. The riders were now easily recognizable. Except for the soldiers he knew every man-jack among the posse riders. He answered Whitmore without looking at him.

"No such a thing as a good day to die. Go get May's bottle."

When Whitmore didn't move, Joe went inside and returned with the bottle. Mather hoisted it, handed it back, and offered a word of advice. "Boy, I know you don't like the stuff but, for your own sake, take one swallow. You'll likely never need it more'n you will today."

Joe took the bottle, swiftly upended it, swallowed once, and had a coughing fit as he held the bottle at arm's length.

Both the older men laughed, Whitmore the loudest. Mather was still a little ruffled with his old friend. He defended Joe. "You didn't do no better your first time. Jem, look yonder."

Whitmore faced around. His grin dwindled, and his voice was soft when he said: "Can you believe it? There's Blaise an' Nicholson from the bank, and. . . ."

Mather snorted irritably. "I ain't blind for Chris' sake. Shut up an' get out of the way. May, are you ready, girl?"

"We don't need her out here," Jem said. "She should go inside."

"I stay," May asserted.

Mather was concentrating on the posse riders when he stated: "With Nicholson along we might need her." Mather did not elaborate, and Whitmore had lost interest.

The posse men were no more than a scant half mile from the yard, and to Jem Whitmore it looked like an army was headed into the place. He lifted his holstered Colt from its housing, let it drop, and repeated that little exercise. Behind him Mather made a derogatory snort but said nothing.

May made a long, slitty-eyed study of the oncoming riders and spoke to no one in particular when she said: "Wish Old Joe here."

That elicited no spoken response; there wasn't a one among the trio who didn't feel the same. The riders were close enough to upset the bull in the corral. He rammed the logs hard enough to make them quiver, roared a challenge, backed off a few feet, and pawed at the ground, throwing clouds of dust over his back.

One of the men in the posse reined around to the far side of the group, keeping his distance from the bravo bull. Mather smiled in spite of himself. That was one posse rider who didn't know a damned thing about cattle. Every hamlet, village, and town had at least one like that.

May squirmed to stand up. Joe put a hand on her shoulder. "You don't get up to them, Ma . . . they take off their hats to you."

It was the mannerly thing to do, but, when

they reined up in front of the porch, not one of them removed his hat. Several, though, had yanked loose the tie-down thongs over their holstered sidearms, and only one man smiled. It was the captain who introduced himself.

"Ma'am, I'm Captain Berthold, U.S. Army. We met before. I'd like to talk . . . palaver . . . with you."

Mather snorted. "She ain't no holdout. She knows English as good as you."

The officer speared Mather with a chilly glance before addressing May a second time.

"Ma'am, it's about some men being shot."

May held to the arms of her chair, looking steadily at the soldier until he reddened and said: "I mean you no harm, ma'am. It's just that we was informed that there's a band of renegade Indians hiding in the mountains down here."

May finally spoke. It was a garbled mixture of several Indian languages. The officer turned to Mather who grinned and said: "Speaks English when she wants to."

The officer persisted. "What did she say?"

Mather could have managed a garbled interpretation, but Whitmore answered: "She said Indians don't trust people with freckles."

The officer's eyes widened. "If she means me, I don't have freckles."

"Not on the face," Whitmore elaborated. "On the heart."

The officer looked at the constable.

Forbes knew what was happening, and, delighting in it, he had difficulty keeping a straight face when he addressed May. "Talk to him, May. There's only five of 'em."

Whitmore spoke again. "Forbes, you know as well as I do that, given a little time, there'll be more of 'em. Tell her straight out why you're here an' what you want."

Captain Berthold looked squarely at May as he said: "Indians belong on reservations. It's against the law for tribes of 'em to stay out."

May responded in English: "You mean me?"

Berthold reddened again. "Not you. Indian hideouts . . . up yonder in the mountains."

"Why you want 'em?"

"I told you. Indians belong on reservations."

"Not them Indians, soldier. They got own reservation. Besides, no Indians 'round here."

Captain Berthold wasn't the only rider whose expression reflected surprise and bafflement.

May whispered to Joe: "Help me up." She used the cane to shuffle over to the porch railing, Joe at her side. She raised the cane to point it directly at the officer.

Joe whispered: "Don't do that." He might as well have been talking to a stone wall. She ignored Joe, and she was not smiling.

"Indians got land," she began. "They got their *rancheria*. They don't make trouble. They know whites. Many whites know them. No trouble. Not any."

The officer cleared his throat before speaking. "Ma'am, you don't understand. The government's set up reservations where Indians have to live. If they leave their reservation, the Army hunts them down. That's the law. Now then, let's move on to something else. Yesterday, three of my men scouted the upcountry. They found no Indians, but they found plenty of their sign. Ma'am, I came out here to ask you to tell 'em that, if they don't all come down where I can count 'em, I'll send for reinforcements. And if the Army is involved, they'll either take them to a reservation peaceably or fight them until there's none left."

Joe looked to the constable. "Forbes?"

The constable was visibly uncomfortable. Captain Berthold had given May a grisly ultimatum.

Forbes faced Captain Berthold. "You're

makin' war talk, Captain. There's only five of you."

Berthold understood the insinuation perfectly. After a moment of hesitation he said: "All right. How about the murders? Crow Colson and Harland, his son?"

Forbes's responded gruffly. "I told you that's a civil matter. The Army's got nothin' to do with it. And for the last time, nobody's turned up Harland's body."

Berthold's anger showed. "Constable, this territory is not a state of the Union. Those territories that aren't in the Union are under Army jurisdiction. Did *you* know that?"

Forbes did not say whether he knew it or not. He said: "You're pushin' for trouble, mister. Except for your soldiers, there's not a man among us that'll let you put him where he might get killed. Law or no law. In town you said you wanted to talk . . . *talk*. Well, do it. Don't threaten."

Berthold's stare at the constable was fully hostile. But he was neither a young man nor an inexperienced soldier. He controlled his anger, saying: "I didn't make a threat, Constable. I simply stated the law. I've palavered with holdouts before. They got to understand the fighting's over. We beat them, and we made them peaceable by reservationing them. Constable, this isn't good. You should be upholding the law with me, not against me."

Whitmore spoke from the porch with his rugged old weathered countenance curled into a snide smile. "Gents. Directly it'll be suppertime, an' May's one hell of a cook." He left out the fact that he had been the one to prepare the stew that simmered in the kitchen.

Among the locals appeared a sprinkling of smiles. The townsmen seemed to be hoping this dispute would end. One man spoke to the Irish sergeant in a needlessly loud voice. "Friend, I don't figure this is our fight."

The sergeant retorted sharply, turning in his saddle: "You was ready to join us on the ride out here."

His fellow blue coats remained quiet, but the members of the posse were showing a distinctive uneasiness. That same loud townsman, who had spoken to the sergeant, spoke again.

"Forbes, it warn't supposed to end up in a fight. In town you said. . . ."

The constable cut the speaker off. "Amos, what I told you was that we got to support the law."

A squeaky-voiced townsman said: "All right. We supported it. Now I'm goin' to be late for supper, an' my wife don't like that."

This time the laughter was general, except for the red-faced captain and his enlisted men.

Berthold addressed the law man: "Well, Mister Constable?"

Forbes did not take his gaze off the quartet on the porch. "Your call, Captain. Bad odds."

A man toward the back of the group called out in an unsteady voice: "Forbes, you best look yonder!"

The attention of all was drawn to the rise of land to the north.

"Son-of-a-bitch!" Mather spit, unable to control his disgust. "Joe?"

At a loss, Joe muttered: "You heard me. I told 'em not to show unless there was. . . ."

A bearded posse man made a dry comment. "What language did you tell 'em in, boy? That's a heap of Indians, an', from what I can see, they're sashayin' their horses back an' forth in the old sign of makin' a fight."

Mather gimped from his chair to the railing near May. He allowed a long moment of indecisive silence to run on before he said: "Boy! Go tell 'em to beat it."

Joe looked at the constable who nodded.

As Joe sprang down the porch steps, Captain Berthold said: "Constable, you knew

249

they would be out here?"

"No, sir."

"But you knew they were fugitives living in the hills."

May spoke from the porch. "They belong here. You don't. Go back. Go home, soldier!"

A whiskered, burly townsman reined around, wove his way between the fellow posse members, neither speaking nor looking back once he broke clear. He rode arrow straight in the direction of town.

The skinny man with the high-pitched voice yelled — "Wait up!" — and also worked his way clear of the other riders. He kept riding at a steady walk following the bewhiskered dissenter.

Joe left the barn by the rear exit, coaxing his animal into a slow lope. He kept at steady pace until he was certain that the up yonders saw him.

On the porch, May addressed the officer. "My husband tell me horse not chair. If you no ride, get down!"

No one moved. Gritting his teeth, the captain resumed watching Joe's progress. At this blatant insolence, the Irish sergeant swung from the saddle. Standing beside his mount, he removed one gauntlet, stroked the horse's neck, and smiled at May.

Slowly, one by one, the local men dismounted. The remaining three soldiers were the last to do so. When the captain realized he was the only man left in the saddle, he, too, dismounted.

Mather nudged May. "Tell the doctor you need to see him."

May singled out the sparrow-like medicine man and spoke. He handed his reins to another rider and passed Forbes and the officer to reach the porch. Mather nudged May again. "Take him inside to see to your hurt."

For the first time since the meeting had begun, May smiled, jerked her head, and led Barry Leger into the house.

Mather hitched slightly closer to Whitmore and addressed the constable.

"Forbes, take 'em back. This here palaver is over with."

Captain Berthold objected. "Stand fast!" he commanded loudly, then stepped forward, glaring at Mather.

Whitmore had anticipated the officer's reaction, and, leveling a stiff finger at the officer, he said: "Mister, them tomahawks up yonder are primed for a fight. All's I got to do is fire one round in the air. Count 'em, mister. They got you out numbered three to one, an' that's only the ones you see. Captain, remember Mister Custer?"

The captain did not yield, but several members of the posse did, and, without speaking, they mounted their horses and rode in the same direction the other deserters had ridden.

A wolfish smile passed over Whitmore's face directed at the officer. "Count what you got left, mister. I make it nine men . . . not all of them willing to fight. Look back yonder again. That's one hell of a mob of tomahawks. Forbes?"

Eyes fixed on Whitmore, the constable solemnly nodded in the direction of the porch, heaved up into his saddle, and followed the strung-out dissenters heading back to Cumberland.

Whitmore walked slowly off the porch in the direction of the soldiers, who had all remounted, including the captain, and stopped when he came abreast of the captain's horse. He raised one hand to the bridle's cheek piece, turned the horse, and tapped it lightly on the rump.

The man holding Leger's animal looped the reins over the hitch rack, got astride, nodded in the direction of the porch, and started out in a slow lope to catch up with his companions. Within minutes the last of the posse, the last of the soldiers, were heading east, clear of the Jessup yard.

Mather had been on his feet as long as he could be and went to sit in May's rocking chair while Whitmore returned to the porch.

"I wasn't goin' to hurt the son-of-a-bitch. I was just movin' his horse. Besides, I'm hungry again."

Squinting into the distance, Mather commented: "You like roast 'possum? They'll likely have some." He pointed toward the hill.

The up yonders were coming in. Not many, no more than possibly a dozen, but it was clear in that each buck in the group had a carbine balanced across his lap.

Leger returned to the porch, where he joined the others in silently eyeing the oncoming tribesmen. He eventually broke the silence. "Isn't that a girl riding up front with Joe Jessup?"

"May's niece," Mather mumbled. "Only they don't have nieces, only daughters. Doc, you can learn a lot from them Indians."

Joe and Donna were almost in the yard when Whitmore solemnly said: "You know what we done?"

Mather snapped an answer. "Run off a herd of idiots. I'm surprised at Forbes bein' with 'em."

Whitmore ignored that last sentence.

"That officer'll come back after he's called for as many blue bellies as they'll let him have. Lads, this ain't over. It's not even really begun."

Leger groped for a place to sit. He had never encountered what he felt were armed hostile Indians before. He lost some color and fidgeted until Mather growled at him: "You're safer than you ever was in your mother's arms."

As Whitmore stepped off the porch to greet the Indians and direct their animals to the barn and out-back corrals, May appeared in the doorway.

The doctor looked around and scolded. "I told you to stay in bed. Trying to make you do what you'd ought to do is like talking to a dumb. . . ."

"Indian," May finished for him. She smiled, using her cane to clear the doctor from her path. She sat down in the chair next to Bart and said: "She can help."

"Doin' what?"

"Cookin' supper. I can't do it alone. They'll be hungry."

Mather growled. "Indians is always hungry."

May's smile remained. "Joe help, too."

Most of the Indians lingered at the barn or near the stone trough. A few of the older men accompanied Joe and Donna to the house. One was Blue Barrel's successor as spokesman. His name was Manuelito. He was a desert tribesman, a Navajo. He knew Whitmore and Mather. He spoke reservation English that, where he'd grown to manhood, was liberally sprinkled with Mexican Spanish. He was a lean, muscular man, gray at the temples, and if he hadn't crossed the yard beside Jem, he would have been notable for his physical development.

Mather struggled to his feet to greet Manuelito.

When May asked Jem for assistance in getting up, Doc Leger exploded, jumping in front of her chair and telling her in no uncertain terms that she was to rest.

Joe smiled as his mother stopped struggling, smiled at the doctor, and addressed Manuelito: "Bad hurt leg."

He nodded understanding. "We know. Good shot."

May's smile lingered, but it was strained.

Mather's gaze at the spokesman was almost hostile. When he had a chance later, he took the spokesman aside. He asked how he had known May had been injured. The Indian smiled broadly, and said: "Secret." Mather repeated the word and winked. The spokesman winked back.

Doc Leger's obvious discomfort was somewhat mitigated when Joe introduced him to Donna. Without thinking he told Joe she was very pretty.

Donna both embarrassed and startled the doctor when she said in accentless English: "Thank you."

With Leger thrown off-balance, May took the opportunity to get up from her chair. She took Joe by the arm and said she would need his and the girl's help in adding to Jem's stew. Before Leger had a chance to speak, she tapped his shoulder with her cane and softly said: "Dumb Indians?"

Realizing it was a losing battle with May, Leger decided to leave. As he walked down the steps, three Indians approached him. As he mounted, one of the trio, a sinewy old Indian, said: "Come see you." He used both hands to rub his back. "Much sick here."

The doctor forced a smile. "Any time," he said, and left the yard at a walk, convinced he was proving his courage, but the three Indians had already walked into the house where fitful little spits of smoke were rising above the kitchen.

Chapter Sixteen

Omens

The tribesmen departed after gorging on the stew that Jem had made, cornbread, and cold spring water. May tried to talk Donna into staying. Not until Manuelito sided with May did the girl waver. Nevertheless, when the horses were brought out, Donna left the yard among the up yonder people. May could see the disappointment in Joe, and she tried to keep him occupied, helping her, until the Indians were no longer in view.

For three days he said little, did not laugh, and rarely smiled. The day Whitmore decided it was time to turn the bull loose was the day Joe began to rally, and Whitmore had nothing to do with it.

May was shucking snap beans on the porch, occasionally shading her eyes to look for any sign of Joe who had ridden out with Mather. On one of her glances up she saw something that would work magic for Joe.

Two Indians, females, came out of the distant trees walking their horses arrow straight in the direction of the Jessup yard.

May put aside the bean basket, went into the house where she stood by the front window until the horseback women were clearly identifiable. She hurried ineptly to her room where she cursed in good English because changing clothing with one leg firing darts of pain all the way up to her head was not easy. Getting on the ceremonial moccasins was genuine torture. For one thing May couldn't raise the injured leg high enough. For another, the foot of her injured leg was swollen. She finally got her foot into the moccasin but could not tie the thong. Cursing again, she got off the edge of the bed fully clothed and reached for her cane just as the two horses nickered from the direction of the barn.

Donna and her companion, a wizened, very ancient squaw, were dressed in their smoke tans attire. May's similar clothing hung on her, which she ignored.

The women cared for their horses at the barn, washed their hands at the trough, and started for the house where May was sitting again, breaking snap beans in the basket.

Donna called a subdued greeting. The old woman with her waved her greeting. She hadn't been able to sing a chant or a greeting in several years. Her name was Bear Mother. She was, as were most of the up yonder people, a cross-breed, Lakota and Crow. How that could be Bear Mother had never explained. All Sioux — Lakota included — hated Crows, had fought them and plundered them. The hatred was mutual. Neither tribe had ever ignored an opportunity to attack the other.

May did not arise until her visitors were on the porch, then she offered them food, which was declined. May considered their elegant smoke tans and also noticed the tiny intertwined snakeskin bracelet Bear Mother was wearing.

The very old Sioux-Crow woman noted May's glance at the bracelet and got to the point without the further exchange of pleasantries. She asked where Joe was. May told her that Joe had ridden out early with Bart.

Bear Mother sat down, looking disappointed. She twisted the snakeskin bracelet.

May smiled. "It be time," she told the old woman. "Joe be back. Always for supper."

With no alternative, Bear Mother said she and Donna would wait.

May put the bean basket aside, looked at Donna, and gently inclined her head.

Donna shyly smiled and nodded her head.

Bear Mother said: "She ready. Not yesterday. Today."

May took them inside, filled two shot glasses in the kitchen, returned to the porch, and handed one glass to Bear Mother who, ignoring any custom concerning drinking, tossed off her whisky with the aplomb of an old hand.

When May did not offer a refill, Bear Mother asked for another.

May lied. "Bottle all gone."

Joe and Mather returned just before sundown. They saw the Indian horses at the barn, so were not surprised when they found the women, sitting quietly, in the parlor.

Mather manufactured an excuse to make himself scarce, and retreated to his log house. He had noticed that Donna and the old woman were dressed for ritual and knew that it meant there was to be a ceremony. Mather sat down on his bunk, kicked out of his boots, and smiled from ear to ear, not entirely because there was to be a hitching, but because May's cooking skills had never been great and they'd gotten worse since she'd been shot. His few encounters with Donna's cooking had been a pleasant experience.

When Joe sat down in a chair across from May, old Bear Mother ignored him and announced to his mother that she was prepared to perform the marriage ceremony.

Joe looked like someone had just doused him with a bucket of cold water, but only for a moment.

Donna had been watching him, and, when his color faded and he met her gaze, she smiled. So did Joe. May excused herself, went to the kitchen for another bout with the bottle, and returned barely putting any weight on her cane.

There was no big bonfire, no noisy dancing, no speech making as was Indian custom. Inside the house, with only four people present, Bear Woman removed the entwined snakeskin bracelet, took the young people to the window where she invoked a blessing from the sun, and mumbled some words Joe could not understand, while May stood as witness to the ritual. When the ceremony was ended, the two old woman abandoned the girl and her husband, making a beeline for the kitchen.

Joe took his wife by the hand and led her over to the creek where a mother mallard and her five ducklings were rooting along the far shore. None of the two-legged creatures heeded the other.

After nightfall, Mather settled himself on a bench outside his cabin to share his thoughts with the moon.

Whitmore appeared, sat down soundlessly, and said: "You got the jug?"

In a testy voice for having his thoughts interrupted, Bart said: "Under the bunk."

Later, when he had a tinge of fire in his veins, Jem said: "There's two tomahawk horses in the barn."

Mather exhaled a big breath. He would have to finish his moon visit some other night. He explained: "That ol' medicine woman come with the girl from up yonder."

Jem looked startled. "That old witch is a. . . ."

"Marryin' squaw."

"Young Joe?"

Bart looked irritably around. "Well, it warn't me."

Jem went back inside for a moment, returned, sat on the bench beside his old friend, and mournfully said: "Too bad Old Joe couldn't have been here."

A snort was the response from Bart, then: "He pushed them at each other for years. An' how do you know he wasn't here?"

The two became silent. Both straightened at the sound of a mallard duck squawking and beating its wings among the creek-side willows. Both peered into the darkness along the creek.

"Varmint over there after a duck," Jem opined.

Bart groped for his chewing plug, offered it first to Jem before tearing off a cud and cheeking it, as he said: "Me 'n' the boy rode out today. What with them runnin'-iron fellers bein' busy an' all, I was surprised. We're goin' to have as big a drive as we ever had."

Continuing to lean with both forearms on his upper legs, head tilted as though listening in the direction of the creek, Jem said: "The Army's goin' to be comin', Bart."

"What're you talkin' about? They haven't had time yet."

"They're comin' anyway," Jem retorted. "You know that young buck who cuts wood around town?"

"The one ol' Abe Cutler uses on his drives every autumn?"

"That's him."

"Well, what about it?"

"Percy Sullivan give him a silver cart-wheel to steal a letter that soldier officer left at the store to be mailed north."

Bart considered the information. "Why in hell would Percy do that?"

Jem straightened on the bench, leaned back, and replied without haste. "Percy's a figurin' individual. All's I know is what he told me. He give the fellow a silver dollar. That buck snuck the letter away from the store, an' Percy read it."

"What'd it say?"

"It was a pack of lies about the hideouts threatenin' the officer an' his escort. Hundred's of 'em. He said he could lead the Army to the hideout up yonder on the Jessup range."

Bart shifted his cud without speaking for a long time. Jem wasn't a liar. They had known each other for many years. He spat out his cud, looked in the direction of the main house. "I got some thinkin' to do," he said.

When they were inside his cabin, Bart turned up his hanging lamp and asked: "How long'll it be, Jem?"

The big man was perched on the edge of the rumpled bunk when he answered. "It'll take the letter at least a day to reach Cheyenne. Give another day for the Army up there to act serious, plus at least three days for the soldiers to get down here. How long is that?"

"A week, maybe a tad less. If they bring along a wheel gun maybe more'n a week. Why?"

"That ought to be enough to roust folks up."

Bart was sitting down when he snapped: "What folks? Most around here got no use for Indians. Not even tame ones."

Jem was stretched out beneath two moth-holed Army blankets when he matched his friend's sarcasm. "You don' know 'em, Bart. I live in town. Folks been payin' 'em for years to do their plowin', scrubbin', huntin'. You know Frank Nicholson? His wife hires 'em to do her housework. Bart, it's mostly the old hard-shell ranchers that don't like 'em, an' even among them there's some that use 'em at markin' an' gatherin' time."

There was no answer, and in a few minutes Jem heard Bart snoring. It sounded like a shoat caught under a gate.

Whitmore was an early riser, had been for most of his life. He was scrubbing at the stone trough, when he heard a woman giggle. It was too dark to see, but he perked up his ears and eventually he heard a door close over at the main house. He stood quietly, breathing deeply of the dawn air. A noise coming from the barn drew his attention. It was one of the animals wanting feeding, so he busied himself with a few of the morning chores, beginning by flaking

265

timothy hay from the loft.

When he was finishing up, a wizened Indian woman appeared in the entry to the barn. She stood perfectly still, looking owlishly at Jem before going on through to the corral where she caught her horse and led it inside to be rigged out. Jem might as well have been invisible. The old woman talked to her horse, looked for something to stand on, saw the nail keg, led her horse to it, and mounted. As soon as she was seated, the horse moved out. She looked back once, expressionless but with watery eyes. Bear Mother had a hangover.

While he was watching her ride north, Bart sidled up. He followed Jem's line of vision and snorted. "She married 'em sure as I'm standin' here."

Jem did not move as Bart made the gesture of someone encircling one wrist with the other hand. He continued to stare.

Bart laughed. "I got makin's for hoecakes. You hungry?"

They walked together to Bart's house, where he prepared breakfast. As they sat eating, they caught the faint but audible sounds of a chant coming from the direction of the main house. The old men paused between mouthfuls to listen. As Bart cocked his head, closing his eyes to listen, Jem speared the last hoecake from the platter in the middle of the table.

There was a knock at the door. Before either could respond, May opened the door, walked in, leaning heavily on her stick. She tossed a tiny leather pouch on the table by Bart's empty plate.

He looked up, slurped a swallow of coffee from a saucer — a habit from his frontier days that he had never quite given up — and picked up the little pouch. He looked at May, nodded, pocketed the pouch, and asked her if she wanted to join them. She turned and left the log house without speaking.

Jem held out his hand. Bart fished forth the little pouch and handed it over.

Jem tossed the pouch up in the air and smiled as he said: "First chance I get." He went back to eating. When he was finished, he said: "Ain't very much, Bart."

"Ain't supposed to be," Mather snapped back. "You don't want to fill the yard with pups, do you?"

Jem shoved back his chair, ran a sleeve across his mouth, and said — "Much obliged." — and got up from the table.

Bart did not even bob his head. Hospitality was a foregone conclusion.

They went together to the barn where Jem

rigged out the big speckled-rumped horse, led him out to be mounted, and, leveling a finger at Bart, said: "Mind my word. Maybe you don't think so, but by Gawd I know so. The Army'll be comin'."

The sun was high and climbing. Bart had difficulty looking up at his old friend with the sunlight slanting in his face. He nodded, hit the speckled horse on the rump, and returned to his house to clean up the tin dishes.

As he was washing the last of the utensils, he glanced out the window. Although he knew his eyesight was deteriorating, he could make out two riders perched on their horses, eying the Jessup layout. "Son-of-a-bitch! They never let go," he cussed to himself. He buckled his hogleg into place and removed his saddle gun from its pegs on the wall. Bart left the booted Winchester leaning against the wall and crossed toward the house where May was supporting herself on the peeled log railing with both hands.

Without looking away from the distant riders, she said: "Joe right, they no give up." She turned, eyed Bart's holstered Colt and cartridge belt. "What you do with them things?" she asked.

Mather replied tartly. "Nothin', if you keep me here talkin'."

May wagged her head. "Time past for you. For me. For all."

"Like hell it is!"

"See that one on sorrel?" she asked.

Bart lied without any expression. "Of course, I can see him. What of it?"

"It's she not he. Never mind. You stay with May."

Bart started to descend the wooden steps to the yard. "It's been goin' on too long already, May."

She stole a piece of his thunder, when she snorted: "No sorrel. One is bay and one is gray."

Bart looked steadily at the woman without a sound until she faced him smiling, then he cursed under his breath, went to a bench, and sat down, peering intently northward.

May came back to ease gingerly down beside him. "Fat Mexican at Laramie make eye glasses."

"I don't like Mexicans."

"No have to like. Get Joe take you see him."

The distant riders loped around behind an overgrown thicket and did not reappear, so the subject was dropped.

May leaned forward, searching the area around her chair. "Where bowl go? Was here. Snap beans go bad."

Bart twisted around on the bench. "May, that was yestiddy. You didn't have no bowl for snap beans just now, when I come up here."

The old woman continued to search, then abruptly straightened up, saying: "Had 'em right . . . there" — she pointed — "today."

Fishing in a pocket, Bart suddenly remembered he had given Jem the pouch when he'd left. "I give Jem that corn pouch, an' he rode to town," he told May.

She looked up with round eyes. "He got to come back," she said.

"Where's Joe and Donna?"

"Sleepin'. I no bother them. You know?" May blushed.

He knew. "Jem'll be back. I'm goin' to saddle up 'n' go look for them bush-whackers."

There was no mistaking the determination in Bart's face. May knew she would be unable to deter him, so she said: "Go! You live too long anyway. *Go!*"

His temper was rising as Bart limped down the steps. He was one of those people whose anger sometimes required two days to abate. This particular black mood had nothing to do with having a female telling him what to do. It went deeper than that.

He was rigging out when Joe appeared,

himself looking irritable.

"Where the hell you think you're going?" Joe snapped.

Bart turned to face the young man, envying his youth. "There was two riders up. . . ."

"I know. May told me. I'll ride with you. I got somethin' to say, anyway. Where's Jem?"

"Taken that spotted rump horse an' headed for home," Bart said, and eyed Joe up and down. "Marriage don't seem to agree with ya none."

"Marriage is fine," Joe responded. "It's everything else that's bothersome."

Bart stood chuckling as Joe rigged out a snuffy four-year-old with an unsteady eye.

May watched from the porch as the two rode out of the yard. She could tell they were arguing. By the time they had passed out of May's view, she looked toward the east and saw two riders. An uneasy feeling passed through her body. At the same time Donna appeared on the porch.

"Where's Joe?" she asked.

"With Bart."

"Where's Jem?"

"Rode to town."

Donna went to a bench, sat down heavily.

They sat in silence for nearly an hour before either spoke. It was May who said:

"Two days." In a slightly stronger voice she said: "Don't worry. I go get him and bring him back."

"You can't ride, May."

May smiled, this time with a scarcely noticeable twinkle. "Old squaw tough. Like rawhide."

The conversation ended, and, as they sat quietly, a rider came swooping down off the northern hill, making a high, trilling whistle.

May gasped as she recognized Joe riding hell-bent for the Lazy J.

Chapter Seventeen

The Bushwhack That Failed

The pair of horsemen May and Donna had been watching in the east saw Joe's horse galloping in from the north, and they shifted their direction, intent, it would seem, upon making an interception, impossible though it would be considering their position.

The women on the porch sat as spectators, too distant to do more than watch. But May couldn't just watch. She got up, limped past Donna, made it as far as the wide steps leading to the ground, and raised her cane in a menacing gesture as she took the first downward step. The injured leg curled under her weight. She made a squawking sound as she fell, tumbling down the second and third steps, one arm extended trying to stop the momentum of her fall. The extended arm caught only the edge of the lowest broad stair, and May rolled, lost her cane, flashed a startled look up at Donna, and landed in the dirt on her injured side.

Donna forgot everything. She seemed almost to fly to reach the older woman. May ratcheted herself up onto both arms, spat, unsteadily raised her head, and fought to turn it toward the porch as Donna dropped beside her. The young woman slid an arm beneath May and strained to lift her. In spite of Donna's youthful strength, the best she could do was raise her five or six inches. Struggling, Donna managed to get her into a sitting position. When May squirmed, Donna said: "Push!"

It was the sound of someone yelling in the distance that seemed to energize the older woman. Her attention became focused, and she called out: "Joe! Son!"

Donna tried lifting again, but she still lacked the strength. As Joe shouted again, grunting, May pushed Donna aside and got to her feet. She stood like a statue as Donna took her by one arm. May lashed out, almost striking the younger woman. Still Donna hung on, steadying May as she weaved.

Joe entered the yard, dismounting his horse in a flying leap. He closed the distance on foot, his arms extended as he ran toward May.

Yanking free of Donna, May nearly fell as she staggered toward her son, but Joe caught her. The two riders approached, called out, but the trio near the porch ignored them as they worked to get May back up on the porch, to the nearest chair. May sat, easing down carefully, a look of fear in her eyes.

Donna stared at her man, her husband. His shirt was ragged and bloody, his face was twisted. There was blood on it, too. She leaned forward, asking: "What happened, Joe? You're hurt!"

Joe ignored her in his concern over May. Standing back, he studied his mother's face. May had closed her eyes. "Help me get her inside, Donna," he said. Donna obeyed.

As they carried her into the house, May mumbled: "He shoot me, again?"

"No, you fell," Donna explained. She instructed Joe to get the whisky once they had May positioned in her bed. Next Donna cleaned May's face, hands, and arms. She was covering up May, making her comfortable, when Joe returned with the bottle.

The liquor worked surprising magic. May's eyes brightened. She reached for Joe's arm and closed down with a powerful grip. "What happen, Joe? Where Bart?"

Before Joe could respond, Emmet Forbes and Percy Sullivan appeared in the doorway of May's bedroom. "Everything OK?" Forbes asked breathlessly.

Joe glanced at the two men and nodded.

The constable went to bedside where May looked up at him.

"Fell down damned steps," she said, looking to Donna for verification.

Donna nodded, and May closed her eyes.

Joe stepped back and tipped his head, indicating he wanted to speak with the law man outside. They left the room together and went outside.

"Run into some trouble up yonder," Joe began. "Bart's hurt. His horse went down. I had to leave him. He's under a big old pine tree a couple of miles or so north. He was knocked unconscious. All I could do was make him comfortable."

Although worded slightly different, Forbes and Sullivan asked the same question: "Were you runnin' from someone?"

Joe held a handkerchief to his mouth as he replied. "Yeah. One fellow had the fastest horse. He knocked me right off my horse. We tussled for a while. Bart came in to help and got knocked out cold. I got in a kick and a couple of punches before I heard riders. Someone yelled for the guy I was fighting with to clear out. Bart was out cold, so I had to leave him to come for help."

"Who were they?" Forbes asked.

"I'm pretty sure the guy I was fighting was

that Gunn Colson. But I never really got a good look at his face."

Forbes nodded. "How many you think?"

"Three, maybe four. It's a guess."

"How'd you get so knocked up?"

"When I caught my horse, it was cropping grass beside a big old oak. I jumped for the stirrup and went straight into the springy limbs of the oak tree, tore my shirt, got hit across the face."

Forbes nodded and said: "You stay with your ma. Percy and I'll go get Bart."

The two loped their horses a mile or so while they looked for Joe's sign. Once they found his trail, they hastened to find Mather. When they found him, he seemed confused as he was searching for his horse. Most times Mather could have caught it, hands down. Today, the horse would let him get only so close, then it would slyly drift away. It was a common trick with horses, but it only worked well if the pursuer was afoot. Consequently Forbes caught the horse.

As he handed the reins over to Mather, who had squatted down by a tree, the constable said: "You all right?" He dismounted and went to give Mather a hand.

"I'm fine," Bart grunted as he tried pushing up and couldn't. His mood did not improve since he had to accept Forbes's assistance.

"Did you recognize him, Bart?" Sullivan asked. "You sure you're OK?" he added, noting that Mather's hands were unsteady as Forbes gave him a boost up into the saddle.

"Told ya, I'm fit," Mather snapped. "I got a good look at him . . . that bronco Indian cousin from down south. The one named Gunn Colson."

Forbes answered irritably. "I know who you mean."

"He was ridin' a Thoroughbred horse, sixteen hands, if he's an inch. Big bay . . . he don't run, he flies."

Forbes said: "Snug up an' let's ride." He waited until Mather had taken up the slack in the cinch and swung over leather before speaking again. "You liked to scairt the whey out of May 'n' the others."

"Weren't my fault. I slipped, and that damned Colson took advantage of the situation. You wouldn't have a dram would you?"

"Don't carry it with me," the constable answered.

Mather looked to Sullivan who shook his head.

They traveled along easily, each with their own thoughts.

Mather eventually broke the silence. "He come up behind us. I got no idea where he come from. We tried to run for it." Mather frowned. "He knocked Joe out of the saddle. I figured he'd shoot, but he didn't."

Forbes relayed what Joe had said, and Bart wagged his head. He had no recollection of a fight nor did he remember anyone but the man who was riding the big, leggy running horse.

By the time they got back to the ranch, May was on the porch again, bundled in her thick robe. Joe was at the barn. Donna inside, cooking. She called out when she saw the riders coming in.

As Joe exited the barn, he squinted in the direction of the three horsemen. He lifted his hat, mopped sweat from his brow, and started for the house. He was on the porch with May, when a rider approaching from the east raised a large arm and called ahead.

"Jem," May sighed, relief washing across her face.

Jem was astride the big, spotted-rump horse. He rode past the house with another wave, went to the barn where he met up with Mather, Forbes, and Sullivan. There was a brief discussion of the encounter with the Colsons, and then Jem led the way to the porch.

The trudge of the their footfalls brought Donna to the porch, wearing one of May's aprons.

"Cumberland's all roiled up," Jem announced. "The Army's comin'. A whole passel of 'em. Folks is actin' like chickens without their heads."

Forbes leaned on the porch railing. "I always feared something like this might happen."

May whispered to Donna who returned to the kitchen and returned with the whisky bottle that she handed to Bart, who gratefully took a swallow.

The bottle was passed around, May and Sullivan the only ones partaking.

After several minutes of commiserating about the sad state of affairs, Forbes announced he had to get back to town, taking Sullivan with him.

Joe went into the house to clean up and put on a fresh shirt. When he returned to the porch, May rocked back in her chair and smiled. He said: "Seems to me we won't have to stand this much more."

May's smile did not fade as she said: "Your pa's gone. I hurt much. Bart ain't so good. There be Jem, but he be one man?"

Joe said the wrong thing. "Ma, you heard Forbes, the Army's comin'."

May's smile winked out. "Son, that be trouble."

As Joe, May, and Donna sat quietly around the table at supper, Donna said: "Army comes for all us people!" She paused before finishing. "My people will fight."

Joe rose, took her hand, and led off in the direction of the creek.

May watched them go. When they were out of sight, she limped the full distance to Mather's house and hammered on the door with her stick.

Bart opened the door, considered May's expression, and said: "Come inside."

May eased down on a bench, looking at Jem who was struggling to get some kindling to burn in the stove. She barked his name.

Jem straightened up and faced around.

May said: "You got pouch?"

Bart and Jem looked steadily at May without speaking as she held out her hand.

Jem fumbled for the small doeskin bag and crossed the room to drop it in May's hand.

She rose without a word, waited until Bart opened the door, and with the sun a giant red disk in the west went hobbling back to the main house. Inside she lighted two lamps, one in the parlor, the other in her bedroom. She sat down in a chair in the parlor to wait. She was patient, so patient she had drifted off, when she heard Joe and Donna on the porch. She pulled herself upright, and, when they came in, she was waiting and ready.

Surprised to find her still up, Joe said: "Ma, you'd ought to be in bed."

May acted as though she had not heard. She motioned for him to come to her side. He complied, and, when he was next to her, she brought forth the little pouch, poured most of its contents in her palm, and waved her corn-filled hand back and forth in front of him. Joe started to move, but Donna, having moved soundlessly to his side, prevented him from stirring an inch.

May made that sweeping movement again. She smiled, handed the empty pouch to Donna, and then stood up with great effort and limped to the bedroom, grasping at furniture edges along the way to steady herself. As she passed through the doorway of her room, she said: "Have good night. Long sleep."

Joe faced Donna. She had a noticeable pale yellow mist on her dress. He raised his hand to brush her off. She stepped away, smiled, and led him away to his bedroom, now their bedroom, with warm fingers.

He said: "Why did she do that? What was that powder?"

When they were alone, Donna explained. "Corn medicine. Grind very much. Like powder."

"Why'd she throw it on us?"

"Didn't throw. Sprinkle. Corn grow strong and big. Maybe many times."

Joe sat on a bench, looking at his wife. "She wants you to plant corn?"

"No! Married woman have many children."

Joe kicked out of his boots, wagging his head, and was quiet. He winced twice. Donna rubbed him with something from the small medicine bundle she carried at her waist. It wasn't as fragrant as it was pungent. The fragrance came from the oil of crushed bluebells. A mildly stinging and heating sensation came from fireweed and red thistle.

When she had finished rubbing him, Donna walked over to the room's one small window. She heard Joe behind her, but she neither turned nor spoke. A small light blinked brightly for seconds outside, then darkness returned. Touching Joe's shoulder, but not turning, Donna whispered: "There is someone over behind Bart's house."

"Where?" he asked, peering more closely through the window.

"I saw a light, like a match. From behind the log house."

Joe squinted, swore under his breath, and, moving back to his boots, said: "Stay here. Keep out of sight in the dark and stay inside."

When she turned, he was gone. Donna did not frighten easily, but she went to May's room, figuring that, if there were trouble, she would have to help May get up.

Joe left the house by the rarely used rear door, stalked along the weathered outside wall of the main house, his six-gun gripped in his hand. He dropped low and peered around the corner of the house, listening. There was nothing to be heard or seen. The distance between the main house and Bart's was enough to suggest caution, being a wide, open space offering no shelter.

Inside the main house, May, having sensed the presence of Donna at her side, had awoken. She would not listen to any admonition from Donna to stay in bed. So Donna was forced to stay close to her side as she made her way through the kitchen. Someone had left a chair pulled out at the table, and May stumbled over it, taking the chair down with her and cursing in an angry voice. The noise seemed deafening in the dark.

Donna's heart thumped as she helped

May back to an upright position.

May whispered: "Damned clumsy old squaw."

Seconds later two gunshots pierced the silence, accompanied by an agitated call.

May hissed: "White skins!"

A gunshot and a loud curse sliced the air near Bart's cabin. There was no mistaking the bull-like voice of Jem Whitmore. Another gunshot followed, this time emanating from somewhere nearer the barn.

May had taken a few moments to search for the gun that usually was kept in the sideboard in the kitchen and, having found it, made her way to the parlor. She stood poised at the large window, gun aimed. She hesitated to fire, though, recalling the many times her husband had commented on the high cost of windows.

Meanwhile, Donna slipped soundlessly from the parlor, and returned just as soundlessly. She had Joe's saddle gun carbine in both hands.

For what seemed a long period of time, although it was only minutes, a deep stillness settled over the Jessup buildings. Then Joe entered through the front door, wagging his head.

"I saw one running near the barn. Then I heard a horse. You both doing all right?"

May wasn't smiling when she said: "Did not see no one?"

"No, just a shadow. Big . . . big as Jem."

May groped in the darkness for something to sit on. After she collapsed on the settee, she looked in Donna's direction. "Indian . . . ?"

Donna did not think so. "Maybe same ones that go after Joe and Bart."

Someone pounded on the door, shouting: "Joe! Open up!"

Donna went to the door, and opened it.

Jem brushed past her, violently punching another man into the room. "You know this one, Joe?"

Joe bobbed his head without speaking, recognizing Fred Harper.

Jem shoved the captive toward the settee where May was sitting. Harper's close-set eyes flicked from Donna, to May, to Joe. Jem placed his six-gun along side his captive's ear and cocked it. The move brought almost instantaneous reaction.

"I lost my way . . . ," Harper muttered. "I didn't know where I was. It's dark out there."

Jem growled: "You lost your way out of the jail?"

Harper forced a feeble grin at the bear-like built older man. "Yes, sir. I was in the jail-house."

Joe had a question. "How'd you get out?"

Harper cleared his throat and fidgeted before answering. "A Indian feller. Dark as a Mexican. Used a crowbar to bust loose the lock."

Joe asked another question. "You knew him?"

"Yes, I knew him. Name's Colson. That's all I know. If he had a first name, I don't recollect ever hearing it. Dark feller. Looked like a full-blood. Mean. Comes up to help the Colsons make their gather. I heard he was some kind of kin to the other Colsons."

Out of the north came the sound of a whistle. The whistle sounded twice more.

The seated Harper squirmed.

Jem approached the captive, asked — "Who's that?" — and stood towering over him until the intimidated man said: "Robin. That'll be Robin, Crow's youngest."

Jem's features twisted into an ominous grin. "If you're lying . . . ," he threatened.

Harper tilted his head, just barely. When he spoke, his voice was unsteady. "Have it your way."

Chapter Eighteen

The Emergency

What remained of the night was spent in the kitchen with Donna keeping the coffee cups full. May retired to her room shortly before dawn's first paleness began to lighten the yard. It was a short night of sleep for all.

Joe did the chores earlier than usual. He did what had to be done, wishing he'd been born with one eye in the back of his head. But nothing happened beyond a rooster creating a racket from a roost in the wagon shed.

Harper hadn't made an effort to get free of the wolf trap chain that held him fast to a smelly old bedroll May had tossed to him on the kitchen floor. When May and Donna appeared in the kitchen, he held the blankets up close to his chin.

May growled a greeting that Harper returned in the language of the *Dinéh*. She faced him, hands on hips. "Where you lived?"

Harper answered, and she smiled at him.

Then she went about helping Donna pre-pare breakfast, telling Donna in the hodge-podge language of the up yonder people, that Harper came from the south desert country.

Joe and Jem appeared, scrubbed and pre-sentable. Bart was the last one to enter the kitchen. He had not only slept in his clothes, which was not entirely unusual, but he had trouble making his legs carry him to a chair. No one commented, not even Jem who rarely missed an opportunity to nag his old friend.

Donna instructed May to sit, and then she served the food. Bart, who had always been a voracious eater, picked at his food. Jem watched from the corner of his eye, and, when breakfast was finished, he got up and without a word to help Bart back to his log house.

As soon as they were out of earshot, Joe said: "He didn't look good yesterday, and he looks worse today."

Looking unusually concerned, May said: "Bart bad sick." And she was right.

When the sun was high, Jem returned to the house, pulled out a kitchen chair, and dropped hard onto it. "Bart's dead," he an-nounced flatly. "Damnedest thing. I got him back to his house. He just looked at me and said he was tired. I got him in bed. I thought he was sleeping . . . ," his voice trailed off as he sat shaking his head from side to side.

May looked steadily at Jem for a long time. Finally she indicated to Joe that she needed his help in standing, then she hobbled to her bedroom without uttering a word.

Jem leaned forward, both large hands clasped between his knees, his eyes closed, breathing noisily.

Joe took Donna to the creek where they sat on dew-damp grass. Donna made no attempt to talk.

Eventually Joe pitched a pebble into the water and said: "He was. . . . It's like losing kin. . . ." He paused. "Where should we bury him?"

Her matter-of-fact reply was given in almost a whisper: "Beside your father?"

Joe pitched another pebble into the creek, watching the circles of water eddy around the spot where it plunked in. Then slowly he faced Donna and took her hand in his. Her only response was a slight squeeze of his fingers. She thought he was going to say something, but, instead, he jumped up and walked to where the creek willows were thickest. He kept his back to her, and, when she said his name, he did not answer.

The sun — their clock — was nearing its meridian before they started back. For Donna that creekside place would be vivid to her for as long as she lived. The mystery of an eventual birth had been consummated there, also the mystery of a dying.

Jem and Joe dug the grave, waist-deep, near Old Joe's final resting place. A shady area. May rocked in silence during the length of time it took to prepare Bart — getting him in his only clean set of clothing and carrying him to the gravesite. She had done the same with Old Joe, mourned and rocked. Because May couldn't stand for long, Donna had brought a blanket from the house for May to sit on. Jem said a few words. They all said a silent prayer before Joe and Jem covered the blanket-covered body.

They returned to the main house with Donna on one side of May and her son on the other. Jem followed, carrying May's blanket and the two shovels. He left the shovels at the barn, entered Mather's log house, barred the door from the inside, and did not come out until the sound of riders brought him back from his solitary recollections of the many trails he and Bart had shared.

When he finally emerged, he saw Emmet

Forbes and Barry Sullivan tying up over at the main house. Jem was in no hurry. He washed his face at the stone trough, dried off using his shirt tail, then crossed the yard. The visitors were inside by then, and Jem, feeling awkward, knocked hesitantly.

When Joe opened the door, Jem nodded his greetings sullenly. The constable and Sullivan were preparing to leave, heading back to town, with the escaped prisoner, Fred Harper.

No sooner had they left than May said: "Forbes say two companies of soldiers camp north of town. That head soldier with them. Him and that other that sunburns."

Jem nodded. "I heard in town, May. They brought along a wheeled gun, and a supply wagon." Jem said no more. There was nothing to say. The officer had meant every word he had said. The Army had come to gather up the up yonder Indians and take them away.

Jem smiled at Donna, taking her by the arm as far as the kitchen door. "You go tell them," he told her. "Get them moving."

She looked up. "They plan for this now many seasons. They've lived up yonder for a long time. It's their home."

"You're tellin' me they'll fight?"

"Yes."

Jem leaned against the doorjamb, studying Donna. "Tell Manuelito there's too many soldiers. That they have to run. Tell them to brush out tracks. Too many soldiers. Tell them to go hide in the mountains. *Go!*"

He ushered her to the back door, held it open until she had passed through.

When Joe entered the kitchen, the sound of hoofbeats could be heard leaving the yard. "Where's Donna?" he asked.

"Gone, boy."

"Gone where? You didn't send her to warn the Indians!"

"They got a right to know, boy."

Joe swung a chair around and sat on it. "For Chris' sake, Jem!"

"Joe, your folks never liked you usin' words like that!"

Joe looked helplessly at the much larger and older man. "Tell me she'll be OK, Jem."

"Donna will be fine," he assured Joe, who plunked down at the kitchen table.

"Jem, if there's two companies. . . . Why that's more soldiers than the Indians got warriors."

"What'd your pa tell you about dyin'?" Jem said. "You just seen how easy it can be. . . . Ol' Bart would've been in favor of sendin' her. They'll listen to her better than to you or me. Boy, they're like kin. Have been for more years'n I can count. Two, three generations, boy, an' they deserve better'n to be rounded up like sheep an' drove to a reservation."

Joe leaned forward, deep thoughts wrinkling his brow, foreshadowing what he would look like in years to come. Eventually he straightened up, having made up his mind. "I'll go, too," he stated. "I can catch her, if I hurry."

Jem took three long steps and put a ham-sized hand on Joe's shoulder. The pressure of the grasp shot down Joe's arm. "You stay with May. You're all she's got left. You're the head Jessup, boy. Her 'n' your pa took you in, raised you. You owe her that much. You're a Jessup. You want to break that old squaw's heart? You leave her now, an' I'll bet you a good horse she'll die."

Joe raised a cuff to wipe a runny nose. "You're makin' this harder'n ever, Jem."

"All right. You pass me your word you'll stay with May, an' I'll go. Maybe I won't catch her, but I can get up there before they decide to take up the hatchet."

Joe brushed past the large man, walked outside, and squinted off in to he north.

From the doorway Jem said: "Give me your word, Joe."

The younger man turned back, returned

to the kitchen. "An' suppose you can't get 'em to run for it?"

"Then there'll be a fight. You take my word for it, boy. I've fought Indians since before you was born. They been at peace a long time, but, Joe, they ain't forgot how to fight. Now you go set with May. She's just about done in from all these goings-on, an' she'd old, boy."

Joe leaned on his recently vacated chair. "You go," he said. "I'll stay. Jem, look out for Donna."

The large man nodded and left.

On Joe's way to his mother's room he glanced out the front window. Jem was halfway to the barn, and he wasn't hurrying, which annoyed Joe. Jem rarely hurried, on foot anyway, and, apparently, this time he was satisfied there was no need for haste. As he'd told Joe, he knew Indians as well as any white man did.

Even tame Indians like the up yonder people never slackened their vigil. By now there wouldn't be an Indian in sight anywhere. If the soldiers were searching, what they would find was a hastily vacated *rancheria,* maybe a loose horse or two, but not an Indian. As for warning them to brush over their sign, that was as good advice as telling wild horse hunters to set rabbit snares.

Joe told May everything, and she smiled at him. When she said nothing, he pushed his hat back with his thumb and sat down in the chair. May was — for her — sweaty and very pale. Her gaze was steady; otherwise, she was motionless under the covers.

In an attempt to get some kind of reaction from her, Joe finally said: "Right now I sure miss Pa an' Bart."

Her next comment did not make sense, when she gave it, although it would later. "Warrior go away at night. Be alone. You stay. You know picture?"

Joe made a sickly grin. "I'll get the bottle. You need a drink."

She was still smiling, when he returned with a glass of whisky. She made no attempt to reach for it, instead, asking: "Hungry. You hungry?"

Joe hadn't thought of food in hours, but he nodded and left the room again. What he prepared was leftovers from the cooler box. The mixture he created was edible, providing someone was as hungry as the proverbial bitch wolf. He was apologetic when he took a plate to May, but she ate it all.

Suddenly Joe straightened up to listen. "Someone coming in," he said, and hastily left the room.

It was Dr. Leger in his top buggy. As Joe

led him inside, he stopped Joe to ask: "How is she?"

"I just fed her. She don't look pert, but she's. . . . Well, she fell pretty hard . . . and Bart's death. You best look at her yourself."

"What? Bart's dead. What happened?"

"Just died."

Leger stood, shaking his head. "You got a plague going on in this house, boy."

May greeted the physician quietly. Leger greeted May as an old friend, striding quickly over to the bedside. "I hear you took a little tumble, May. How do you feel?"

The old woman shot Joe an angry look. "Feel good," she said to Leger, her eyes still locked on her son.

"May, I've been seein' you pretty regular now. Don't you lie to me. Let's have a look at that hip. Hold still." He slid back the blankets. His fingers slid along the wound as he examined it. It actually seemed to be healing.

Barry Leger studied May's face. He put a hand on her forehead. She was feverish. As he pulled the blankets up over her, he brushed against her lower abdomen. She winced. Without saying a word, his fingers began probing the lower right side of her abdomen. She shuttered. He noted the glass of whisky sitting on the bureau. "Have you sampled that, May?"

"She hasn't," Joe answered from the doorway.

Leger pulled the chair around, put his satchel on the floor, and sat back. "Have you been vomiting, May?"

She nodded. "Can not be," she said. "Joe been dead long time now."

Leger stepped back, excused himself, and quickly left the room. He hurried to the porch, Joe following a few steps behind. Outside, a huge grin lit Leger's face, and he said to Joe: "I'm sorry. I had to get out of there before I laughed. You aren't going to believe this, but your mother thinks she's pregnant."

Joe's eyes widened, otherwise, he showed no expression as he waited for a fuller explanation.

"For her sake I wish she was," continued the doctor, turning serious. "She's got a bad case of appendicitis."

Joe's expression did not alter. "How bad? Can it kill her?"

"It can. But, if you an' May agree, I'll try takin' it out. Joe, it'll likely kill her if it isn't taken out. A week, maybe tomorrow."

"Is it from a bite, Doctor?"

"No, nothing like that. Its cause isn't important. The decision's got to be made right away, Joe. They can burst an' that'll kill her."

Joe glanced around, wondering how much more could go wrong. Finally he nodded his agreement and ushered the doctor back to May's room.

May listened as Leger explained the problem. When he finished, her gaze went to Joe. "Son?"

Joe saw an intense fear in her face that made him shudder. He forced the words out. "Ma, the way I see it, there's no choice. But you got to make the decision, not me."

"Both make, Joe."

He tried to smile and said: "Can't waste time, Ma."

She looked from Joe to Leger and back again. Slowly she nodded her head after which she said: "You?"

His mouth too dry to speak, Joe also nodded his head.

Dr. Leger was looking at May when he asked Joe to get hot water. Plenty of it.

Once Joe was out of the room, the doctor took May's hand and squeezed it. He had come to admire her greatly over the last weeks. He explained what he was going to do, answering the few questions she had. Her last comment indicated the direction of her thinking. "I die you say I tell you. From me to you. Joe belongs to everything. All of it, you hear? You do that for me?"

Leger swallowed the lump that had formed in his throat. "I promise. But I won't have to do that because you're going to be fine."

By the time Joe returned with an old large wash pan filled with steaming hot water, Leger had May just about ready. He gestured for Joe to set the basin on the chair. His instruments were laid out on the bureau. Then he went to work, first putting a small cloth over May's mouth and nose. He asked Joe to fetch some clean towels and rags, all he could find.

When Joe returned, he put the clean cloths on the chair. He watched the doctor wash his mother's abdomen. As he worked, Leger talked. "You got to be prepared, Joe. For anything." As Leger began making the incision, he heard a crash behind him. He glanced around to find Joe on the floor. Shaking his head, he returned to his work, continuing to talk.

Barry Leger was a meticulous man, which was fortunate. If the slippery, hot organ he lifted out of May with caution had burst, which was possible, May would have died. He put it aside with the same care he used in birthings, pausing one brief moment to look upward before finishing up the operation — the gentle cleansing and closure.

When he was done, he arranged the covers so he could see the wound, stepped back, swallowed the contents of the glass on the bureau, and sat down to admire his handiwork. He knew there were a dozen reasons why May might not recover. But there were the same number of reasons for her *to* recover. All of his sixty-five years he had heard Indians were tough. If May Jessup ever needed the benefit of her heritage, it was right now and for the week ahead.

He considered attempting to bring Joe around, but thought better of it, at least until he had cleaned up. So he went to the kitchen to get more water.

When he returned, May was exactly as he had left her. However, Joe had revived on his own. He was leaning against the bureau. Leger addressed the young man as he busied himself picking up the rags and washing his instruments. "She'll sleep, Joe. Folks come back different. You stay with her. Maybe all night."

"Did you ever do this before?" Joe asked.

"Four times like this . . . in a house. Three other times in hospitals. That was many years back. I wouldn't have done it this time if she hadn't been as close to having this thing" — he lifted the organ he had wrapped in some rags — "burst. Joe, I got to get back to town. Carry my satchel out to the buggy with me." The doctor carried the bloody bundle of rags.

Outside, Leger asked: "Got a feedbag we can put this in? Then you can bury it or burn it, I don't care. Just don't leave it around."

Joe went to the barn to find an old bag, and then he helped the doctor place the soiled items in the bag.

"Primitive, Joe, but it couldn't be helped. If an infection don't set in . . . peritonitis or something else . . . I'd say in ten days or maybe a tad less she'll be up and around."

They clasped hands before Joe spoke. "If you'll wait a spell, I'll get you some money."

Leger climbed into his buggy. "Next time you're in town will be soon enough. You take care, Joe. Those soldiers aren't here for the climate. I'll come back and check on May in a day or two. I left some medicine on the bureau. Give her a dose whenever she's been up for a while, it'll keep her quiet." A flip of the buggy lines and Leger was off.

Joe watched him leave the yard and then went to the barn to get a shovel. He checked on May before going out back to dig a hole.

May was semi-conscious. She had to work at smiling at her son. "Doc gone?" she asked.

Joe nodded. "You're going to be fine, Ma. But you just have to stay in bed for a while."

May smiled weakly now. "No hurt," she mumbled.

Joe took the bottle Leger had left on the bureau and poured a small amount in the glass on the bureau. He held the glass while May sipped. "Ma, I want your word you'll stay in bed."

Her smile lingered, her eyelids seemed weighted. "How long? Who cook, clean?"

Joe smiled to himself. "We'll get by. There's five, six tins of sardines in the cupboard. Besides, Donna will be back."

May lifted her hand as if to emphasize a point. Words came out of her mouth in a slur. "Got . . . belly . . . gripe."

"Ma, you just been cut into and opened up."

May's only response was a huge grin.

Joe kissed her lightly on the forehead before leaving the room.

The new day wore along at the Lazy J. Most of Joe's time was spent doing chores, checking on May, and worrying about

Donna and Jem. He was in the kitchen, cleaning up a few dishes when he heard the first echo of hoofbeats. They were still off in the distance, but his ears had always been fine tuned to that sound. As he headed toward the door, May called for him.

No sooner had he crossed the threshold into her bedroom than she said: "You hear, Son? Horses."

"I heard it, Ma," Joe replied, trying to sound calm even though he wasn't, fearing it might be the soldiers.

"What we do?" May asked, throwing the blankets back as if she was going to jump out of bed. A look of pain washed across her face as she lifted her shoulders off the bed. She fell back.

Joe rushed across the room. "Ma, I'll take care of it." His hands shaking, he poured a dose of medicine in a glass and forced it into May. "You don't move! You hear me, Ma? You don't so much as wiggle a finger."

Even that small exertion had been too much for May. Her breathing came hard. "If soldiers, fetch head man here," May muttered, her eyes closed.

"I'll bring him. Now you lie back an' don't move. Doc Leger said you'd have to stay down for at least a week. He meant it this time." As her breathing evened out, Joe reiterated: "Ma, I want your promise. You don't move from this bed."

With the corners of her mouth turning up slightly, she whispered: "I promise, Son." That was one thing Old Joe had been adamant about. A promise was never broken.

Walking through the house, Joe heard them clearly now. Many horses, many riders. As he stepped onto the porch, the Army entered the yard, leaving a dust banner in their wake. Joe had never seen so many soldiers before in his life, although he had heard stories. He gripped the peeled-log porch railing as one soldier who looked no older than Joe approached the house holding a little swallow-tailed guidon. The soldier next to him was the same Captain Berthold who had been here before. On the captain's far side was the ruddy-faced, muscular soldier with reddish hair. He had three reverse chevrons on each upper sleeve. None of them smiled as they reined to a halt.

Chapter Nineteen

They Are Coming!

Captain Berthold's expression was one of pure satisfaction as he glared at Joe. He had said he would return, and he had. This time with a small army in support. He was in no hurry to achieve vindication. He offered the man on the porch a needlessly exaggerated bow from the saddle before addressing him.

"Part of my command is scouting," he announced. "Young Jessup, where's your mother?"

Joe answered curtly. "In bed. The doc just operated on her."

There were some murmurs and expressions of surprise. The red-maned sergeant asked: "Last night?"

Joe nodded. "She's not to leave her bed for a week or more."

The sergeant gave a round-eyed look at the captain, who said: "You mean . . . here in the house?"

"Yes, sir. If you figure to talk to her, you'll

have to get down an' come inside. But I can't promise she'll make sense or even hear you. She's in a bad way yet."

Shaking his head, Berthold dismounted. He handed his reins to the sergeant, Mallory, straightened his coat, and climbed the steps.

As Joe led the way, Berthold asked where the pair of old men were, and Joe told him one had died, they'd buried him. The other one, he explained fumblingly, was out with the cattle.

May appeared to be sleeping as they entered the room. Berthold remained in the doorway while Joe walked across the room to the bed. With trembling hand he touched her shoulder, whispering: "Ma, you awake?"

Slowly May's eyes blinked open. She glanced around the room as if trying to get her bearings. Several minutes passed before her eyes settled on Berthold. "You bring soldiers," she said. "Why?"

Clearly made uncomfortable by the situation, Berthold removed his cap. "Ma'am, you know why," he responded, taking a step into the room. "I told you we'd be back for the renegade reservation jumpers."

May's color deepened. "No reservation jumpers."

Berthold had no intention of arguing, so

he said: "Indians, ma'am. Call 'em what you want. They're Indians, and, accordin' to the law, they got to be reservationed. You know that. We discussed this before." He paused.

"No help," May inserted at this point, clearly angering Berthold.

His face reddening, the officer continued: "You can prevent trouble by telling me where they are, or you can lie in that bed an' pray they don't resist when we find 'em. They can't win. The Army'll fight them to a fare-thee-well. Those that survive will be taken up north to a stockade. From there to a reservation. Ma'am, if you want to save 'em from gettin' hurt bad, you best tell me where they are."

Berthold despised the idea of talking with this old squaw, but he was due for a promotion and a successful campaign without bloodshed would work to his advantage. The previous night in the confines of his quarters he had come to the decision that he would be polite with this woman, even wheedling, if he had to. But at the moment he was finding it difficult.

"Missus Jessup, from what I learned in Cumberland yesterday, these Indians could field maybe twenty fightin' tomahawks. I got better'n sixty soldiers. Think on it. If it comes down to a fight, by law, I don't have to take prisoners. Do you understand what I'm saying?"

May's dark eyes shot venom in Berthold's direction. "You brave man," she began. "Threaten old squaw. Tell you there be many warriors. Squaws fight, too."

Berthold bristled at the insult. "Are you telling me your Indians want a war?" he asked.

For the first time May smiled but without the usual warmth of the act. "Mister Soldier," she said quietly, "no soldiers come into our country that we not know it. Not for many miles."

Berthold looked at Joe. "Do you know where these renegades are?"

Joe replied truthfully. "No sir, I don't. Them mountains run for hundreds of miles north, east, and west, an', if they don't want you to find 'em, take my word for it, you won't find 'em."

"Mister Soldier . . . ," May began.

Berthold stopped her. "Captain, ma'am. Captain of the Fourth United States Mounted Infantry." No sooner had these words left his mouth than the sound of a bugle resonated through the air.

May smiled and said: "Mister Captain, why you so stupid to have bugle make noise?

How you win when that stupid?"

For a long moment all were silent.

The call — "Captain!" — broke through the air as the red-haired sergeant entered the house and ran into the bedroom. He looked past his commanding officer, his eyes settling on May. "Cap'n, they found 'em. Martin blew his horn . . . came from the northwest."

Berthold jerked his head and followed the Irish sergeant out of the house.

Joe looked around the room. "Ma, I gotta see what's going on. Remember now, you stay in that bed."

"Where are you goin', Son?"

Joe did not say where he was going, but turned quickly, kissed May, and left the room without either of them commenting.

Outside, Joe found the soldiers scattered about the yard. Berthold and Mallory were conferring in the shade of the porch. Joe positioned himself so that he could catch some of what they were saying. What he learned, before the two noticed him and shifted out of hearing, was that the captain had detailed a bugler to accompany his party of scouts with orders to sound off if the scouts found Indians or any sign of them. The bugler had sounded, not because the patrol had found holdouts, but rather because they had seen one Indian, had made a capture, and were now heading into the Jessup place. It seemed also that they were convinced that a large party of holdouts were traveling west in order to escape the Army.

Joe made his way across the yard where he discovered four troopers playing cards inside the barn, out of reach of the hot sunlight. They interrupted their game to watch as Joe led a horse in from the corral, cross tied it, and prepared to saddle up. One of the four, an unkempt, thick man, rose as he watched Joe. Finally the soldier approached Joe to ask him where he was going and whether he had the captain's permission. Joe continued to rig out the horse without either looking across the saddle seat at the soldier or speaking. The soldier stood by as Joe bridled the horse, then stepped forward and yanked off the bridle.

This time Joe acknowledged the soldier when he said: "Boy, you're not goin' nowhere without you got the captain's permission."

Joe took two steps backward, yanked the tie-down loose over his sidearm, and said: "Move away from this horse."

Two of the card players came up off the ground. One, a tall, sinewy man took several silent steps, grabbed Joe by both arms from behind, whirled, and violently flung him toward the saddle pole. Joe fought for balance with his left hand while his right hand dropped toward the holster. The saddle pole prevented Joe from falling backwards, but nothing impeded his forward collapse. As he was falling, the tall, wiry soldier caught him along the slant of the jaw with a rock hard fist.

Joe went face down, out cold. The tall soldier bent over, took Joe's six-gun, shoved it in the front of his britches, and addressed the man who had caught Joe from the far side of the saddle pole. "Get the captain."

The man left the barn at a fast clip while the remaining three stood around Joe. The tall man massaged his right fist.

The captain arrived, a grin pasted across his face as he espied Joe sprawled in the dust. He listened to several versions of the events, then snapped an order to — "Prop him against the wall and get a bucket of water."

A drop of blood showed on Joe's lip, but still he did not move. The ice cold water brought him around. As he came to, he felt his jaw, blinked until he could clearly make out the officer, then wiped his mouth on a sleeve. He studied Berthold and finally asked: "You hit me?"

The soldier massaging his hand shook his head. "Not him. Me 'n' Arnie. Captain, he was fixin' to saddle that horse and leave. I asked if he had your permission. He didn't answer, and the fight started."

Berthold stood, legs spread wide, looking at Joe. "What did you figure on doing, Jessup?"

Joe's lip was swelling. "I was goin' up yonder."

"Why?"

"Because my wife's up there."

The soldier who had grabbed Joe from behind seemed to be uncertain now whether he had done the right thing or not. "I didn't know about the wife, Captain," he said. "I figured he might be fixin' to ride off 'n' warn them tomahawks."

The officer ignored the speaker and addressed Joe. "Is that what you were going to do, Jessup? Warn them?"

"I . . . was goin' for the constable."

The captain made a crooked smile. "The constable livin' with the Indians now, is he? Anyway, he's got no authority here, Jessup. This is Army business. The Army and the Indian agent up at Fort Laramie." Berthold paused and seemed to be sizing up Joe before he barked another order. "Tie him. Chain his ankles."

As the soldiers searched for rope and

313

chain, the officer sank down to one knee in front of Joe. "Where are they, Jessup?" he asked, and then waited patiently for a response. When none was forthcoming, he continued: "Listen to me. You help us find 'em, or so help me I'll put your ma on a horse, take her to Cumberland, and lock her up in the jailhouse."

Joe's eyes blazed. "You'll kill her. She was just cut open. Doc Leger took out her . . . gizzard."

Berthold laughed. "People don't have gizzards. Boy, you been too long away from civilization."

"Appendix," Joe corrected himself, remembering the word. "You can't move her, and you know it. If you even think about it, I'll. . . ."

"You'll what?" Berthold asked. "You and your mother are both in defiance of the law. You tell me where we can find those hideouts, or I'll personally tie her astride a horse." The officer straightened up to his full height. "I'm waiting, Jessup. We haven't got all day. Where can we find 'em?"

At that moment a beard-stubbled enlisted man came running breathlessly into the barn. "Cap'n, scouts is comin' in from the northwest. Looks like they got a female Indian with 'em."

"Watch Jessup," Berthold ordered no one in particular as he hurried from the barn. So no one followed the order, all four men heading for the door. To a man, the soldiers under Berthold's command stood watching the riders close the distance. No one spoke until that Irish sergeant noisily cleared his throat and expectorated. Then a soldier, leaning on the corral, said: "Sure as hell that's a female woman with them."

At this Joe heaved himself up against the barn wall. His jaw hurt like hell. As he walked past the old nail keg, he kicked it. The top spun off, and, although Joe continued to walk toward the door, he noticed a sheaf of papers flop to the floor out of the keg. He walked over, picked them up, shoved them in his pocket, and continued on through the doorway.

"Cap'n, we got one!" yelled one of the scouting party who rode out front as they approached nearer the yard.

The echo of that shout had scarcely died when a large man on a large, muscled-up horse swooped out of the west, waving a Winchester saddle gun, and heading straight for the scouting party. He let out a blood-curdling yell as he pulled to a stop in front of the stunned group of scouts and leveled his gun.

The soldiers in the Jessup yard watched with their mouths hanging open. Joe smiled as he recognized Jem. He watched with amazement as one of the scouting party leaned to yank the carbine from his saddle boot. At the motion Jem gave his Winchester a powerful up and down jerk. On its downward stroke the gun fired. At the explosion two horses carrying soldiers bolted. Jem cocked his carbine again and shouted to the man, leading the captive on a horse: "Pass me that lead rope you blue bellied son-of-a-bitch!"

The soldier snapped the lead shank, jerking it to make the captive's horse turn. It was then that Joe saw that Donna was their captive. Jem snatched the lead from the soldier's hand, and the two took off.

In the yard, Berthold stamped his foot, cupped his hands around his mouth, and shouted to the patrol to shoot the man and his animal but not to hurt the prisoner.

Not a one of the scouts obeyed until Jem and Donna were close to being out of short gun range.

A few soldiers shouted encouragement to the fleeing man and woman from the yard while Mallory made mental note of the turncoats. A grizzled corporal, his shoulders shaking with laughter, wheezed out: "Crazy! Crazy as a coot!"

Mallory stood by at attention, awaiting the order to pursue from his commanding officer. But Berthold stood fixed as he watched the fleeing riders approach a spit of spindly trees and disappear among them. Any hope of an easy campaign and a subsequent promotion disappeared as well at that moment for Berthold.

"Mount up," he told the men half-heartedly.

A lopsided grin pasted across his face, Joe approached Berthold. The officer's attention was trained on the scattering of soldiers now gathering, mounting, or riding out after a pair of fugitives they could not see.

"They'll never catch 'em," Joe commented. "But if they could, that big feller leading my wife could break half their necks."

Berthold turned slowly. His face was pale, his eyes registered disbelief. He walked out a way and scoured the west. After several minutes he said: "Where'd that man come from? And how could one man do what he just did?"

Joe had an answer, but he wasn't about to voice it.

May only had four words for Joe, after he told what had happened. "Go after her, Son." Then she leaned back in the bed. The pain was excruciating.

Joe was torn between staying with his mother and going after his wife. He tried to conceive of a way to do both. It was an impossible situation. He continued to administer the medicine Leger had left behind in an effort to keep May in a stupor so she would not hound him about going after Donna. Most of the time he paced through the house or walked around the yard, cursing his lot.

Evening's shadows began to blanket the yard. By twos and threes Berthold's men returned to the ranch. As their numbers multiplied, they began setting up camp. Joe stayed inside the house, catching snatches of conversation often followed by muffled laughter. The atmosphere of camaraderie and joviality abruptly changed once Berthold arrived back on the scene.

Some time later there was a knock at the door. Reluctantly Joe answered it. As he looked into Berthold's eyes, Mallory and another soldier grabbed him by the arms and jerked him out onto the porch. They then carried him to the barn where four soldiers were posted to guard Joe.

Chapter Twenty

The Standoff

For hours, as he scoured the hills looking for the hideouts, Captain Berthold had been stewing about how his report on the activities in and around Cumberland would look in relation to a promotion. He cringed each time he thought of having to relay having lost a prisoner to a wild man who had come charging out of nowhere to effect a rescue while he stood by with two companies of mounted men whose purpose was to prevent such a thing from happening. He had plans to remedy the situation.

Berthold conferred privately with Mallory and then went to the barn to confront Joe.

"Jessup!" he shouted as he entered through the wide doorway. Then to the quartet of soldiers surrounding Joe: "Hold him tight, men. I may rile him up a bit with what I have to say." Berthold stepped up close to Joe and grinned, saying: "You're mother's in a bad way, Jessup. I'd hate to see anything happen to her . . . anything that would compromise her condition." He paused. "As her loyal son, it's up to you to make sure she continues in her convalescence. So, I'm giving you until sunup to find your wife and the man who took her and get them back here. Otherwise, I will be forced to take your mother into Cumberland. And it won't be an easy journey . . . I assure you."

"You bastard!" Joe shouted at Berthold. The soldiers holding him struggled to maintain their grip as he twisted and tried to jerk free.

"Did you understand me, boy?" Berthold said softly through a clenched jaw.

"I'm not leaving my mother here alone with an animal like you," responded Joe.

The soldiers held fast to Joe but stared at their commanding officer in disbelief at the words that had passed from his lips over the last several minutes.

On the other hand, Joe had no difficulty. He had accurately assessed the officer upon their first meeting. He knew he wouldn't think twice about killing May. She was an Indian. A full-blood. Promotions were hard to come by nowadays.

"I'll watch after the boy's mother while he's gone, Captain," the man to Joe's left said.

Joe glanced at the man. He intuited a kindness in the sun-burned face as well as growing contempt for his commanding officer.

"I'll go. But if I find that you've hurt my mother. . . ."

"That's up to you, isn't it?" Berthold said before Joe could finish his sentence. "Release him."

"I'll be on my way as soon as I say good bye to my ma," Joe said, shaking his arms to release the tenseness. He knew May, in fact, would be relieved to hear that he was going after Donna. He hoped that she would not understand the gravity of the situation.

Joe reined to the right and put the horse into an easy lope. He could feel the eyes of Berthold on his back as he hooked over into a faster, mile-eating run. He followed the route of Jem and Donna up to the spit of trees. It was nothing but a hunch, but his guess was Jem had taken Donna into Cumberland. The farther he rode, the more confident he became that he was on the right trail, since the night was clear and the moon was full and bright and he could, upon occasion, discern the tracks of two horses heading for town.

At one point he came to a sudden halt

when he saw that the pair of horses had met up with a large party of riders — Joe guessed about fifteen. The trail indicated the group had continued on in the direction of the Lazy J. Perplexed, Joe lifted over into a lope in the opposite direction, following the two sets of hoof marks toward town.

The farther he rode east, the more confident he became that the party of riders had come from town. Had he followed his usual route to town, he might have met up with them. But, since he had also been confident that Berthold would send men out to follow him, he had been following the circuitous path that Jem had taken to throw off any trailers. He only hoped that this party of riders was led by Forbes. Over the last several weeks Joe had become convinced that Forbes was an honest man even if somewhat ineffectual. Joe smiled to himself when he realized that this makeshift posse, if that's what it was, might, indeed, meet up with Berthold's soldiers. That, he thought, would be an interesting interception.

By the time he had Cumberland's rooftops in sight both Joe and his horse were weary. He slackened his pace as a pair of mounted men approached him, coming from town. Joe set his horse up when they were a matter of a hundred yards away. The man in the lead he identified as Hank Morgan, a rugged older cowman, one of the ranchers dead set against Indians, but, oddly enough, one of the stockmen who occasionally hired Indians — at one-third pay — to help drive his gather to the shipping pens.

When the distance had diminished to less than thirty feet, Morgan stopped, planted both gloved hands on his saddle horn, and called ahead in his gruff voice: "Joe, boy! That damned Army's huntin' your hideout Indians. They left about sunrise, headin' for your place."

Joe regarded the older man steadily — their families had never been particularly friendly — and said: "They're there now. Plenty of 'em." As he spoke, other riders arrived from town. "Doc Leger operated on Ma. She's in a bad way, and the captain is threatening to bring her into town." Joe stopped, his voice beginning to shake in anger and fear. "He'll kill her, Hank, unless I bring back Whitmore and Donna, May's niece . . . my wife. You seen 'em?"

By now Morgan had a contingent of nearly a dozen stockmen gathered around him. They listened in silence. In response to Joe's query about Jem and Donna, Morgan shook his head, saying: "Damned Yankees!"

Joe twisted, fearing that this interruption would allow Berthold's men to catch up with him. He told as much to Morgan and the others.

"Don't you worry none," Morgan announced, bringing his arm up. "We'll take care of them . . . and any others that threaten you or May." He turned in his saddle and addressed the others. "Men, let's move." As he straggled past Joe, Morgan leaned over and said quietly: "I expect you know where to find Jem and your woman."

Joe wasn't sure, but he thought he winked at him. "I think so," he said in reply. "Thanks."

"All right, boy, you go find 'em. We'll take care of this bunch."

Morgan spurred his horse and let out a howl. A significant number among the group responded with like calls. If Joe had been older, he might have recognized the hollering as the Rebel yell. The war was but a dim memory in the minds of many in this group of men, former Secesh Confederates, and an opportunity to grasp a moment of glory warmed their blood and triggered vivid recollections of youthful dreams.

The first sense of relief he had felt in the last week or so washed over Joe as he pointed his horse toward the south, the lower end of town where Jem had his cabin.

When Joe dismounted near the barn to hide his horse, Jem appeared on the tiny stoop in front of the house, a big-bore old buffalo rifle filling his hands. "Joe, boy, that you?" he bellowed.

"It's me," Joe called back.

At the sound of his voice Donna came running from the cabin, crying out her husband's name.

Jem grounded his rifle and went to join the reunion. Then the trio adjourned inside the house.

"How many behind you, boy?" Jem asked.

Joe shrugged his shoulders and told of the events that had occurred since Jem had left, including his meeting with Morgan and his party of riders.

"Ranchers got no use for Indians unless they need cheap workers. But that's only part of it. There's folks like me who remember the war. Blue uniforms just naturally makes their hair stand up. Boy, by the time the Army had spent a few days here, the locals had held a number of meetings. A lot of 'em don't like the idea of soldiers telling folks what they can and can't do. Boy, them Indians is *our* Indians!"

"I'm still worried about May. Jem, she's

alone and helpless. And that Berthold . . . never met a meaner bastard." Joe slumped back in his chair, having run out of hope again. "So, what do we do, Jem?"

"You and me head back to the ranch. Donna stays," Jem answered, and pushed up off the bed where he was sitting, there being only two chairs in the room. "I'll go over to the livery and get you another horse. Give you two a little time alone."

"Donna'll be safe here?" Joe asked, looking up at the old man's face.

Jem picked up his old buffalo rifle and grinned. "She'll be fine, boy. Just fine," he said, and left the cabin.

No sooner had Jem closed the door, than Donna grasped Joe's hand.

He smiled at her and stood up. She came into his arms, and they held each other.

"I'm worried about May, Donna," Joe whispered.

"I know. I know," Donna said, then slowly let go of him. As Joe turned to pull out the chair, Donna saw the papers he had picked up in the barn sticking out of his pocket. "What's there?" she asked, pointing.

"I don't know," Joe replied honestly, as he pulled the papers out. He unfolded the five or six sheets and began reading. "Bring over the lantern," he said to Donna, sitting down on the chair, his attention totally absorbed by what he read. Donna brought the lamp to the table and placed it in the center of the table. Then she sat down next to him.

"What is it?" she asked, her brow wrinkling with concern.

"Good news, for a change," he said, nearly gasping with joy. "But I gotta get back to the ranch." He stood up, and was nearly to the door before he caught himself, and, turning around, returned to Donna. He embraced her, kissed her, ran his fingers through her glossy hair. "Don't worry," he comforted her, and then he was gone.

He was saddling the horse Jem had been riding earlier in the day when he heard him returning from the livery. "We gotta make time, Jem!" he called out.

The first glimmer of the new day was just beginning to show as Joe and Jem neared the ranch. During the ride Joe had explained what he had discovered in the papers. They had discussed a number of ways to deal with the problems that they would face at the home place.

The two had been silent for the last ten minutes when Jem said: "Imagine how many times we sat on that keg, never even knowin' what we was sittin' on." He laughed loudly. "You know, Old Joe got madder than a hornet once when I mentioned I was goin' to chop it up . . . I wanted to use the metal bands that was around it. Imagine!"

As they topped the last hill that would put them in full view to anyone at the house, Joe took several deep breaths. Seconds later he saw the spread. He was shocked. Never had he seen so many horses in the yard and corrals. Plainly, Morgan and his group had arrived, and, from the looks of it, others as well. When you added in the Army horses, well, it was close to a hundred.

"What say we have us an auction," Jem joked as he, too, looked down on the yard with amazement.

Someone must have spotted them because suddenly there was flurry of activity in the yard, and the attention of everyone in the yard seemed to be directed at the two riders.

Neither slowed as they approached the yard. They rode directly to the hitching rack in front of the house, raising clouds of dust as they abruptly pulled to a stop. Joe dismounted hurriedly, throwing his reins at one of Berthold's men. The soldier looked at the sergeant who nodded without taking his eyes off Joe. The horse was led away.

Joe nodded at Mallory, as he mounted the

steps, asking: "Where's the captain?"

The sergeant studied Joe, remaining quiet. It was a tall man next to him who answered. "Inside," he said.

"Didn't you forget someone?" Mallory said as Joe walked through the doorway. Joe didn't bother answering.

Jem was only a few steps behind Joe.

The two went to May's bedroom, Joe pausing briefly in the doorway before striding quickly over to the bed. Quite a crowd had gathered in the small room, including Forbes, Frank Nicholson, the banker, and Captain Berthold.

May appeared weak and pale. She smiled weakly once she realized it was Joe at her side.

"Ma, I'm back. Everything's going to be OK. I promise. How ya feelin'?"

"Tired, Son." Uttering even two words seemed to exhaust May, and her eyes fluttered shut.

As Joe kept his eyes on May, he said through grinding teeth: "So help me Berthold, if you've done anything to hurt her. . . ."

"I think that matter is in your hands. Did you bring the woman?" Berthold responded.

"Now, hold on, Berthold," interjected Forbes.

"You stay out of this Forbes!" Berthold snapped, his temper obviously getting the better of him.

Jem, who had remained in the doorway, stepped into the room as the tension mounted. "What say we take this outside. We got a sick woman in here," he suggested.

"Woman? You mean squaw, don't you?" shot Berthold.

"Outside," Jem asserted.

"He's right," Forbes added. "Let's go."

Joe stayed behind as the men filtered out of the room. He brushed a stray hair from May's face and leaned over and brushed her cheek with his lips.

When he emerged from the house, the heavens were brightening. But in the yard dark words were being exchanged between Forbes and Berthold. Mallory, standing to the left of his commanding officer, occasionally put in his two cents' worth. Joe stood back for several minutes before he jumped into the fray. Finally he stepped into the midst of the group, saying: "Hold on, just hold on!" When he had their attention, he continued: "I think this can be settled. . . ."

"What about the woman?" Berthold interrupted.

"You'll understand, if you let me speak," Joe shot back, irritation mounting in his voice. His eyes traveled from face to face — Berthold, Forbes, Mallory, Jem, and Frank Nicholson. "Mister Nicholson," Joe began, "I'm asking you to hold your peace until I've cleared up a few other matters. But I promise I'll get to you. Now," he paused and took a deep breath, "it appears Old Joe Jessup, the man I'm proud to have called father, was a far wiser man than most of us considered him to be." Here Joe paused and reached into his pocket. "It seems" — he shuffled through the sheaf of papers — "we're all fighting about something that was dealt with a few years back by Joe."

Berthold jumped in. "What are you talking . . . ?"

"Let him say his piece," Jem shouted, stepping toward the captain.

"When Old Joe had a survey done, he found out he owned a lot more land than he thought he did . . . including most of that mountain up there . . . the land where the up yonders live. And that land was put in trust with the territory for the up yonders, for Blue Barrel's people, his heirs and assigns as this here paper says. So rightfully that land is vested by the territory as a reservation. The papers look legal . . . they've been signed and recorded. An agent for the Bureau of Indian Affairs signed it, too. I don't know how Old Joe did it, but he did. It says so right here. Look 'em over." He extended the papers toward Berthold, who yanked them from Joe's hand.

Joe continued. "Captain Berthold, I'm afraid you and your Army were used by the Colsons who wanted this land. It wasn't the up yonders causing trouble. It was the Colsons themselves. They didn't know about this paper. Nobody knew. They just took advantage of the situation when Crow got shot. I'm not sure who killed Crow. Hell, it could have been one of their own did it. It could have been anyone. A lot of people sure hated him." He paused and glanced significantly at Jem, laughing. "Hell, maybe it was Ma." At this everyone laughed. "But," Joe continued, "a killing in Cumberland is out of your jurisdiction, and I don't believe it's a military matter, wrong as it was. Or, if those are the kinds of things the Army deals with now, maybe you can find out who's been putting a running iron to our cattle the last several years."

At this, Forbes said: "Got some news on that, Joe."

"So, you see," Joe added, "Captain Berthold, you and your men are here on a trumped-up mission. Like it or not, you're plumb in the middle of a feud between my family and the Colsons. I hate to say it, but somebody at your end made a mistake, somebody who was unaware of the arrangement Old Joe Jessup made several years back with the territory."

"My orders were to find hideouts and herd them north," Berthold stated. "I just follow orders."

"Well, maybe that's *your* mistake."

The captain's gaze drifted to the soldiers scattered about the yard, some sitting, some standing, all caught up in the confrontation that was playing out near the house. Berthold's look returned to Joe and he rasped: "Indians can't own land." Then, after handing the papers back to Joe, he ordered the men under his command to mount up. "You haven't seen the last of me, Jessup," were his parting words as he turned to leave the circle of men.

The soldiers reacted swiftly. When an underling brought up Berthold's horse and saluted, the captain pulled on his gauntlets, took the salute, and passed orders on to Mallory. After he had mounted, Berthold took one last look at the house, fixed an angry glare at Joe, and led the contingent out of the yard.

Hank Morgan let out a satisfied Rebel yell as they departed. The rest stood silently, unable, it seemed, to let out a sigh of relief for several minutes. Then suddenly chaos broke out as the townsmen came up to congratulate Joe. It was the general opinion that today Joe had become a man, had stepped into Old Joe's shoes. In fact, there was so much commotion that no one noticed the arrival of Doc Leger.

As the newcomer was filled in on the events, he seemed pleased, but his concern was for his patient, and, after shaking Joe's hand and commending him on a job well done, he entered the house to check on May.

Joe watched him through the doorway while well-wishers patted his back and began arguing among themselves as to the high point of the morning. "Excuse me," he said, "I'd like to go check on Ma."

Immediately Nicholson began blustering: "What about me? You still own the house and this land" — he pointed, indicating the land around them — "don't you? I got a claim with your pa's signature on it for the money I gave him. It's right here." He patted the various pockets of his suit coat.

Joe smiled and reached for the sheet of paper he had tucked back in his pocket. He handed it to Nicholson. "This here paper's got your signature on it. It says my pa paid off that loan, Mister Nicholson. If you'll look closely, you'll see you signed it paid in full."

Nicholson now scoured his pockets for a handkerchief with which to wipe his brow that had burst forth with drops of sweat. "Where'd you get that paper?" he asked.

A grin brightened Forbes's face as he stepped forward to take the paper. He studied it for several seconds, then announced: "Seems you got no claim, Frank. That's your signature, ain't it? Besides, you didn't want this land for yourself. You wanted it so you could sell it to the Colsons. Always the businessman, hey, Frank? Well, the Colsons won't be buying anything real soon. As a matter of fact, you might want to think about buying up the Colson land and selling it to young Jessup, here. You see Fred Harper is willing to talk about the running-iron business that the Colsons had going on Jessup stock. Told me where I can find another running iron to match the one I got stored in my office that Sullivan brought me. Also, I've had word on Harland Colson. He's on business up north. Looks like he may have made himself scarce to help the Colsons make their case to the Army. As for who killed Crow, well, maybe

Joe's right, maybe it was May."

Again, everyone within hearing distance laughed at the absurdity of the statement as they pictured the old woman lying in bed in the house.

As Joe stood listening, Jem slipped in next to him. He put his hand on Joe's shoulder and said: "The men are right, boy. Old Joe would be proud."

"Thanks," was all Joe said, but he smiled. Then he went into the house.

When Joe entered May's room, he found May awake. She and Leger both held a glass with a finger's worth of whisky in them.

Upon his appearance, Leger lifted his glass, smiling and saying: "We're toasting to your success."

Joe shook his head, grinning. "I'll take that as a good word on Ma's health," he commented and then kissed his mother on the forehead. "It looks to be over, Ma."

"She needs to stay in bed for some time, Joe," Leger broke in, "but I think she'll come out of this in fine shape." He directed his next statement to May: "But you have to take it nice and easy, you hear me, May?"

"I hear," May said weakly. She cocked her head and studied her boy's face. After several moments of observation she said: "Look tired. Look old, Joe." Then she smiled.

Joe slept till near supper time. He woke hungry as a horse, and, after finding Jem asleep in the parlor and the yard free of people, he made himself a dozen eggs and a strong pot of coffee. Then he went to May's room. She was staring out the window when he entered.

"Where Donna?" she asked.

"She's safe, Ma. In town, at Jem's."

Her eyes widened. "Get her," she said. "Now."

"I planned to Ma," he responded. "Anything you need or want to know before I go?"

"Yes . . . when bring back your woman?"

"Now, Ma, now," Joe said, thinking to himself that it was going to be hard to keep May still for a couple of weeks.

Joe left the house, rounded up a horse, thinking they'd have their work cut out for them with the gathering starting soon. He didn't push his horse as hard in the direction of town as he had pushed it leaving town hours before. But the time flew by.

By the time he rounded that last bend that would take him into town, he saw that the lights of Cumberland were flickering and flaring. The saloon was filled with stockmen who lived in the outlying regions and were celebrating their victory over the blue coats. They would lie over in town this night and head out come daylight, no doubt nursing painful headaches.

At Jem's cabin Joe put up the big horse and pitched it a thick clump of timothy. His legs seemed heavy as he trudged toward the dwelling that housed only one small lantern. He could feel Donna's happiness at seeing him in spite of her reserved demeanor. Sitting across from each other at the table, he told her the significant events, figuring he could explain in detail another time. She seemed most enthused by the news that May would be all right.

Weary to the bone, Joe got a horse from the livery once they had shared a cup of coffee. The moon was still in the full phase of its cycle as they traveled back to the home place. They rarely spoke, although they exchanged timid smiles every so often. Each was occupied with their own thoughts. Joe about hiring some of the up yonders for the upcoming gather as well as the possibility of hiring Jem on to take Bart's place on the ranch. Donna wondering whether their first child would be a girl or a boy. By the time the Lazy J was in view, she had decided that, if it was a girl, it would be named May. If it was a boy, it would be another Joe.

About the Author

Lauran Paine who, under his own name and various pseudonyms has written over nine hundred books, was born in Duluth, Minnesota, a descendant of the Revolutionary War patriot and author, Thomas Paine. His family moved to California when he was at an early age and his apprenticeship as a Western writer came about through the years he spent in the livestock trade, rodeos, and even motion pictures where he served as an extra because of his expert horsemanship in several films starring movie cowboy Johnny Mack Brown. In the late 1930s, Paine trapped wild horses in northern Arizona and even, for a time, worked as a professional farrier. Paine came to know the Old West through the eyes of many who had been born in the previous century, and he learned that Western life had been very different from the way it was portrayed on the screen. "I knew men who had killed other men," he later recalled. "But they were the exceptions. Prior to and during the Depression, people were just too busy eking out an existence to indulge in Saturday-night brawls." He served in the U.S. Navy in the Second World War and began writing for Western pulp magazines following his discharge. It is interesting to note that all of his earliest novels (written under his own name and the pseudonym Mark Carrel) were published in the British market and he soon had as strong a following in that country as in the United States. Paine's Western fiction is characterized by strong plots, authenticity, an apparently effortless ability to construct situation and character, and a preference for building his stories upon a solid foundation of historical fact. *Adobe Empire* (1956), one of his best novels, is a fictionalized account of the last twenty years in the life of trader William Bent and, in an off-trail way, has a melancholy, bittersweet texture that is not easily forgotten. In later novels like *The White Bird* (Five Star Westerns, 1997) and *Cache Cañon* (Five Star Westerns, 1998), he has shown that the special magic and power of his stories and characters have only matured along with his basic themes of changing times, changing attitudes, learning from experience, respecting nature, and the yearning for a simpler, more moderate way of life.

The employees of Thorndike Press hope you have enjoyed this Large Print book. All our Large Print titles are designed for easy reading, and all our books are made to last. Other Thorndike Press Large Print books are available at your library, through selected bookstores, or directly from us.

For information about titles, please call:

(800) 223-1244
(800) 223-6121

To share your comments, please write:

Publisher
Thorndike Press
295 Kennedy Memorial Drive
Waterville, ME 04901

Muhlenberg County Libraries
117 S. Main
Greenville, Kentucky 42345